AN EVENING'S ENTERTAINMENT

"I can see why you're so sure of yourself," Shafer said. This was the moment; he was going all in, just not with his chips.

"I been doing this for ten years. Shouldn't I be?"

"It's because you haven't played this game straight."

He'd actually said it. If Tom hadn't known it was coming, he'd have sat there like a man just struck by lightning. He would've questioned his ears. But he'd known. Shafer's plan wasn't to cheat; it was to call Tom a cheat.

"It's been a while since someone said something like that to me," Tom said, getting to his feet, and Shafer got up too.

That seemed to wake everyone up, and Mr. Carroll hurried forward, alarmed. He cleared his throat, but Tom raised a finger to stop him from saying whatever he'd been about to say.

"I wouldn't get involved, Mr. Carroll," he said politely. "There isn't a player in this room who isn't ready to fight for his name. You wouldn't want to be the man to try to stop me."

He turned to Shafer and, gesturing toward the double doors to the deck, asked, "Shall we step outside?"

Tom wouldn't have thought him a terribly strong man, but Shafer flipped the poker table like it was nothing. Everyone fell back as it crashed down, cards and chips flying. . . .

RALPH COMPTON

CALVERT'S LAST BLUFF

A Ralph Compton Western by
E. L. RIPLEY

BERKLEY
New York

BERKLEY
An imprint of Penguin Random House LLC
penguinrandomhouse.com

Copyright © 2020 by The Estate of Ralph Compton
Penguin Random House supports copyright. Copyright fuels creativity, encourages
diverse voices, promotes free speech, and creates a vibrant culture. Thank you for buying
an authorized edition of this book and for complying with copyright laws by not
reproducing, scanning, or distributing any part of it in any form without permission.
You are supporting writers and allowing Penguin Random House to continue to
publish books for every reader.

BERKLEY and the BERKLEY & B colophon are registered trademarks of
Penguin Random House LLC.

ISBN: 9780593102381

First Edition: October 2020

Printed in the United States of America
1   3   5   7   9   10   8   6   4   2

Cover art by Chis McGrath
Book design by George Towne

THE IMMORTAL COWBOY

This is respectfully dedicated to the "American Cowboy." His was the saga sparked by the turmoil that followed the Civil War, and the passing of more than a century has by no means diminished the flame.

———◆———

True, the old days and the old ways are but treasured memories, and the old trails have grown dim with the ravages of time, but the spirit of the cowboy lives on.

———◆———

In my travels—to Texas, Oklahoma, Kansas, Nebraska, Colorado, Wyoming, New Mexico, and Arizona—I always find something that reminds me of the Old West. While I am walking these plains and mountains for the first time, there is this feeling that a part of me is eternal, that I have known these old trails before. I believe it is the undying spirit of the frontier calling me, through the mind's eye, to step back into time. What is the appeal of the Old West of the American frontier?

———◆———

It has been epitomized by some as the dark and bloody period in American history. Its heroes—Crockett, Bowie, Hickok, Earp—have been reviled and criticized. Yet the Old West lives on, larger than life.

———◆———

It has become a symbol of freedom, when there was always another mountain to climb and another river to cross; when a dispute between two men was settled not with expensive lawyers, but with fists, knives, or guns. Barbaric? Maybe. But some things never change. When the cowboy rode into the pages of American history, he left behind a legacy that lives within the hearts of us all.

—*Ralph Compton*

PROLOGUE

I T WASN'T NATURAL, this chill in July.

There was no danger of frost, but the air was sharp enough to feel as though there should have been. The mist rising off the river was as thin and fine as lace, but there was so much of it that the far bank and the hills and buildings beyond were lost in the white and pink of dusk. The smell of woodsmoke was everywhere, mingling with the murmurs of a city trying stubbornly to stay warm with the sun going down.

It was a lucky night in Omaha if the wind brought only the smoke and the scent of the river and nothing from the stockyards and the slaughterhouses. There weren't many things in life that really came down to luck, but the mood of the wind seemed to be one of them. Folks liked to bemoan their bad luck when things went south, but Tom found there was often something those folks could be doing differently if they really wanted to. The wind was another matter, though. You couldn't do much about the wind.

He chose to enjoy it while it was on his side, taking in plenty before going into the oily, lathery air of the barber's parlor. The man in the chair was just getting to his feet, clearly the educated sort, with a funny hat and enough mustache to make it difficult to notice anything else about him.

Tom took off his hat and waited. There was nothing but exhaustion in the barber's eyes, yet his hands looked steady enough.

The customer paid for his shave, and the barber nervously brushed off his spotless apron every second or two. He didn't realize he was doing it, and he didn't realize he had those raccoon eyes, either.

"Thank you, sir," he said, bowing the customer out of the shop. "And good evening." He was a Greek by the sound of it.

Tom took his place in the chair, which gave him a view of a trio of sketches on the wall: one of a man, likely intended to be the barber; one of a woman, likely his wife; and one of a boy, who was likely the artist. The drawings weren't much good, but Tom didn't blame the fellow for hanging them. He'd have done the same.

Whether due to fatigue or disposition, the Greek didn't try to converse. He'd barely begun to work when the door opened, and Dan Karr came into the shop, looking as though he had something to say that mattered. If he did, it would have been the first time.

He paused dramatically on the threshold, letting in the chilly air and sweeping his hat off dramatically. "Tom Calvert," he said.

"Dan."

Dan's eyes were the same as always: deader than Lincoln. "I heard it was you on that stage last night out of Sioux City."

The stage hadn't come from Sioux City, but it wasn't worth mentioning.

"Who'd you hear that from?" Tom asked, curious. The barber had a very sure hand with his razor, and it was the best-smelling lather Tom had ever encountered. The only thing that would have made it better would have been Dan leaving. He probably hadn't heard the rumor anywhere; he'd probably just seen Tom climb out and go into the hotel.

Dan ignored the question. "Is that a new suit? Where you going to play tonight?" he asked without waiting for an answer to his first question. He knew damn well it was a new suit. Now he let the door fall shut and ducked his head at the barber, who politely kept quiet. He knew who Dan was; everyone did. For a long time, he'd managed to stay in the shadows, but it was shooting that bank robber Victor Wells that had done it. It broke open Dan's reputation like a sudden thunderstorm. Now people wanted to buy him drinks and hire him to chase bounties.

Dan liked to wear his pistol high and near his belly, where his coat would never hide it. It was his way of making his intentions clear. Tom had always been of the belief that a man could be talkative or useful, but not both. Dan was an exception; he would talk until you were sick of him, but still do the job he was paid for.

Who was paying him now? He was wearing a new suit himself.

"The Six Table? Or the Jewel?" Dan pressed.

"Neither," Tom told him, sensing a sneeze coming on. He held up his hand, the barber obligingly withdrew the blade, and he got ready, but the sneeze didn't come. "Pardon me," he said, settling back again. "I won't play in Omaha at all. I'll be on Bert's boat."

The look that came over Dan's face wasn't surprise when it should have been. Something was wrong.

Tom didn't let anything show. "Dan?" he prompted.

"Tom, you know that ain't Bert's boat no more," Dan said, frowning.

Tom blinked. It was a bad tell, but nothing could stop it. "Oh?"

"It belongs to Mr. Carroll from Saint Louis."

Tom considered that. "I was there not two hours ago," he said. "The fellow took my invitation, same as he ever did. My things are aboard already."

"Carroll ain't changed nothing, Tom." Dan shrugged and put a little tobacco in his cheek. "You'll still have your game, I'm sure. I just mean it ain't Bert's no more, that's all."

"Did this happen fairly recently?"

"I suppose."

Tom sighed. There wasn't any helping it; Bert probably wasn't inclined to notify him, and even if he were, how would he go about it? He didn't know where Tom was at any given moment.

Carroll. The name was familiar, but Tom had never met him.

He squinted, trying to remember. "Is Carroll in wheat?"

"Among other things. You know old Jeff Shafer's on that boat."

"Is he really? He isn't busted yet? I didn't realize his wife had any more money for him to lose."

"New wife," Dan replied, stifling a yawn.

Tom sighed. "What happened to the first one? She seemed nice."

"I don't know, Tom. I don't keep up with him. I only know he's on the boat and in big, flaming humor."

"She must be rich."

"He wouldn't waste his time otherwise. Is it true what I heard about you in Springfield?"

Tom groaned. "Most likely. She was there."

"That pretty Chinawoman?"

"She isn't from China," Tom snapped. It wasn't the first time he'd told Dan that.

"Then where is she from?"

"Japan."

"What's that, then? Like a state in China?"

"How the hell should I know, Dan?" As though either of them knew the first thing about China. Dan probably didn't even realize China was to the right of Africa.

"Did she take your money again?"

"She did," Tom grumbled, and the barber narrowly avoided nicking him. "Twice more now. That makes four times she's robbed me. If I was a bank, I'd have closed by now."

"You seen her again after Charlotte?"

"Oh, she turned up in Yankton as well." Tom wanted to rub his face in frustration. "I thought I had her figured, but she just took it all again and quick. It was only nineteen hands."

"Is she a cheat? Can't see how she could be. Ain't nowhere to hide no cards in that dress."

Tom knew that. "She's no cheat," he said wistfully.

"Are you broke, Tom? You could save her some trouble and just buy her something nice."

Tom glared at him. "Look at me, Dan. I'm not in the gutter. But yes, what do you think I mean when I tell you she took it all? Then I went to pay her a compliment, and she laughed at me."

"At *you*?"

"Yes. And why not? If she can know my mind at the table, she can know it anywhere." Tom felt wilted. "I don't need to worry about her here, though. She's still up north. She'll have to get what she can while she can. People are talking, and a lot of fellas won't play with her. They'll say it's on account of her race, but that's a lie. They'll take anybody's money if they can get it, but they can't get hers. She's too good. Won't be long before she won't be able to find a table to sit at. That or someone'll shoot her in the back."

"What about you, Tom?"

"I need to get a little something for myself first." He sighed. "Then I suspect I'll try again."

Dan just shook his head, looking incredulous. It probably struck him as odd that Tom would choose to lose his money to that woman rather than spend his time on easier prey. That was all right; Dan didn't need to understand.

The barber was finishing, and he wiped away the last of the lather. Tom rubbed his chin; the shave wasn't perfect, but it was awfully close for being so quick. He paid the man and picked up his coat, checking his watch.

"Thank you, sir." The barber ducked his head.

"Thank you. What's the name of this? I like how it smells."

The barber cleared his throat and showed Tom the bottle. For a moment, he didn't understand; then he did. He didn't know how to say that word, either.

"Where's it from, France?" He scratched his head.

"I do not know, sir."

All the same, Tom got out a bit of paper and his piece of charcoal and wrote the letters down, peering at them for a moment.

"It's real nice," he said.

The barber smiled appreciatively. Dan was still standing there, as though he had nothing better to do, which was all but certain.

"When you say you mean to try again," he said, watching Tom shrug into his coat, "do you mean to best her at cards or marry her?"

"Both if I'm able. But I'd like to do a little winning first, Dan. Weddings cost money."

"Does she like you?"

"I think she does. Hard to be sure. She's awful good."

It was the truth, even if people had a way of thinking that a man who played cards for a living might have been less than honest. He wasn't lying, though, and he rarely did. There was no getting around the winning; he'd have to do it. There were things to be done, but none of them would come free, and it had been a tight squeeze just to pull together enough money to be able to play tonight.

It didn't matter what color another player's skin was or if he was a man or a woman.

Anyone's money would do the job, and Tom Calvert had a plan.

PART ONE

WINNERS AND LOSERS

CHAPTER ONE

ANYONE WOULD KNOW at a glance that *Newlywed* was no longer in Bert's hands. She'd never been exactly shabby, but Bert's priorities leaned away from making her pleasing to the eye. Keeping *Newlywed* clean, freshly painted, and crewed by respectable-looking men would have bitten deeply into Bert's ten cents from every dollar to change hands on his boat. He'd always managed to keep it just decent enough that people with money wouldn't turn up their noses at the prospect of a hand, but it had never gone beyond that. No one was fooled into thinking it was a classy joint, even if that was the way Bert had liked to think of it.

Things were different now. Her hull, her paddles—every inch of the steamboat was lovely white with yellow trim. There were banners, streamers, and decorative lamps. *Newlywed* lit up the river and the evening, tingeing the mist and the water gold. It was impressive that that was all it took to make what was in Tom's estimation the humblest paddle steamer on the water into something remarkable.

However warm it looked, none of that warmth reached him. He was in the shadows between the cobbler and the barrel maker, watching in silence. He rubbed his hands together and waited, drawing back out of sight as two men rode by on horseback.

He'd recognized at least half the people going aboard, but there was only one who gave him pause: Pollock. He was a player out of Reno, and he wasn't much talked about, but Tom had sat down with him three times. Not once had he walked out with a profit. Pollock didn't just know how to get money; he knew how to keep it. He was such an easy fellow that most folks didn't mind seeing him win.

It was all right, though. One of the others to go aboard, in the company of no fewer than three girls in silly gowns, was Franklin McCall. McCall was every gambler's favorite opponent: a man with enough money that there was no danger he'd ever run out and the sort of disposition that rendered him able to lose it regularly without getting sore.

Tom hadn't seen Russell yet, but he'd be there as well, and there was no telling what sort of trouble he'd be. If he was sober and things were going well with his wife, he'd likely be the big winner in the end. If not, he'd be good for a few easy dollars.

There was some kind of luck at play already; Tom's new suit would've been overdressing for Bert's boat, but for the new *Newlywed*, it was just enough that he wouldn't stand out. Even Red Parker looked decent;

the last time Tom had seen him, he'd been using string for suspenders.

Tom had seen enough, and it was getting to where he'd be pushing the limit of being fashionably late. He straightened up and went into the open, impressed by the relative quiet. Omaha had tripled in size in the past three years, but it wasn't like some other places that got to be this crowded. It wasn't as loud yet, and there was still a little clean air in it, at least close to the water, where the wind had room to move.

The welcome waiting for him was a warm one, with porters in uniform, and he even spotted a woman dressed as a maid.

Three well-dressed men, and one well-dressed idiot, were also waiting. It was easy to tell which one was Mr. Carroll: surely no one else would wear a white dinner jacket on a paddle steamer on the Missouri. There was enough wax in his mustache that it could have doubled as a candle, and enough gold in just the chain of his watch to buy a few good horses. The two other gentlemen were strangers to Tom, but he knew their type, and he wasn't worried. He'd never loved the ground rocking underfoot, but there was no helping it; there was money to be made here.

And the fourth man, well, everyone knew him.

"Dan," Tom said dryly in greeting, shaking his hand.

"Tom," Dan replied as though they hadn't seen each other just a few hours ago. Tom had to admit, Dan had come a long way. It seemed he had a bit of a poker face himself; he hadn't given any indication at all that he intended to be on this boat. Carroll must have hired him for his gun.

"Mr. Calvert," Carroll said, and there was some real warmth in the words. Indeed, there was a good deal of warmth coming from them all. If you were going to lose money, it was best to do it with a smile. "I'm very glad to meet you."

Tom sensed it was true; there wasn't any lying in his eyes, only confidence. Tom supposed if he had enough money to just buy a steamboat, he might come off like that himself.

"You as well, sir." He shook readily. "It was news to me today that *Newlywed* belonged to you."

"It's just a whim," the other man replied, waving his cigar. "My wife was so taken by the card games on the Mississippi that she wanted it all for herself. I'm coming around to seeing it her way." He shrugged and looked down at the lanterns lining the boat. "Good feelings and good cheer, you know."

That was true enough until the wrong man started losing.

"Well, it was kind of you to honor Bert's invitation to me," Tom told him.

"You're very welcome, Mr. Calvert. I've seen you play."

"Oh?"

"In Topeka."

Tom stiffened. "Topeka," he replied, taken aback, and the deck seemed to rise a little extra underfoot. The lanterns swayed in the breeze, and the laughter and voices from inside were suddenly very far away.

"What was that man's name?" Carroll asked, chewing his cigar.

"Can't say that I remember," Tom lied.

"You only gave him what he deserved. You did not

do one thing that I would not have done myself," Carroll assured him. "He dug his own grave. However, we aren't here to greet you because we're enjoying the weather. I'm afraid that with my wife being here and all, I'm not allowing any firearms onboard."

"I hope you took Red's," Tom told him frankly.

"All," Carroll said, smiling.

"Fair enough." Tom pulled back his coat, took out the pistol tucked into his belt, and handed it to Dan.

"Is that a habit of yours," Carroll asked curiously, "not to wear a holster? It was the same in Topeka if my memory serves me."

Tom shrugged. "Just like every other joint I ever walked into, Mr. Carroll, I'm here to play cards, not to shoot anyone. I have this one too," he added, giving Dan a look. The other man had been staring expectantly, as though challenging him not to mention the tiny gun in his waistcoat. Tom pulled it out, holding it out in his palm.

Carroll raised an eyebrow and took it, holding it up to the light to admire the pearl handles and the engravings on its two barrels.

"I wager you won this from someone," he murmured. "It doesn't seem like the sort of thing you'd choose."

"I did. I keep it for luck. It isn't even loaded," Tom said, waving a hand. It was true. He'd have a better chance of being elected president than hitting anything with that toy.

Carroll tipped the barrels open and peered in, finding the chambers empty. "Well, Mr. Calvert, if there's one thing I've seen for myself, it's that you have a cool head. I wouldn't try to confiscate your luck."

Tom snorted. "I'm not superstitious. More than luck, I keep it for the memories."

"Won it from a woman, did you?"

"As you said, it's not the sort of thing you expect a man to carry."

Carroll grinned and tossed it back. "Have a pleasant night tonight as well, Mr. Calvert."

"Thank you, sir. I plan on it." Tom tipped his hat and went aboard.

Newlywed was even more difficult to recognize up close. There were more than just paint and decorations; walls had been added and removed, and now there was carpet inside. Just the smell of the dinner being cooked down below was enough to push cards out of Tom's mind.

A man in a suit took him to a cabin, which was cramped but still better appointed than most hotel rooms. Tom had always liked Bert, and he'd enjoyed playing cards on this boat, but he wouldn't miss him or the way *Newlywed* had been in the past. There'd always been a moldy smell that had clung to the boat no matter what season it was. That was gone, which was a pleasant surprise.

Tom's things were already there, and he was half surprised they hadn't been unpacked for him, not that he planned to stay more than a single night. The boat would reach the Nebraska camp by midmorning, and he'd go ashore there and find a stage that could take him to Topeka. He was *not* superstitious, and he would not avoid Topeka because of what had happened there.

The man's name had been Colin Adams, he'd been a sore loser, and it had been a fair fight. There was nothing more to say about it. So Carroll had been among the onlookers; Tom wouldn't have guessed. At any rate, that had been nearly six months ago, so it was time to go back and take whatever money Topeka had to offer. Then to Wichita to do the same there before swinging back north. He'd never been any farther west than Reno, and it was high time he saw what was waiting out that way.

He pulled back the drapes and peered out at the river. The sun was nearly done for the day, but so were the clouds, so it would be a clear night. A good night to be out on deck if it wasn't so cold. He'd never seen chill like this in July in all his life.

Rubbing his hands together, he patted himself down, patting a few extra times where his gun would've been. It didn't bother him not to have it; it was just a different sort of feeling. Nothing would happen at a game like this, but there was no blaming Carroll for being cautious. He was new to this business, and he'd probably heard stories.

And he'd been there in Topeka to see what had happened to Colin Adams.

Raised voices startled Tom, and he turned toward the door.

"You think I don't know a liar when I see one?" a man shouted.

Well, that was new. The first hand hadn't even been dealt, and people were already calling one another cheats. Tom opened the door and went out to find a big man, well-dressed, towering over a terrified boy.

The boy wasn't half as well-dressed as the man, and he was clearly a hand aboard the boat; there was coal on his hands and face and oversized sleeves.

And his eyes were so full of lies, Tom couldn't help but feel bad for him.

"I did not steal anything," the boy said, raising his hands as though he expected to be hit. It was jarring how well he spoke, being so small, thin, and ragged.

He spoke his words well, but he didn't *choose* them well. He shouldn't have denied stealing; he should have denied being a thief—but whatever his grift was, he was so bad at it that there was no saving it at this point. Not that Tom approved; he certainly didn't.

"I know you didn't! I caught you before you could do it!" the man roared.

"What was he doing?" Tom asked curiously, and the big man turned on him.

"He was in my room. I seen him."

"I was bringing a towel," the boy blurted.

"With them hands?" the man asked disdainfully, eyeing the coal stains.

The boy swallowed.

"Where's the towel?"

"It's there, mister."

Indeed, in the next room over, there was a folded towel on the table. It even had a few grayish smudges on it where the boy's fingers had been. This was the worst game Tom had ever seen, bar none, but at least the boy had made some sort of effort to sell whatever it was he was trying to pull over on this man. He looked only about thirteen, so it would be a while yet before he had enough brains to do much more than find trouble.

The big man wasn't convinced, and rightly so. The boy had fully intended to steal from him.

"You look familiar," Tom told him. "I saw you on

the Mississippi, didn't I? Aboard Sawyer's boat. You were serving drinks. You ought to be more careful. Misunderstandings'll get you killed. The wrong fellow thinks you're doing wrong on a night like this, and you're liable to get a bullet, not a paddle."

The big man scowled, slammed his door shut, and locked it. He stalked off without another word. He was more concerned with the cards bluff than with a boy who *might* have been a thief. He'd gotten his temper under control fast; Tom had never seen him before, but at a glance, he looked like trouble.

Tom stifled a yawn, but the boy was still there, giving him a funny look. Tom sighed and leaned in, lowering his voice.

"If you're going to steal, don't do it at the *beginning* of the voyage," he murmured. "Wait until you got somewhere to go with what you get." He saw the look on the boy's face and smiled. "Why do you want to steal anyway? Boat like this, you're probably paid a dollar a day. Isn't that enough for you?"

The boy looked uncertain, and that gave it away. He wasn't being paid at all. He probably wasn't even supposed to be aboard. What had his plan been? Had he even had one?

There were a lot of things Tom could have said.

Instead, he shook his head and gave the boy a pitying look.

"You do what you have to," he said, locking his own door. "But for what it's worth, I'll tell you this isn't the right boat to try your first grift on."

He left it at that. This was no business of his; the boy was no threat, and if he wanted to take a risk, well, Tom had never let anyone talk *him* out of that.

CHAPTER TWO

Looking like a classy joint wasn't enough to make it one.

A night's entertainment for real people of means would have been more leisurely, but the dinner and all that were just formalities; they were what you did. No one wanted to play cards on an empty stomach, but they *did* want to get on with it.

The boat was barely underway, and Mr. Carroll's people were already bringing out food and gently ushering the guests to the tables in the dining room. There were twenty players Tom could see, and he recognized more than half of them. That meant four tables. The host wouldn't pressure anyone to do it, but there would be an expectation that the last man standing from those tables would sit for an encore tomorrow. A reporter or two were mixed in with the rest of the people, and there were a fair number who appeared to be along just for the sake of being there.

Tom had run into their kind before, and he didn't particularly mind an audience, though having bodies all around meant he'd have to devote more of his attention to spotting inventive cheats.

In summer this room was usually stifling, but tonight it was agreeably choked with warmth and perfume. Tom took a chair at a table where Dan was seated with two women who were certainly in Mr. Carroll's employ. So that was the nature of his investment in the boat; not only would he take his piece of the winnings, but these onlookers had paid for the privilege to be here. His gains wouldn't end there; even after the winners and losers were sorted, the winners would have the opportunity to send a little of the money Mr. Carroll's way in exchange for good company.

It seemed like a tidy way to turn a profit, but it probably wasn't as easy as it looked. Tom had no head for business; if he had, he'd have been a banker in the city and not a gambler on the road.

"I think he's done a fine job with it," Dan remarked as Tom sat down. "Don't you, Tom?"

"I don't care for all the yellow," Tom replied, placing his napkin on his lap, then putting his hand over his wineglass as a boy tried to pour.

"It's cheerful. Ladies, this is Tom Calvert."

Tom smiled and nodded obligingly; then he spotted Shafer. He was at the other end of the dining room at Mr. Carroll's table. The two were speaking to each other.

"Is that worry I see?" Dan asked before taking a sip of wine. "I never knew you to be afraid of Jeff Shafer."

"The man's no good at cards, but he's a hell of a salesman. Look at his wives."

"Look who he's here with," Dan countered.

Tom did so. There was a woman with Shafer, but she wasn't his wife; she was dressed rather similarly to the women with Dan, in a dark dress with too many ruffles that no married woman would ever touch. At a glance she looked slightly too pretty and a good deal too sensible to be with a man like Shafer, but money had a way of making these things happen.

Tom turned back to Dan. "Did she catch your eye?"

"I guess not, Tom." Something was funny to Dan, but he wasn't planning to say what, and the waiters were serving food. The dinner looked lavish, and the guests likely had Mr. Carroll's desire to impress Mrs. Carroll for that.

Russell turned up, taking the seat next to Tom.

"How'd Deadwood suit you?" Tom asked, shaking his hand.

Russell scowled. "Not as well as I hoped. Most of them don't bring the gold to the table. They use it all on women, and there's nothing left over. It's an ugly place, it smells, and I can't say that I recommend going there."

He was sober all right.

"Are we at the same table?" Tom asked.

"You worried about me, Tom? You robbed me blind in Kentucky."

That was true, but Russell had apparently forgotten that they'd played in Kansas City since then. Tom had profited both times, but both times Russell had been so drunk that Tom and Dan had had to carry him to the hotel afterward.

Not tonight. Tonight would be different.

"How's Scarlett?" Tom asked cautiously, watching the other man shake out his napkin.

"Hasn't touched the opium since January."

However inconvenient that was, Tom couldn't find it in himself to be disappointed. Russell's weaknesses benefited him, but his struggle with Scarlett and that stuff she drank had been going on for too long. Tom was tired of the pain that went with it, and he wasn't even married to the woman. Good for her. Good for Russell.

Tom still didn't want to play against him at his best.

"We'll have a good game tonight," Russell went on, and Tom realized he was being read. What was worse, Russell was trying to make him feel better. "Lot of talent," Russell added, glancing around the room, now filled with voices and the clinking of silverware. "It'll be a late night, I know. Winners won't sit until tomorrow."

It looked as though Russell already had things figured, and he was giving Tom an out: challenging him to win his table, then simply go with those winnings rather than risk them at the winners' table.

On the one hand, that was *exactly* what Tom had planned to do from the start; easy money was the only money he was interested in. It was flattering that Russell was already declaring him the winner at his table.

It was also an insult and a vicious one.

Did Russell have the audacity to *assume* he was the better player, when he liked to behave so modestly and even forget the last time they'd played together? Did he know so much that it was all a foregone conclusion? Did he know Tom's thinking?

That was a big head on those average shoulders. And was that a smirk or just his jowls?

Dan wasn't smiling anymore, and neither were the ladies.

Tom snorted. "You got me all wrong, Russell. I'm a gentleman." He smiled, brushing his lapel ironically. "All this? It would be rude to stay less than two days. You aren't calling me rude, are you?"

Russell's brows rose. "Oh, no. No, Tom. I wouldn't do that. I like living too much. At least, most of the time."

Dan let his breath out.

Tom twirled his fork. "I'm relieved."

"So am I. Sure was nice talking to you, Tom."

"My pleasure, Russell."

They watched him get up and leave the table. Tom sighed, and Dan shook his head.

"You ain't even got cards in your hands, and he's beating you," he said, trying not to laugh. "Now you have to play him."

"I *know* what he's doing. Thank you," Tom snapped.

"Start the night off losing."

"It's about time I stopped worrying about him." Tom went back to eating. "It's been almost a year since he's played me sober. I'm the better player now, and there's a good chance he's worse. He spent six months all but pickled."

Dan nudged the girl beside him. "You let him take it all from you, and you won't be able to have any company."

He knew perfectly well that company was the last thing on Tom's mind. All the same, Tom's reputation for doing impulsive, boneheaded things, like losing to the same Japanese woman over and over and letting himself be baited into overstaying by fellows like Russell, was well deserved, and Dan knew it.

But Tom knew better than to let his thoughts go to women when there was still winning to do. Dan was just in an irksome mood, and who could blame him? He'd stumbled into a real nice place here, being paid a couple dollars a night to eat and watch cards in comfort. Supposing something did happen and he had to toss someone overboard, Dan wouldn't be bothered. He wasn't afraid of anyone walking God's earth, let alone anyone on this boat. Someday that would get him killed, but not here.

And on the subject of people wanting to get themselves killed, that *boy* was simply fearless.

He was back, cleaned up noticeably and carrying a tray of desserts. How in the world had he swung that? Who had he spoken to? Who had he convinced that he was meant to be here and working?

Tom's hat was in his room, but if he'd had it, it would've come off for the kid.

Best not to stare, though. People would see him looking and start to pay attention to the boy. Tom went back to his food, wondering how long he could ignore the way Dan was looking at him.

"What's on your mind, Dan?" Not long apparently.

"Never saw you take one lying down that way."

Tom grimaced but kept eating. Yes, he easily could have tipped that the other way, once he had seen Russell's intent. He could've brought up Scarlett or insulted Russell or even just reminded him that they'd played in Kansas City and how that had ended. That would've been enough to put Russell on his heels, and if Tom was vicious enough, maybe even weaken him later in the evening. Calm heads, not smart ones, made money at the table. Taking a man's calm away was the closest thing Tom knew to a sure thing.

"Why didn't you push him back?" Dan pressed.

"Truthfully?" Tom wiped his mouth and put his napkin aside. "I didn't feel like it."

But that was with regard to Russell. There was another man present Tom didn't like quite so much, and if there was a showdown with Russell on the horizon, he'd have to make sure he had the money to pay him with.

Tom pushed back his chair and got up.

"Ladies," he said, and included Dan in the sweep of his eyes. The gunfighter just sat there with his wine, smirking. Tom checked on the boy, who might as well have been invisible. That was one advantage to having such a pitifully slight build, he supposed.

Threading his way through the tables, he gave nods and smiles where appropriate. It was an odd thing: there were so many acquaintances in this room yet so few friends.

There was Russell now sitting at Pollock's table. What did he have in mind? Did he want to sabotage the other man? Or did he intend to do the same as he had with Tom and make certain he would remain for the winner's hand? Was Russell really that confident? Probably not; he was more odd than arrogant. For all Tom knew, these little chats weren't calculated at all; they were just Russell's asinine notion of being sociable.

Tom, meanwhile, had no interest in being sociable as he approached Mr. Carroll's table.

Shafer threw his fork and knife down and stiffened the moment he noticed Tom.

"What do you want, Tom?" he asked bluntly, a sour look settling on his face. His mustache was conspicuously missing, and there were no fewer than three cuts on his cheek. Maybe this wasn't necessary; maybe he had enough nerves already if he couldn't even afford a decent shave.

"That's no way to greet a friend. I'm just surprised to see you here. That's all."

"I play cards, Tom Calvert. Same as you."

That was a worthy attempt for Mr. Carroll's benefit, but they weren't anything alike, and Shafer knew it.

"Well, I thought you might have a laugh," Tom told him, his smile in place, "if you knew that ten thousand I took from you in Saint Louis? It wasn't even a week before I lost it all to Miss Ayako. Every dime of it."

Shafer didn't laugh, of course. The money he'd lost hadn't been his, and as he liked to spend his time ranting about his dislike for Mexicans, it was likely he wouldn't much care for the money going to a foreigner.

His face was getting red.

"My luck just isn't what it used to be, I suppose," Tom went on good-naturedly, scratching his head. Of course, luck had nothing to do with dirty tricks like this.

He noticed the way the woman beside Shafer was looking at him. What was that in her eyes? Recognition? Of course it was; Tom recognized her as well, and he nearly jumped in surprise.

"Holly," he said, breaking into a wide and completely unplanned grin. "Is that you?"

She blanched but then tried not to laugh, and Tom felt a stab of guilt. Holly wouldn't have been the name she was going by, most likely.

"No," he amended quickly, straightening up. "I've mistaken you for someone else, and I beg your pardon."

That was the polite thing to say, but everyone at the table had understood him.

If Shafer's face got any redder, he wouldn't make it to the card table. If he couldn't form words, he sure as hell wouldn't be able to play. Normally Tom wouldn't have been quite this brazen about provoking him, but why not?

Mr. Carroll had taken everyone's guns.

CHAPTER THREE

$\sim$

ONE WAS ALL right, two were better, and anything more was too expensive. That was the sort of crude thing that Dan might have said when he'd had a few whiskies and was feeling wise. It wasn't true about women, and it certainly wasn't true about poker chips.

There were three chips left next to Tom's hand on the table, and they looked mighty lonesome.

Shafer, meanwhile, had a crowd gathered behind him, including Mr. and Mrs. Carroll. Even more plentiful than his friends were his chips, which stood in stacks taller than his whiskey glass.

It wasn't that Shafer had won that money; Tom had merely lost it while he took the measure of the table. To his right was Red Parker, who was a decent fellow, if rough around the edges. His language and manners made him a poor fit in this place, and in truth, he wasn't quite a good enough player to sit at this table.

He would be one day, if his temper didn't get him killed.

To Tom's left was Cyril Long, who had been Tom's equal a year ago but had clearly let his game slip.

And over there next to Shafer was a new man, one with a big, bushy beard and little spectacles on his nose. He was older than Tom and Shafer combined, and his fingers shook when he held his cards.

He was the reason Shafer had all the money; Tom didn't know that man, who very creatively called himself Mr. Smith, but Smith was trouble. It was impossible to know in a single evening if his peculiar behaviors were an elaborate grift or if he really was some tremendously skilled player from overseas. His accent, which might've been German, was suspect, but Tom was no expert.

At any rate, Smith had ruined everything. He'd sat down at the table with the rest of them and landed like a big tree on a small cabin. Tom wasn't afraid of every stranger he met at the table, only the ones he couldn't get a feel for.

And no one could get a feel for Smith.

"You need a drink, Calvert?" Shafer asked, and there it was—it had peeked out all evening, ready to show itself: real confidence. There was nothing like a mountain of chips to make a man think he had the upper hand, and it was usually true. It certainly was tonight; Shafer had every advantage, though probably not the sense to use them.

"You know I don't drink." Tom took two cards and placed them facedown.

Two more were slid across the table to him.

There was a hush; not in the whole room, as someone was laughing at Pollock's table, and there was a gasp from Russell's, but here—here they were quiet.

Tom knew there was a reason he was here and not in New York City. He wasn't the best gambler to lay down money, but he was damned if he wasn't *one* of them. And he'd been showing it for long enough that there were a fair few people who knew his name. Yet here he was, at nine o'clock at night, about to bust on an old steamboat with a new coat of paint.

These people were right to find that interesting.

He looked at Smith's eyes, all but hidden by his glasses and eyebrows. The man even hunched his shoulders and kept his face down, where the light couldn't get to him.

Was he an actor here to take the smooth road to easy money, throwing everyone off and playing the people, not the cards?

Tom was inclined to think that was exactly what he was doing. Since those first few hands, Smith had acted like clockwork. He knew how to play poker like a sensible man, but there was a reason you didn't see sensible men gambling. That was a way to play, not a way to win.

It had taken nearly two hours, but Tom was finally sure. Smith was no threat. Red Parker had showed more insight during this game than he had, and Red was only about as good as Shafer on his best day.

Tom picked up the cards and threw his last thirty dollars onto the pile. The bet was forty.

"You need to fold, Calvert," Shafer told him.

"Over ten dollars?" Tom tossed his derringer the table, where the polished metal and pear the light. "Any objections?"

"I object," Shafer said at once, but he was the only one.

"Play it," Red said, his eyes on the little gun.

Mrs. Carroll was enjoying this at least.

And there was another face, one a bit lower than the rest, crowding for a look. It was that idiot kid. Well, he was still in one piece—good for him. This ought to be prime time for the boy to be doing his stealing; everyone was up here and occupied. The *cash* was all locked up, so he didn't have a prayer of getting that, but nearly everyone on this boat was well-off; there were *plenty* of valuables for the taking.

If the boy would just grab some and swim for shore, he'd be long gone before anyone would ever notice. Of course, Tom was no thief and never had been. Maybe stealing was like cards, and there was more to it that wasn't obvious to a layman.

There was also the detail that it was awfully cold out there, and anyone who went into the water would stand a good chance of freezing if they didn't get out and build a fire quick.

Enough. Tom had his own problems; the boy had already caught one more break than he was due, and he was on his own.

Tom put down three kings and took the hand. He tucked the derringer into his pocket with his watch. Sev ᵈ to breathe again as he scooped in the ree hundred dollars, but to Shafer it thousand. His face had locked up ᵘldn't move. He'd been one face n home. *That* was an even bigger lling in Mr. Carroll's presence or the fact that Holly was at another table entirely, watching another player.

Shafer could usually handle himself in a game, but now he'd taken two body blows and still hadn't managed to land anything on Tom. Every time he had taken a hand and Tom's money with it, he had expected to see something, but Tom hadn't given him anything. Dan wasn't going to tell anyone that Tom was as close to broke as he'd ever been. As long as Tom gave the impression that none of it mattered, Shafer believed it and seethed at his own circumstances.

Temper had no place at the table or anywhere; that was what Tom would preach, even if he didn't practice it. If Shafer ever learned that lesson, he might start to win once in a while.

Tom took up his cards, watching Smith. There were nerves behind those spectacles; Tom was sure of it.

Mr. Carroll was watching with naked fascination, and the room was getting quieter by the minute. The night was still young, but a lot of money had changed hands and not just at this table. By the sound of it, Russell was giving everyone a good show.

Red overplayed, and with luck and that blunder on his side, Tom collected again. Now the table was reeling. As a game took shape, players had a way of figuring where it was going. When it became clear they were wrong, that could be frightening. Tom remembered the feeling; the only way to fight it, to get those nerves out of the body, was to stop trying to see the future. It wasn't the hands to come that mattered; it was the hands that had already been won and lost. Those were the hands that shaped the spirit of the table.

No one could know the future, but if you paid attention to the past, the future would look better for you.

Smith was realizing he was out of his depth.

Shafer was growing angrier by the second.

Cyril was still solid, but Red knew where he stood.

Tom had just won a small hand and then a big one, but all he let anyone see was boredom.

The cards slid across the table, and Shafer's third glass of whiskey was empty. Red was asking for another, and it would have been best if he didn't stop there.

Mr. Carroll had previously been drifting around with his wife, being seen and taking in as much as he could, but now he was rooted to this table. Did that mean Tom had become more interesting than Russell? That would be the day.

Shafer folded, and so did Smith. Red and Cyril stayed in.

Was it worth it with only two pair? The momentum from this win would be enough to put Shafer into the ground; his game was already tilted, and he was close to capsizing.

Tom raised, Red folded, and Cyril made a mistake.

It was easy to think that the night was the game, that streaks and patterns had meaning, but they didn't. If you lost a hundred times in a row, you weren't due to win; your odds were the same as they had been the first time and every time after. The night wasn't the game; the night was a series of games, each one a fresh opportunity.

Cyril thought Tom was pushing his luck, but jacks and tens still beat fours and eights.

Tom brought in the chips and yawned.

"Aren't we entertaining you, Calvert?" Cyril asked.

"Don't be like that. You aren't entertainment."

"What are we, then?" Shafer asked.

"You?" Tom raised an eyebrow, picking up his cards. "You're a bottle, Jeff."

"A bottle?"

Tom shrugged. "You know. I take a bottle and put it on the fence. Then I shoot it." He tossed a few chips into the middle. "To keep my aim sharp. I still haven't figured how I'm going to handle Miss Ayako, but I'm thinking on it." He scratched his cheek.

"You practice your aim a lot, Tom?" Red asked, taking only one card. He was bluffing.

"Lot of sore losers out there, Red. Smith, you still alive over there?" Tom asked suddenly, and the bearded man startled. It was the first time anyone had spoken to him. He hadn't actually been taking too long to play, but Tom wanted to be absolutely sure where he stood.

He'd seen a man like this once before in a gold camp. An actor had come from England, and finding no interest at all in his recitations, he had quickly run out of money. He'd seen how easily it could change hands at the table, and thought he could bluff his way into better circumstances. He had two good nights before they figured him out. He probably could've gone farther if he'd had the sense to try another town, but sooner or later, he'd have sat down with someone with a little skill.

Smith stayed in; he probably had good cards.

This hand wasn't worth it. Tom folded, and Red's three nines took it, but not before Shafer inexplicably pumped the bet. Were only three whiskies enough to put him in this kind of sorry shape? No, that wasn't it.

Shafer was pulling himself together—that was what it was. He'd realized his nerves had gotten to him, and if he couldn't fake calm, he could create it. If he *acted* as though he was in control, it would become true. Tom had seen a few guys do this before. Every player had his own way of getting into the right sort of mind for the game. He didn't much like Shafer, but the man had a right to play the game however he pleased.

It worked; he came into the next hand much more level and pushed Tom high before losing, and he did it with a good hand. Tom collected the chips, but it was Shafer's win; he'd done everything right. If he played like that all the time, this table would be a good deal more interesting.

Smith went bust not long after, and Tom felt a hint of annoyance. He'd let Shafer have all that early money to keep it from going to Smith in order to feel him out. Time spent on caution was never time wasted, but still, you couldn't get it back.

A predatory look came into Cyril's eye, and he couldn't hide it in time. Tom caught it and folded.

Red was falling behind, and Shafer didn't like it; he needed Tom to be the next one out of the game. Shafer had pulled himself together, but he still must have dreaded the thought of facing Tom alone. He'd never had to before, never even come close. He'd always pulled out or been shut out before it ever got to that point.

Tonight he had a shot or at least decent enough grounds to believe he did.

Red gave in to resignation and started to play more cautiously; that would be the end of him. It took only one good hand to get back in, but you wouldn't get that hand if you were trying to defend yourself. Maybe in a battle, there was some good in taking the defensive, but not in cards. He was on his way out, and there was little danger of him coming back. He had another thousand dollars, but it wouldn't last him half an hour.

Tom took two more hands, and the scrutiny on the table was growing. What was more, Shafer's nerves weren't matching pace. He wasn't nearly as worried as he should've been.

He laid down a full house, and Tom gave up four hundred dollars gladly. It was a small price to pay for what he learned: Shafer had something up his sleeve. Not literally; Shafer didn't have the guts to try a cheat like that. He knew damn well that if he ever did, Tom or anyone with a shred of decency would kill him on the spot, with or without a gun.

But he looked like he still thought he had a chance. Even after three—now four—whiskies, he should've had a sense of what was coming. He should've had it more or less worked out that this was Tom's table. Shafer wasn't like Red, though. Shafer *ought* to figure it out and still do the right thing: play like he meant it, nerves and all. And he'd lose his money, but at least he could do it with some self-respect.

"You know," Tom said, picking up his newly dealt hand and considering the cards, "I think I will have that drink. Kentucky bourbon."

A man ducked his head and walked off to get it, and it was right there for all the world to see: hesitation in Shafer's eyes. The other man should've been heartened by a show of nerves from Tom, but he wasn't.

Shafer appeared to be on good terms with Mr. Carroll; did he think he could cheat with the rich man's blessing? It wasn't likely. Mr. Carroll had just started this thing up, and if it got around that he was a bad actor from the jump, there wouldn't be even a second night of poker. He wouldn't risk that. Or was he so ignorant of cards that he thought there weren't enough meaningful people here to expose him? Or did he think they wouldn't have the guts? He *was* an important man and a ruthless one—everyone knew his reputation.

And he didn't have a reputation for being stupid. If he'd been in Topeka that night six months ago, then he knew cards and players as well. He wouldn't knowingly make enemies of people like Tom, Russell, and Pollock. And Dan worked for him, which meant that Dan thought Mr. Carroll was all right.

No, whatever Shafer had in mind, Mr. Carroll wasn't behind it.

All right, Shafer wasn't planning to cheat. What did that leave? Tom probably didn't have long to think about it.

CHAPTER FOUR

THE FEELING OF dread, years ago, when Tom had first caught himself absently toying with his stacks of chips was a memory he'd never let go of. It had been like a punch to the gut. There was satisfaction in identifying another man's tells, but nothing hurt worse than noticing one of his own.

Of course, once you noticed it, you had no excuse not to stop it. And he had. Now there were stacks of chips beside him, and he didn't touch them. He didn't touch the glass of whiskey, either; it had been sitting there for an hour, and it had served its purpose.

Red sighed. He had six hundred dollars left. He gazed at Tom for a long moment, then pushed it in.

Tom showed and took it.

Red sat back, and several people applauded. After a long moment, he stuck his hand out, and Tom shook it. He got up and left, leaving Tom with Cyril and Shafer, whose stacks were getting low. Cyril had managed not to lose money so far, but most of what Red and Smith had lost was now with Tom, and a good helping of Shafer's as well.

Tom took no pleasure in making Shafer miserable, but he didn't lose any sleep over it, either. He'd done it enough times that he was used to it, and yet he'd never seen the other man this way. Shafer was *conflicted*. It was strange, and Tom felt bad for him.

"Is it getting late yet?" Tom took out his watch and consulted it.

"I can go till dawn," Cyril said. He'd noticed Shafer as well, and it puzzled him.

"You never saw me try to leave early," Shafer said, and it was mostly true. He did a good job saying it as well, but there was a single point of sweat there on his forehead, and even after all this time, he still didn't seem to be aware of the way he would swallow constantly when he was upset.

The night was getting on, but the spectators weren't yawning; now that players were starting to bust and leaders were emerging, they were even more keen. Tom was already hearing murmurs about the winners' table and what the buy-in would be. There hadn't been anything in writing about it, so they'd hash it out tonight, if anyone even wanted in. Tom didn't *particularly* want to linger, and he might not be the only one, but that would be a discussion for later.

Cyril took two big hands, Shafer was the bigger loser for them, and Tom came up lucky with four threes off the draw. He bet high, but no one took the bait.

Shafer's chips were dwindling, though.

"Reckon we'll have to up the ante again," Tom said to Cyril, putting his cards down, "if we're to stay awake."

"I wish you wouldn't talk about me like I wasn't here," Shafer said, and he was no actor. He'd honed his poker face, at least to a point, but the rest of him wasn't cut out for it. Anyone who knew him would know he was all out of sorts. Of course, most of the people here didn't know him.

"You won't be for long," Tom told him tiredly, his eyes on his cards. "But I'll come tuck you in after Cyril and I get finished."

It was about the most vicious thing he could've said, and Tom did a quick count of his chips, then Cyril's. The quiet had deepened a bit; several onlookers were visibly taken aback. Some tables were downright chatty, each of them a little party, but not this one. Red had talked only when he was winning, and Shafer was the same. Cyril was always quiet, and Tom opened his mouth only if it was going to help him win. Smith hadn't said anything because he'd realized how badly he had miscalculated, and he'd spent the whole night terrified out of his wits. Tom didn't have much sympathy for him.

"What's the matter, Shafer? You forget how to ante?" Tom gave him a meaningful look and accepted his new hand.

"I can see why you're so sure of yourself," Shafer said. This was the moment; he was going all in, just not with his chips. "Tom Calvert."

"For God's sake, Shafer. I been doing this for ten years. Shouldn't I be?"

"It's because you haven't played this game straight."

He actually said it. If Tom hadn't known it was coming, he'd have sat there like a man just struck by lightning. He would've questioned his ears. But he'd known. Shafer's plan if he lost hadn't been to cheat; it had been to call Tom a cheat.

Tom wasn't a Christian man, but sometimes it was good practice to do the Christian thing regardless.

He hesitated for a moment in the sudden quiet that had spread. "Shafer," he said, rubbing his face, "I believe I didn't hear you correctly."

"You heard me," Shafer said.

"It's been a while since someone said something like that to me," Tom said, getting to his feet, and Shafer got up too.

That seemed to wake everyone up, and they moved back, but Mr. Carroll hurried forward, alarmed. He cleared his throat, but Tom raised a finger to stop him from saying whatever he'd been about to say.

"I wouldn't get involved, Mr. Carroll," he said politely. "It's not the prettiest part of the business, but it isn't up for negotiation. There isn't a player in this room who isn't ready to fight for his name. You wouldn't want to be the man to try to stop me."

Mr. Carroll took that in, and his wife clutched at his arm. A couple of his men were nearby, and they were still armed, but he calmed them with a look. Mr. Carroll might not have expected a fight on his boat, but he knew better than to think he could avoid one now. Tom had given Shafer a chance to take it back, and he hadn't done it.

Tom knew why, but did Mr. Carroll? It didn't look like it, but he was a shrewd man and not an easy read himself.

Cyril laid his cards down carefully, just as Tom had done. He pulled his chair back and moved out of the way.

"Shall we step outside?" Tom asked dryly, gesturing toward the double doors to the deck. It was interesting to be in this situation aboard a boat, but more than interesting, it was inconvenient. His night had just gotten that much longer, when what he really needed was to rest up for tomorrow.

Shafer just did it without a word. The fact that he didn't say anything just made it all the more startling. Tom wouldn't have thought him a terribly strong man, but Shafer flipped the poker table like it was nothing.

Tom and everyone else fell back as it crashed down, cards and chips flying, and the sensible corners of Tom's mind just kept going about their business. He'd counted the chips, but had Cyril? And they couldn't very well play the hand now, so how would they proceed? He was thinking about details when he needed to think about other things, like why Shafer would have *done* that.

Tom knew, of course. The table had landed upside down, shaking the deck. Shafer had done this because he'd used something sticky, resin by the smell of it, to stick several cards to the underside of the table in Tom's spot. Tom was playing in shirtsleeves with those sleeves rolled up, as always, so it was really about the only way to paint him as a cheat.

Shafer stared at the place where the cards had been before Tom had found and discreetly removed them half an hour ago. It wasn't pity that Tom felt, though it was something like it. It seemed unlikely that Shafer genuinely wanted to fight, so his notion must have been that if Tom's cheat was revealed, the room would take his side. And it very well might have, and that could have gone very badly.

"How are we going to finish the game now?" Tom asked sourly, folding his arms.

Shafer didn't have an answer. He was speechless. And after Tom's warning to Mr. Carroll, no one else was going to say anything. Seconds that must have been agonizing for Shafer crept by as he stood, hands shaking, redder than the paint on the face cards.

Tom just looked at him.

This was an escalation. Shafer had always been an unpleasant man to be around, but never, to Tom's knowledge, had he done anything more dishonest than take advantage of lonely women with more money than sense. If he couldn't be a threat at the table, he wanted to be a threat in another way. What he didn't realize was that Tom wasn't in the business of being grifted.

Shafer wouldn't be the first sore loser who Tom sent down below, and Tom doubted he was lucky enough that Shafer would be the last. It wasn't what he'd hoped for, stepping aboard this boat, but griping wouldn't make it any better.

There were too many people in this room whose opinions mattered for Tom to put Shafer down now. He'd be justified, but it wasn't good for business if he was seen that way too often. Mr. Carroll in particular didn't want to see it. And his wife might *believe* she wanted this excitement, but she didn't really want to see this up close.

No, dealing with Shafer in front of all these people would be very bad for business.

And business had to come first.

Tom took a step toward the other man, who was rooted to the spot. He reached out and took a handful of Shafer's lapel and pulled him close but warily. Shafer appeared to be frozen, but he might not have been, and he might very well have a knife.

"Do you have any last words, Jeff Shafer?" Tom asked, sounding every bit as bored as he had at the table.

"I," Shafer said, drawing up and gulping. He raised his hands and set his jaw, a drop of sweat running down his face. "I made a mistake. I was wrong, Calvert."

That was good to hear. Probably good for his soul too, though the Almighty wasn't known for his love of gamblers. Especially bad ones.

"Is that an apology?" Tom cocked his head.

"Yes!" Shafer flinched at the slightest movement, in this case Tom letting him go. He narrowly avoided crashing into the people behind him.

"Then I accept," Tom told him, taking out his pocket watch and glancing at it.

Shafer stood there.

"Well?" Tom pressed.

"What?"

Tom held up his watch and gave it a little shake. "Hadn't you better clean up this mess you made?" He indicated the table and the chips. "I recall the accounts, and I'm sure Cyril does as well. We still have cards to play. Wouldn't be right to let one mistake ruin it. Hell, Shafer, we all make mistakes."

There wasn't a chance that Shafer would endure the humiliation of picking the table up; he stalked away, and Tom let him go.

Cyril was a few paces off, eyes calculating. He'd probably already put it together, but he wouldn't say anything to anyone as long as Tom didn't. And Tom wouldn't; that would only make things messier than they already were.

Mr. Carroll's help appeared to put the table right, and Tom helped himself to a glass of water and a small sweet pastry from a passing tray. He *wanted* coffee, but his nerves were still stirred up, and that would make him jumpy. The card table was the wrong place to be jumpy. Well, at least he wasn't quite so sleepy now.

Shafer had to be dealt with, but not before the game was over. The game *had* to come first. In his mind, Tom saw Shafer as a portrait on the wall, and he threw a curtain over it. He wouldn't think of him again until the work was done. Shafer would still be there, but Tom needed all his concentration if tonight was going to end the way he wanted it to.

The table was back, and the accounts he gave were the same as Cyril's. They took their chairs, and Mr. Carroll appeared, looking understandably worried.

"Mr. Calvert," he said.

"Yes, sir?"

"I thank you for resolving that matter in a gentlemanly way."

"No need. Thank you for being a gracious host. I expect we'll deal a new hand," he said, glancing at Cyril, who nodded agreement. "And Mr. Shafer's account will serve as our ante; he won't be coming back this evening, and he's left money on the table."

Carroll nodded slowly. He'd been around cards a long time, but he was new to running the show, and this was a situation he clearly hadn't thought about.

"I can't imagine anyone would object to that," he said.

"Well, now," Tom said, smiling. "where were we, Cyril?"

"Your luck was just about to change, Tom," the other man replied.

And they picked up their cards.

CHAPTER FIVE

Tom pushed both doors open and went out into the cold.

It was as still as the grave; the wind couldn't even be bothered to stir the hanging lanterns. That made it a little less frigid, but he had his coat back on now. After rubbing his hands together, he shut the doors behind him and joined the four figures gathered around a little stove on the balcony. The boat creaked, but the water was so calm that the boat scarcely moved.

Russell was there, an empty beer glass in his hand. And Pollock, as expected, was working on a plate piled with cake. Mark McLaughlin had come out on top of his table, beating out Pete Gibbs, and the fifth winner was a stranger to Tom.

"God Almighty," Pollock said, peering at his watch in the light from the stove, "what took you, Tom?"

"I thought I had him," Tom yawned, scratching his

chin. "He thought he'd had it too, and he was ready. He drew for the inside straight. I don't know who was more surprised: him or me." Once it was clear he wouldn't be inching his way back into the game, Cyril had started to bet a little more aggressively, and luck had been on his side. It had taken Tom more than another full hour to get all that money back.

But he had, and that was no surprise to anyone.

"Sir," Tom said, putting his hand out to the stranger.

"Mr. Tom Calvert," the fellow said from behind his red mustache. "Carl Poplin."

Tom had heard of him. "I'm glad to meet you."

"And you as well. You're a kind man."

"Hardly." Tom brushed himself off. He hadn't really taken mercy on Shafer; he'd only given him a reprieve. Once they were out of polite company, that score would have to be settled.

"Boys, it's late," Russell said, shaking his empty glass.

"Hell, Russell, who made you president?" Tom asked, and Pollock choked on his cake.

"I'd agree that it's late in the evening to be holding elections," Poplin said dryly. "Mr. Carroll ain't hiding that he wants us for another night."

"He sure ain't," Pollock grunted. "I believe he might pay us if we unionize."

Tom grinned. "I'm inclined to humor him, but I *am* a little risk averse at the moment," he said.

Russell snorted. "It's all right, Tom. I'll wager no one set foot on this boat to have a big night."

That was a relief to hear; Tom *wanted* to walk away now. The buy-in had been three thousand dollars, so each winner was now holding fifteen. They could potentially agree to have a seventy-five-thousand-dollar table tomorrow, but it didn't look like there was much appetite for that.

Poplin ran his hand through his hair. "I could stand to do five."

"Five sounds good to me," Tom agreed readily. They'd all leave the boat with at least ten in their pockets, and someone would go home with twenty-five. *That* was a good two nights of poker for an out-of-the-way game like this, and a nice start for Mr. Carroll's little venture. In fact, there was a chance they could talk him into chipping in a little himself so the stories of the pot could be that much more colorful.

And that would be a good game. Tom looked at the four of them. It would be anyone's game, not like tonight, where there had been only a single upset. There was no saying who'd get that money tomorrow. Tom was afraid of Russell the same way that Shafer was afraid of Tom, but that didn't mean he'd lose. And the only way to put that fear to bed would be to step up and make something happen. He wouldn't do that by being a coward and clutching his fifteen thousand like it was his first win. It was only money; he could always win more.

"Is that settled? We'll each sit with five thousand?" Russell asked, raising an eyebrow and looking at each of them.

"I'm good for it," Tom replied, and Poplin nodded, looking pleased.

"All right," Pollock said.

Mark sighed. "And I'll look like a spoilsport if I ain't there," he grumbled. "I'll sit."

Poplin drained his glass and tossed it overboard. "All right, boys. We got us a game."

They shook on it and, tired and shivering, crowded

back into the boat. It was still warm but much quieter. Any cardplayer would've found the showdown between Tom and Cyril fairly exciting, but it had been the last of the night and stretching on endlessly. Most of the guests had started making for their beds as midnight grew near.

There were a few of Carroll's people still cleaning up the dining room and no one else in sight. Tom stopped one of them from taking away a tray of cured meats and cheeses, and took it for himself. He never ate too much before an evening game, and his stomach was grumbling. It had been a long night, and even the old cabins aboard this boat would've seemed welcoming, spiders and all.

There wasn't the same money and prestige on this boat and this river as there would be in the bigger games on the Mississippi between Saint Louis and New Orleans, but those boats couldn't be any more comfortable than this one. Whether it was Carroll or his wife, they'd outdone themselves.

Tom made his way down to his cabin, only to find a familiar figure in the corridor.

The kid was still dressed as though he belonged on the boat, and the clothes were only a little too big for him. Tom hesitated, but the boy was between him and his room.

"Mr. Calvert," the boy said by way of greeting.

Tom looked over his shoulder, then approached, chewing ham. "Kid, I don't know that I want to be seen with you, not knowing what you've been up to."

The kid swallowed, licking his lips and looking around suspiciously. "Yes, mister. Um, and I don't know . . ." He trailed off, showing nerves.

Tom frowned. "What's the matter with you?"

"I don't know," the boy went on suddenly, drawing himself up, "that I want to be seen with *you*." He spoke as though his words were supposed to mean something.

Tom's brows rose. "Oh?"

The kid gave him a meaningful look and nodded vigorously, lowering his voice. "On account that there might be someone nearby who means you harm, mister."

The boy was bad at about everything he tried his hand at, including communication, but Tom still understood. He sighed and nodded.

He had helped the boy out before, and the kid wanted to return the favor. That was fair enough.

He nodded. "I understand."

The boy smiled at him, then hurried off. He'd been waiting here just to deliver that warning? Tom snorted and, shaking his head in wonder, went to his cabin. The second Shafer had gotten out of earshot, of course he'd have been talking about all the things he'd like to do and perhaps even intended to do—after all, Tom had been wrong, dead wrong. He never would've guessed that Shafer would stoop low enough to try something like that, and that could've been a very costly miscalculation. If he hadn't gotten it figured and found those cards, there was no saying what might've happened when Shafer flipped that table. Tom's reputation was only slightly less important than his neck, and Shafer had gone after both.

The temptation to go visit him right now was strong, but that was a bad idea.

Tom closed his door and locked it, then pulled off

his coat and took a breath. There was plenty of time to sleep; he'd be well rested in time for the game tomorrow. Shafer would get off the boat first thing in the morning, and he might well anticipate what Tom was going to do, so he'd have a head start. That was all right; Tom wouldn't chase him. Shafer was a bad player, but he was still a player, so no matter what, he'd always end up at the table. Their paths would cross again, and when they did, Tom would make sure Shafer would never do anything like this, or anything at all, ever again. It was that simple.

He set down his tray and gave in to sloth, lying back to eat like a Roman lord in a painting. And why not? The river outside and the creaking of the boat were a good lullaby, and his neighbors were quiet.

He wouldn't count on winning tomorrow. Most likely he'd leave the boat with ten thousand, and he'd need three times that much before he sat down with Miss Ayako again. That would take time, unless he had a run of remarkable luck. Nights like this didn't come along often; it was easy to find big-money games and easy to find weaker players, but it wasn't often you found them both at the same table. When a good hand came along, you took it. When a chance like this showed up, you didn't question it. Would there be another? It didn't matter.

There was a knock at the door.

Tom swallowed his mouthful of cheese and swung his legs out of bed. It was probably Carroll; he hadn't been around when the game finally wrapped up, and that was unusual. On the other hand, he was new to this business, and it was late. Tom got to his feet and stepped to one side of the door.

"Who is it?"

"Fiona Bannon, Mr. Calvert," a young woman replied.

Tom reached for the lock but hesitated. He hadn't requested any companionship, but it wasn't unheard of for it to be offered gratis under the circumstances. He hesitated a moment longer, then covered his mouth as another yawn came on.

"Ma'am, I'm tired," he said truthfully. "But thanks all the same."

"Sir, I only need a moment of your time." She sounded nervous.

Tom had heard only one set of footsteps, and they'd been light ones. Whoever she was, she was alone.

He turned the lock and opened the door.

This woman had been in the dining room tonight, but she hadn't been one of the girls in low-cut dresses trying to get noticed by the players with the biggest stacks of chips. She'd been right there next to Mrs. Carroll all night, whispering and giggling and wearing a dress that had probably crossed an ocean to be here tonight.

That dress was torn, her hair was a mess, and the fear and nerves coming off her were like heat from a furnace.

A little while ago, he'd had time to spare. He'd worked out Shafer's game well before he needed to.

This time, it took him just a moment too long.

She screamed, and Tom had already grabbed for her, hoping to cover her mouth before she could do it—but he wasn't fast enough. She gave him a hard shove, and without really meaning to, he grabbed her arm. The girl was so slight that he couldn't possibly stay on his feet, and he toppled back into the room as heavy footsteps thundered up the corridor, and the girl stumbled past him to catch herself on the bed.

Tom fell, hitting his head and seeing enough stars that it looked as though there were two Shafers coming through the door, and they each had a gun in hand. Where had he gotten a gun? Maybe the same place he'd found the audacity to do something like this.

Maybe Tom had never given Shafer enough credit. He had all this nerve, and maybe some good sense to go with it; maybe he *realized* he was a dead man and had chosen to make the first move. He'd even done it in a way that might justify what he was about to do.

Tom groaned as the muzzle of the pistol came to bear on him.

"Tom Calvert, what have you done?" Shafer roared.

CHAPTER SIX

SHAFER WAS NO better at this showmanship now than he'd been a few hours ago. The words were stilted and false, but they'd been loud and heard by many, and that was all that would matter.

It would be suspect for Shafer to go from fool to hero in the space of an evening, but a little suspicion wouldn't sink him, and Tom would be dead. That made it a good exchange from Shafer's position. No one could argue that.

Tom jerked the rug from under the other man's boots, and Shafer managed not to fall, but the gun went off.

The shot boxed Tom squarely on the ears, and as they rang and his eyes swam, something warm touched his cheek. He looked over to see the woman there, with a bullet hole where her eye had been and not much left of the back of her head.

Her body thudded to the floor of the cabin, and Shafer made a noise like a gasp.

Tom's hand found purchase on the table, and he shook his head to clear it. Nausea wasn't the only thing he had to push aside to move forward, but it was by far the biggest. He lurched to his feet and Shafer scrambled into the corridor, slamming the door. Tom wasn't having that, and he barely heard the other man shouting about how Tom Calvert had just shot an innocent woman; his ears were still ringing, and he didn't care.

Tom kicked the door off its hinges, but Shafer had already gotten out of the way and was fleeing. Tom stepped into the corridor, and Shafer would've had a clear shot, but he couldn't very well take it; enough people were bound to notice that *he* was the one with a pistol in his hand, not Tom.

As the thought entered Tom's head, and people started to poke their heads out of their rooms, Shafer ran right into a suddenly opened door. If there wasn't a woman lying dead in his cabin for no damned reason at all, Tom might've found humor in that.

Shafer rebounded and hit the wall, along with the oil lamp mounted on it, knocking it free. He caught himself on his hands and knees as the lamp shattered, and that startled him enough to leap away from the sudden flames.

Tom started forward, and as a few people with sense shut their doors, more opened them. Red Parker started to emerge from his cabin, half dressed, and Tom just shoved him back in and closed the door as he passed. This was none of Red's business.

He scooped up the fallen pistol and hurried past the

flames, following the chaos that trailed behind Shafer and his panicked shouts.

Tom had a temper, though it didn't poke its head out often. He hadn't felt even a touch of it when he reached under the poker table and found those cards there. He'd been too surprised, most likely. Impressed, even. He hadn't learned the hard way that temper didn't belong at the table; it had never been a problem to begin with. He was always too focused on the money to give a thought to how he *felt* about what was going on.

This wasn't like that.

One of Carroll's men clattered down the steps ahead, his pistol in his hand. "You put that down," he warned.

Tom heard the words, but he heard them in the same way he heard a sermon on the rare Sunday that he sat for a service. These words weren't anything that would ever matter to him. He kept walking, and the man raised the pistol.

"He went too far," Tom told him, and it was strange to hear the words come out so calmly. "Move out of my way."

Only he wouldn't. The man went to cock the pistol, and Tom shoved it aside and kicked the other man's legs out from under him. There wasn't much room in the corridor, much less on the stairs; the man was big enough that he couldn't properly fall. Worse, Carroll wasn't hiring just anyone off the street. This fellow was big and strong, and this sort of trouble wasn't entirely new to him.

He hit back, and Tom ducked, flipping the pistol to give him a blow to the head with the handle, only the man caught his arm. Tom rammed his knee into his groin, and that set the bigger man back. Tom dealt him a headbutt, then heaved him down to fall into the hallway in a tangle.

With that, he was climbing, and there were quite a few people out of bed now.

And a strong smell of smoke, but Tom didn't much care about either of those details. More trouble waited on the next deck, more housecoats, nightgowns, and confusion. He pushed through the puzzled people, only for a strong hand to catch him by the arm.

It was Dan.

"What in the world is going on, Tom?" the other man demanded, not a trace of sleep on his face. His eyes were searching; he must've heard Shafer's shouts.

Good. Then Shafer *had* come this way.

Carroll was suddenly there as well, eyes wide. "Yes, put it out!" he was shouting at someone.

"He went too far," Tom repeated. Those were the only words he had. There was more to say, but that wasn't going to happen; Tom was done talking. It would've been too far even if Shafer's stupidity hadn't killed that poor girl.

A piercing scream came up from down below. One of the women fleeing the fire must've gone past the room and seen the body. Couldn't blame her; she'd been a pretty girl. Not anymore.

Tom pulled free, and Dan grabbed him again.

"Tom," he began, and Tom hit him hard enough to put him to sleep for a week. Dan crashed into Carroll, and both men went down in a heap. There were more screams, and a bullet went by his head close enough that he felt the tiniest sting to his earlobe.

He whirled and fired rapidly, aiming much too high

to hit anyone. The people dashing around didn't deserve to be shot, but he had to make the shooter think twice. Was it Shafer or one of Carroll's men?

Tom's money was on Shafer. He shoved a man out of his way and went into the hall, seeing doors bang shut on the other end of the room. Coughing, he stumbled after, feeling a touch of a cold draft. His head swam, and he didn't know if that was his anger or the smoke, but it would take more than that to slow him down.

There was a bang behind him, but this was no gunshot, just the note that came before it. He twisted around to see the door bounce back from where it had hit the wall when Carroll's man kicked it open.

Tom fired in midstep, and the other man's pistol fell to the deck as blood streamed down his arm. There was still enough of his brain left standing to know it wouldn't be right to kill Carroll's guards. Carroll's poor taste in friends couldn't be blamed on them. At least, not unless they didn't take the hint.

With that, Tom went on.

Smoke was coming up between the floorboards. They'd gone one way toward the front of the boat, and then Shafer had come back toward the stern. Their rooms and the fire were right down below. That was why there weren't any people here; they were all making for the fore to get away from the worst of the smoke and the flames.

And what was Shafer's plan? He'd have one, wouldn't he? He must have liked making plans, as he'd made and executed two already just today.

Eyes red and burning, Tom shouldered through the doors and onto the rear deck. He recoiled, shielding his watering eyes from the blinding moon, bright and low in the black sky. His waistcoat protected him from the icy wind about as well as a bedsheet might have, and though his hands turned to ice, his knuckles were still white on the revolver.

Shafer was there, and Tom had never seen a man so wild and terrified. There was no telling if it was Tom who had him scared or the sight of what he'd done, but either way, maybe for the first time in his life, Shafer had a levelheaded notion of what was coming.

Had this all come about because of Holly? Because Tom hadn't set out to embarrass the man that way; that had been pure chance, *real* chance, not the kind of chance you saw at the table. How was he to know Shafer had brought a girl from a bordello, let alone one Tom had met in the past?

No, that wasn't it. Shafer hadn't dreamed up his plot at the table in the space of just an hour; he'd been cooking that up since long before Tom had even set foot on the boat.

Not everyone saw the world the way that Tom did. Not everyone could put it all away and let the table be the whole world. Tom could laugh at anything, but there were men out there who couldn't. He *knew* that what was a joke to him might not have been a joke to Shafer. Tom had a notion that he wasn't the easiest man to deal with. He *had* set out to needle Shafer tonight, after all.

It did not justify what the other man had done.

Shafer was saying something, but the wind was blowing now, and with the ringing in his ears, Tom couldn't hear him. A few sparks swirled in the dark, and Shafer backed away, but there was nowhere to go.

He caught the railing at the stern and glanced at the dark water, then raised his hands.

Tom was close enough to hear him now.

"I was wrong, Calvert," he was saying.

"Yeah," Tom replied, nodding. "You said that earlier."

"I can make it right."

"I don't need you to do that. I'm going to do that myself."

"I was wrong, Tom!"

"Keep saying that," Tom told him. "Maybe in hell it'll do you some good." He shoved the muzzle of the pistol into Shafer's belly and pulled the trigger. The shot echoed out into the night as Shafer fell back, shocked. He clutched at his bleeding belly and gave Tom a blank look.

He made a noise.

"No," Tom told him. "Don't die here. Then we'd have to waste a coffin on you." He grabbed Shafer by his coat and shoved him overboard, watching him splash into the dark wake behind the steamboat.

It was too dark to hear, but there was only the one splash. Shafer wouldn't ever come up, not in water that cold with a bullet in him. Purely out of habit, Tom tucked the gun into his belt, just as he would his own.

In the dark, he looked down at his hand, which shook badly. It wasn't nerves; it was temper. He shook his head in disgust. It wasn't dignified. It was all wrong. A man like Shafer shouldn't have been able to make him feel this way, or act this way, to be perfectly honest. Calm was just another word for control, and this had taken all that away. In a strange way, he felt *robbed*.

The worst part was that the temper wouldn't go. Shafer was dead, and Tom still seethed. The boat was on fire, but his blood was even hotter. Grinding his teeth, he turned away from the railing to find that he wasn't alone.

Carroll was there, and Dan, and another of his hired men, and a few others Tom didn't know personally. There was no gratification for him in the looks on their faces. This wasn't their business, and he didn't much care how they felt about it. Shafer was sinking to the bottom of the Missouri, and Tom didn't feel a thing but the cold. By now Shafer would be gone, and in Tom's accounting, that made it a quick death. More than Shafer had deserved.

"He shot that woman," Tom called out over the wind, and he had to put up his hand as the wind changed, bringing billowing black smoke toward him. Though his eyes burned and watered, he could still see that the fellow next to Dan had his hand on his pistol.

Dan was rubbing his jaw where Tom had hit him.

"The gun is in your hand," Carroll shouted back.

No, it wasn't; it was in his belt, but that wasn't the point.

Tom looked as hard as he could, but the smoke and the dark and the twenty paces that separated them were too much. He didn't know if Carroll had been in league with Shafer. Had they been friends or allies? Anything was possible. Carroll was rich and powerful, but that didn't mean he had good judgment. Had he simply been taken in by Shafer's game? Shafer had always been better at playing people than cards. Was Carroll a decent man who'd found himself in the company of a scoundrel?

Tom's anger wasn't leaving, but his exhaustion was coming to join it.

"He slandered me two times," he said loudly enough to be heard, "and tried to murder me."

"I do not know that!"

"Mr. Carroll, Tom already won fair," Dan pointed out cautiously. "He's got no reason to be looking for trouble. And Shafer wasn't right tonight. We all saw that."

"I trust Jeff Shafer," Carroll said stubbornly, and Tom felt his eye twitch. He'd already lost his temper; it had run off so suddenly and fast that there hadn't been a hope of catching it, so he couldn't very well lose it again, could he? It was already gone. It hadn't gone off alone, though. It had taken other things with it, like good sense.

Carroll didn't have a reputation for being a fool, but he was one. He'd just put it out there for everyone to see.

"Then you and your stupidity can keep him company," Tom said tiredly. He pulled and fired. The bullet should've gone right between Carroll's eyes, but there was no bullet.

The hammer had fallen on an empty chamber.

CHAPTER SEVEN

It wasn't as though it was the first time he'd made a mistake.

It didn't seem fair, though, the way that he'd spent so long trying to slow down. Sometimes you had to be quick, but *most* of the time, it was better to be slow and easy. Better not to do things on impulse without thinking them through.

For a long time, he'd told himself that thinking was the best thing he could do, but then he'd been too slow. Too slow to stop that girl from screaming, too slow to grab the railing and vault over as shots cracked out over the black water, spooking bats from the trees on the riverbank and filling the air with the stench of gunpowder.

It wasn't lost on him that if he'd been a little slower, a little more thoughtful, he might not have *needed* to go over that railing.

But he couldn't change the past. This could go with

everything else on the pile of things that couldn't be taken back. It didn't do any good to dwell on that, but at the same time, there wasn't much choice but to regret them.

Regret was a feeling, though. And Tom didn't have much of that because of the cold. Inconveniently, it wouldn't do to simply freeze, as one was inclined to do in times like these.

There was mud beneath him, and that didn't seem quite right; he'd hit the water in the widest part of the river, and he couldn't have done any swimming under the circumstances. The current hadn't brought him here; the current didn't have teeth.

They were chattering in the dark, not just Tom's, but someone else's as well.

Something was happening, but he was so numb that he couldn't tell what. The blinding moon swam as someone dragged him arduously out of the water. Tom wasn't a heavy man by any means, and he was only of average height, but his rescuer struggled as though Tom were a giant.

Something obscured the moon, but it was all a blur. He was underneath trees, the bare limbs waving and scratching in the dark as the knifelike breeze whistled by. The sound came and went, and he didn't know if it was his ears or the wind. He was thinking, though only slowly. And his mouth didn't even work as well as his brain, but he used them both regardless.

"Matches in my pocket," he said, and it wasn't a great speech, but it took as much work as one. Or it felt like it did. He tried to gesture, but his arm was so weak and clumsy that it likely wasn't much help in the dark.

But someone was touching him, and it was the first

time in his life that he didn't mind the notion of someone going through his clothes. The teeth kept chattering in the dark, and as though it was someone else's problem, he listened to the sounds with sympathy. Whoever it was, they were as cold as he was, and trying to find a dry match to light kindling with icy, numb fingers would be a miserable chore.

In time, a light appeared. It grew and became flames, and the snapping of branches filled the air as someone ineptly tried to build a fire, using all the wrong fuel by the sound of things: damp branches and ones that were still green. Steam rose from Tom, but there was smoke as well. He was too frozen and spent to be bothered or even curious.

The fire grew, and as the numbness faded, the pain crept in. Not only from his icy body, but from his right leg. Something was there, pressing on it, making it hurt even more.

He remembered those two shots, and that flash of fire as he went over the side. Who had hit him? Dan? Or the other fellow?

It had to have been the other fellow. If Tom was still alive, then Dan had missed, and Dan would have only missed on purpose.

Sitting up didn't feel likely, but he could open his eyes. The boy from the boat knelt over him, pressing both hands and some cloth to his leg, maybe his own waistcoat. The boy's skin was white as a sheet, and his lips were blue. His terrible haircut was even worse, stuck to his face as it was.

He looked about as bad as Tom felt, but *he* didn't have a bullet in him. Well, neither did Tom—it had gone through—but all the same . . .

"It's all right," Tom managed to say. "You can leave it."

The boy looked uncertain, but if that big vein in his leg had been hit, Tom would've been dead a good while ago. He was no doctor, but he knew that much.

After a long hesitation, the boy drew back his bloody, trembling hands and put them out to the fire, glancing worriedly at Tom. What was he so worried about? The *boy* would be fine; he just needed to warm up. He didn't have this fiery, throbbing wrongness in his leg that Tom had, though that wasn't the most gracious thing to consider. He wasn't so far gone that he didn't know the kid had saved his life.

He watched the boy huddle by the fire, or tried to, but his eyes were getting heavy. He wasn't sleepy, and he certainly wasn't comfortable, but he was fading fast.

"Mr. Calvert?"

He was polite, even if he wasn't the brightest. Why would he do that? Jump into the river to pull Tom out? He had no cause to do that.

"The boat's gone," he said.

Of course it was.

The pain was about as bad as it would get now, though there was a tingling in his fingers and toes, a bit of the warmth trying to come back. The boy pushed more sticks onto the fire. Once it was big enough, it didn't matter if he'd built it up correctly or not, and the blaze was growing.

Tom lay perfectly still, his jaw set. He had never been shot before, and it was a good deal more painful than he'd have thought. It wouldn't have been any better in good weather.

"Which side of the river is this?" he asked quietly,

though the words came out as barely more than labored breaths.

"The west side," the boy replied.

Tom tried to think. There wasn't much else to do but think, lying there in the dark. How long had they been aboard the boat, and how much speed had she been making? He had enough brains left to ask the questions, but not to find the answers. And it seemed foolish to think about tomorrow when tonight wasn't by any means settled.

He couldn't think about tomorrow, but he could see past it in a way.

He could see San Francisco or at least what he imagined it would look like. He could see himself in a white suit. He imagined a fine gambling den, the sort of place that figured in his future, and stacks of notes and chips alike.

And Miss Ayako in her strange dress that covered every inch of her, and didn't even cling too tightly, but he could look at her, and he wouldn't have a chance of keeping his mind on his cards. It had always bothered him, and now it always would, because if that den was real and Miss Ayako was there, he wouldn't be walking into it. Not next month, not next year.

Was it true, though? Was she really such a great player that he'd never had a chance? Or was it that he simply couldn't take his eyes off her, couldn't mind his own cards? Was that why he walked around singing her praises all day? Because he admired her so much, or because if she was that good, he must not be that bad?

"Mr. Calvert? Mr. Calvert?"

That brought him back, though he wasn't sure

where he'd gone. The warmth in his body was trying to come back like the glow in an ember, and the night was a blanket of knives, the cold piercing him as his leg ached.

"Yeah?" he groaned.

"Why did you help me?"

The kid said it, but those were Tom's words, because that was Tom's question. He wasn't sure why he hadn't asked—maybe because he wasn't sure he'd like the answer.

His eyelids were heavy but no longer frosted. He saw the boy looking at him. Even just breathing had become a chore, but Tom did what he could, and he answered the question honestly. That was the best way to do it.

"I don't know, kid."

CHAPTER EIGHT

Rough, panicked hands shook Tom awake.
Fire might have kept death away, but the cold
had never really left. He hissed, shivering, and his
body did its best to curl up of its own accord, but it
couldn't with his leg so stiff. How could his leg be on
fire this way and the rest of him be like ice?

The boy's face bled into the air, which was hazy and
pale in the light of dawn. One eye, two noses—the
numbers changed as Tom's eyes played tricks on him,
but the expression didn't. The boy was in a panic.

"Mister," he was saying.

Tom made a noise. It was meant to be a word, but it
didn't quite take shape. He would've pushed the boy
off; he didn't like being touched to begin with, but he
didn't have the strength. He was sweating, and that
didn't seem right. Why was it cold like this?

The boy vanished, and leaves crunched while the wind made the branches rustle.

Tom just closed his eyes and let his teeth chatter.

It was dawn but the world was dark, and the earth was rising up and shaking him. He was back aboard *Newlywed*, going after Shafer, but Dan was there, only this time it went differently. Instead of Tom being the one to throw a punch, it was the other man, and Tom fell and kept falling in the dark.

It hadn't been right to hit Dan. He'd regretted it the moment he had done it, but that hadn't slowed him down any. That had been real regret, not the same as what he had felt when he turned the gun on Carroll and pulled the trigger. He'd known it was a mistake, but he hadn't *regretted* it.

He didn't care much for regret, especially since it seemed to smell like a horse. When he opened his eyes, that was what he saw: chestnut fur and grass and rocks, and there was a rising and falling like ocean waves— and then concerned eyes.

The boy was there, trotting along beside the horse, watching him worriedly. Tom knew he wasn't at his best if he was draped over a horse and thinking about Dan of all people, but he just couldn't get it figured out. *Why* was the kid so worried? Did Tom look that bad? Of course he did, but why should the boy care any?

"He's dead already," a voice said, and Tom opened his eyes without remembering closing them. He squinted at the bearded face, which was squinting back, maybe out of necessity. He was an older man and apparently blind. "You see, son? He's already dead." Rough fingers prodded Tom's head.

The boy was there as well, wearing the only face he seemed to have: that worried one.

"I do not believe he is," he said hesitantly.

Tom was there, eyes open, looking straight back at the man. The horse whinnied and shuffled, and Tom nearly slipped off. The man made to prod him again, and Tom swatted feebly at his hand.

"Oh," the man said, taken aback. "I guess he ain't."

It wasn't long before he wished he was, and it was hard to say which was worse: the wound or the fever. But it wasn't the wound that made the passing ground seem to look like swaying, rippling waves of green and brown that made him sick to his stomach. No, the worst was the boy, with his fretting and hovering as though it would make one lick of difference to him what happened to Tom.

The fever couldn't take all the credit. His pride was also in there, making sure he didn't get too comfortable. No one could outrun a bullet, but he'd gotten into the habit of thinking that getting shot was something that happened to *other* people.

He'd said the words more than a few times over the years: *it wouldn't be my first mistake*. This was the first time he'd ever been surprised to find that it hadn't been his last.

"I'm wet," he said. It was true.

"Yes, mister," the boy said patiently from the dark. "It's raining."

That would explain it.

The best game of cards he'd ever played had been on a night when the whole sky had broken loose, like that story from the Bible in which all the people drowned. It rained so hard that sitting by a window was like sitting by a waterfall. Tom hadn't heard drops or a patter; it had just been a pounding scream for hours on end. The water had hammered that hotel like he'd hammered Dan's jaw.

Tom didn't have a lot of friends, except the spiders. There were two of them dangling. And one was lowering itself on a thread, coming closer to him. The room came into focus, more or less. It was small and dim, and he was tucked into what could only loosely be called a bed. There were blades and saws and traps hanging on the walls, and a fair number of skins on hooks from the ceiling.

And the spiders. Tom shifted, intending to knock them away, but the boy was right there beside him. He'd been dozing, but now he came awake.

Before Tom could say a word, the kid saw the spiders and recoiled, toppling out of his chair and crashing to the floor. That was enough of a surprise that Tom nearly forgot what he was doing, but he sat up and brushed the threads away. He wasn't quite sure what you said in a moment like this.

The boy, face red, picked himself up and brushed himself off, though he needed a good deal more than that. He needed a bath, and Tom wondered if that wasn't the first sleep he'd gotten since the boat. He rubbed his eyes, and there was a vague sense of time, but it was hard to be sure.

"Has it been one day or two?" he asked, moving gingerly and wincing. The pain was nearly enough to put him on his back again.

The boy cleared his throat and righted his chair. "Two days, mister."

That explained the strange but intense combination of hunger and nausea. And thirst; Tom's voice was a croak. He needed a bath just as badly. What was he even wearing? Nothing? He groaned. The notion of a bad morning wasn't new to him, but he'd never had one like this. It probably wasn't even morning.

He settled on a position, up on his elbow a little, and for the first time since he hit that water, things were clear. They weren't good, but he saw them as they were.

The boy still wore that worried face.

"Kid, looking at you, I'd think you were the one who'd gotten shot," he said.

There *was* some relief, and that was interesting. But the boy was still stretched thin over something. Tom could feel a bandage on his leg, and it was clear he'd been cared for.

"You found a doctor for me?"

The boy nodded. It was chilly, but he was sweating.

"What's wrong?"

"I do not have money to pay the physician." He swallowed. "Or the man who owns this bed."

For a moment, Tom could only look at him. Then he sniffed, cleared his throat, and shook his head. He peered around the little shack, and that was what it was—a trapper's shack. There were his clothes, filthy, spread about on the floor. That was probably where they'd fallen when the boy and the doctor had stripped him.

Tom squinted at the boy. "You really aren't a thief, are you?"

There was no answer for that apparently. Tom groaned and reached down for his waistcoat and trousers. There was his belt, and there was his pouch. Untouched. He snorted. Had it not even occurred to the boy?

There was money in the pocket of his waistcoat with his watch, and even his derringer was still there in the other pocket. He pulled them all out to find his watch mangled beyond recognition.

And a hole in his pocket.

"Oh, my," he said, letting out a long breath.

The boy tore his eyes away from the money in his hand. "What is it, mister?"

Tom held up the watch. "Maybe Dan didn't miss after all." He sighed. "I reckon I must've hurt his feelings. I wish I could tell him I'm sorry." He tossed the ruined watch away and thumbed through the money. The boy was scared. He'd pulled Tom out of the river, built a fire to keep him alive, talked some stranger into carrying him—somewhere—and now talked more people into helping. But he had *no* talent for the grift and no instincts to speak of. How had he done it? Tom had a hunch, and it made him want to laugh. The boy was small, he had an innocent face, and he didn't have to act much to look scared and clueless. He'd probably told the truth, and luck and pity had picked up the slack.

It could've gone the other way, though. One man would see a poor kid he'd want to help; another would see an easy victim. It looked like that hadn't occurred to the boy.

At least one of them had some good luck left. No, that wasn't true. Tom wasn't kidding himself: his luck hadn't run out; he'd just come into it. That was why he was still alive and without even being robbed. That was the *least* the boy could've done after saving him. As far as Tom was concerned, the boy would've been within his rights to help himself to anything on Tom's person and take off without a word. Tom still would've been grateful.

He shook his head. "Where are we, kid?"

"I do not rightly know, mister. We are north of where we came ashore, but not yet returned to Omaha."

"Well, I owe you one." Tom held out the money. It was about fifty dollars. Not much money to him, and certainly not much in exchange for his life, but by the look of things, it was more notes than the boy had ever seen in his life. "Pay whoever needs paying. The rest is yours. What's your name?"

Embarrassed, the boy took a moment to answer. "Ash—Asher Smith," he replied, eyes down.

"I'm grateful to you."

"You killed that man." Asher was giving him a more direct look now.

Tom grimaced. "You saw that?"

"You killed him because he did you wrong?"

"I was angry," Tom said truthfully. But then he nodded.

Asher nodded too, a serious look on his face. "I understand," he said.

Tom snorted, but he didn't know what to say.

"Were you a soldier?"

"What, kid?"

"I saw you with the gun. And you hit that man," Asher went on deadly serious. "Have you been to battle?"

Tom's brows rose. "No. No, kid. I play cards." He winced at a particularly nasty reminder from his leg. "But getting money's only half the game. The other

part is keeping it. That and you make the worst enemies at the table. Any decent poker player needs to
know how to handle himself. I'm not a soldier."

Asher took that in, looking at Tom very directly
now. He nodded, still with that strange look on his
face. "You know how to fight," he said.

There was a man in a box in Topeka who would
agree. One in Springfield too. And now Shafer made
three. Moving was painful, so Tom didn't shrug.

"I guess so, kid." He didn't know what else to say.

"What will you do now?"

Tom groaned and glanced at the ceiling, wary of
more spiders. "I made a mistake," he said, and Shafer's
voice was in his head, saying those same words. "I expect everyone on the boat'll think me dead." A moment went by, and he sighed. "That's for the best. Mr.
Carroll isn't the forgiving sort. I'll lie low a while. Not
much choice." He smiled. "I won't be seeing Miss Ayako
for a while now."

"Who is that?"

"A woman I admire."

"Are you to be married?"

Tom turned and looked at Asher as though he were
insane. "While I would like that very much, no. I don't
think she sees me that way." He rubbed his face. "And
I don't know that she ever will. It's all right. I just like
her, is all, but I can't go anywhere near her *now*. That'll
just get me killed and make trouble for everyone."

"I am sorry."

The boy meant it. Well, not all of it—his name
wasn't really Smith, for example—but he genuinely felt
sorry for Tom. That was nice of him. As for lying about
the name, Tom couldn't blame him for that. Even if he

had no affinity for the work, the grift had been on Asher's mind when he boarded that boat.

The boy was running; that much was clear. So was everyone else in the world: some away, some toward. It wasn't always easy to know the difference. This kid was educated but ignorant, polite but apparently willing to take both chances and liberties.

"It's all right," Tom told him. "If you can't make the play that'll help you win, sometimes you can make the one that'll help you not lose. I should hide. It's as simple as that."

There was a tap on the doorframe, though there was no door, just several thick blankets. The doctor didn't wait; he just brushed on through and drew himself up, immediately bumping his head on a hanging trap. Swearing, he focused on Tom.

"How do you feel, son?"

"Like someone shot me in the leg, I guess."

"Wasn't a lawman, was it, Mr. Calvert?"

"It was not," Tom replied before the words sank in. He didn't do anything as obvious as look at Asher. If there was a bright side, his hunger was gone, replaced by a whirlwind of nausea and cold. "Though I believe my name is Billings."

"No, your name is Tom Calvert. I heard what you done in Topeka."

Tom groaned. It wasn't Asher's fault at least.

"And the boy introduced you," the doctor added.

He cringed. So it was, then. Tom took a deep breath. "At any rate, I feel as though I'll live."

"You might, provided you stay off it and change that bandage every day. Now, if you see colors that ain't right or it swells, you heat your knife and cut it open.

Then you pour this on it. Then you bandage it tight."
The doctor knelt and handed him a bottle. "And the
same should it open for any other reason." He touched
Tom's forehead. "Fever's gone, and you're lucky, but it
ain't enough to be lucky. You're lucky and young, but
you had still best lie still a while. You hear?"

"I do," Tom said.

Real lucky. If this doctor knew Tom Calvert was
still alive, that meant other people likely would soon.
That made Tom a dead man.

CHAPTER NINE

IT WAS A camp for trappers, and there wasn't much to it. A whiskey hole with girls and a few beds, a livery, and something of a store that had no walls and was really just a tent. It should've been sleepy and sparse, only it wasn't.

There were a crowd of wagons and a staggering amount of cattle. They didn't belong, and they were clearly just passing through, but the noise and the smell were appalling.

That was what Tom was able to tell from his bed anyway. The sun was starting to set out there, and it was getting chilly.

The boy knocked politely and waited for an invitation to step inside. He had some bread, which he offered to Tom.

"Kid, why are you still here?"

Asher seemed taken aback by the question. "You

have to stay off your leg." He gestured toward the door. "You cannot go for things, Mr. Calvert."

Tom opened his mouth but stopped himself there. It was too late for an assumed name. There was no telling how many people the boy had spoken to, and Tom wasn't about to ask. The kid didn't know any better.

"You don't owe me anything more," Tom told him. "You didn't to begin with."

"I want to talk to you, Mr. Calvert."

"Go on and do it, then. Before I die."

"What?"

"Nothing." Tom gestured invitingly.

"What do you plan to do now?"

"You heard the man." Tom settled back. "Can't do much walking. And like I told you, I'll need to be quiet."

Asher just nodded, that grave look on his face. It didn't look right; it was a stupid expression for such a young face, though it also appeared well practiced. Someone had taken the time to teach this boy how to speak *very* politely, and then apparently they hadn't taught him anything else at all. You didn't ask a man you didn't know a question like that; it just wasn't done. And Tom wasn't in the business of being curious about other people, but he could hardly help it. He didn't ask, though.

The boy leaned forward, clasping his hands. "I mean, where do you plan to go?"

"I haven't thought that far ahead yet," Tom told him. Even if he'd had an answer, the kid liked to talk so much that it'd be wiser not to share it.

"Have you heard of a place called Friendly Field?"

"No. Where is it?"

Asher scowled. "I do not know exactly. I know it is

to the west. My hope is that as I go, I will find someone who can tell me how to get there."

"You got kin there?"

The boy swallowed. He shook his head but saw Tom's face. Tom wouldn't voice the question, but he didn't have to.

"I have heard it is a good place," the boy said.

"That's where you're trying to go?"

"Yes."

"You'll pardon my rudeness, but if you wanted to go west, what were you doing on a boat going south?"

Asher scowled. "I was . . ." He trailed off, glaring at Tom for a moment. "I did not realize that was where it would go."

So maps hadn't figured much in his education, it seemed. That was all right; maybe if Tom knew maps a little better, he could tell the kid where Friendly Field was, but he'd never heard of it. "Mr. Calvert, it must be a very small settlement. No one I have spoken to knows it. If no one knows about it, it seems unlikely that any-one would look for you there."

Tom took that in. "Yeah," he said, face expectant. "That's a thought."

"Mr. Calvert, I would like you to come with me."

Tom had sensed this coming, but he still didn't un-derstand it. "*Why* would you want that?" He looked at his leg, mercifully covered by the blanket, and ges-tured, shaking his head. "I'm a cripple. I'll be lucky if I ever walk right again." It hurt to say, but it was true. "Why do you want me around?" Because he *did* want Tom around, or he wanted to be around Tom. No one had forced him to do any of this, and no one was keep-ing him here now.

"It is a good proposition," the boy went on, and where he wasn't confident, at least he was earnest. "You would be on the move and away from whoever you might want to avoid. And you need help. You need it, Mr. Calvert. I am able. I can help you until you are well, and I am willing to do it."

"For what?"

"I cannot make my way alone. Not safely." He did have some sense, then. Maybe that moment on the boat, when he would've been in real trouble if Tom hadn't stepped in, had really gotten to him. Had that been the moment that he had realized he was in over his head? It would explain a lot.

"And I would like you to teach me," Asher said.

"Teach you what?"

"To fight. And shoot a pistol like you do."

"You'll get more use out of a rifle. And fighting's only what you do when things've gone wrong, kid. You're better off learning to make them go right."

"I know what I want to learn," the boy said stubbornly, a hint of irritation in his voice. He was even trying to make himself sound a bit gruff, but his voice hadn't even begun to change yet. It was sad.

"Why not learn to play cards?" Tom asked tiredly. "There's some money in that at least. You're a little small for fighting."

Small but maybe not quite as young as he looked. He chose his words like he was a little older.

"Done," the boy said, eyes burning. He hesitated for an awkward moment, then stuck out his hand. "Teach me to play cards, then. And I will help you till you are well."

Tom snorted. He eyed the boy's hand.

So that was what he'd been after. He'd clearly given this some thought when he'd been outside.

"Put that down, kid." Tom indicated with his eyes, and Asher lowered his hand, frowning. "We haven't gotten to that part yet. I have to move soon. I don't know how long it'll take Carroll to find out I'm still alive or what he'll do, but it's not a risk I need to take. If he sends someone after me, I have to have as much of a head start as I can."

Asher nodded.

"But," Tom went out, taking a deep breath, "I need to heal. I can't ride. I can go by stage, or I can go by wagon, and that makes things complicated."

Asher's face fell. "Do I have enough money to buy passage?"

"That's the wrong question. Do you know where these cattle are going? And those wagons out there?"

Asher shook his head.

"Go out there and find out."

The boy got to his feet.

"And, kid," Tom said, "you're not Asher Smith. You're Asher Calvert. You're my nephew."

Asher hesitated, then glanced back. "Does this mean we have an agreement?"

"Maybe. Go on, now. We're losing daylight."

CHAPTER TEN

⌒

T HE KID WORKED fast. They hadn't shaken on it yet,
but he knew he had Tom hooked. Laid up and
hurting, Tom couldn't very well pick and choose how
to get out of this camp. A willing pair of hands to help
was a proposition he couldn't turn down. Asher was
smart, even if he didn't know much.

The cattle belonged to Seth Fulton, and they were
going to Oregon. This Fulton family had money and
something of an entourage. A fair number of people
related to their outfit were traveling with them on the
drive rather than just getting on a train.

At Tom's instructions, Asher sought out the man
leading the party. His name was Breeden, and he'd led
the way to Oregon five times.

"I've heard of Fulton cattle," Tom told Breeden
when he was standing over Tom's bed in the little shack

with Asher watching quietly. "Big in Texas, aren't they? What do they need you for?"

Outside, notes from a harmonica were coming and going in the wind.

Breeden just folded his arms, stooping slightly because the shack wasn't tall enough for him. "Seth Fulton's a solid man, and he's run a dozen good drives. But this ain't him. What I got on my hands is his sons. They know their cattle and their ropes, but they ain't never traveled over land like this."

Tom chewed on that. The cattle couldn't have come from Texas; there was a deal of some kind going on, but the bigger picture was clear enough. Fulton was expanding, and he'd sent his sons to secure the livestock and get them to the new land.

"The boy said you were looking to join us. We ain't really that kind of party," Breeden said, but he said it politely.

"I'm laid up bad, Mr. Breeden. I'm not looking to join you, not exactly. I just want to explore my options. I'd like to go west, I'd like to go reasonably quickly, and a wagon's the best way for me to do it." Tom couldn't buy a train ticket; if Carroll wanted to be thorough, that was the first thing he'd look for.

"As I said," Mr. Breeden replied, holding his hat in his hands and looking apologetic, "I got four young men who are good at cattle and nothing else. And they and their kin are all right. They have what they need to make it. But I also got a contract for a crowd of Norwegians that don't. Half of them don't speak ten words, and more than half of them don't have two nickels to rub together. And I have to get them there, every last fool one of them. Me and my right hander, and that is all. We won't get no help from them Fultons. I can't take on deadweight."

"I wouldn't ask you to do it for free," Tom told him frankly.

It *was* a good prospect. You wouldn't expect to find Tom Calvert tucked away on a cattle drive. It was a long road, and it would go slowly. He could heal in a wagon with no one the wiser.

Breeden looked skeptical, but Tom held his gaze firmly.

"My nephew has no experience on the trail," Tom admitted. "But he isn't stupid. We'll be all right. And if we need help, I am willing to pay to get it. I don't have my hand out to you, sir."

The tall man scratched his short graying beard for a long moment. He twirled his hat on his finger idly and looked at Asher. Tom wasn't trying to hide his cards; he was letting Breeden know that he had the better position. This wasn't a time to bargain ruthlessly; it was a time to foster some goodwill.

"There is one thing that occurs to me," Breeden said finally. "A week ago a man died on the trail. One of the Norwegians. I still do not know why. He was not ill." He sniffed. "One morning he just didn't get up. He was traveling with his daughter."

Tom frowned. He wasn't sure where Breeden was going with this, but it wasn't the direction he'd expected things to take.

"Now she's alone, and she can't handle her wagon or her team. Wouldn't even know where to start. Matt's done it up to now, but his contract was up yesterday." He stopped and waved a hand. "It don't matter. The story don't matter. You buy that wagon from her and that team. I have another family that will take her if she has money in her pocket. This way she can stay with her own people and not be destitute. And you would have a wagon and a team." He shrugged. "And there ain't no reason you couldn't come with us if you could provision yourselves and turn your own wheels. It would need to be a fair price," he added. "I won't let you rob her."

Tom took that in. Mr. Breeden was a generous man; he might just as well have taken a bribe, then gotten a good price on that wagon. He wasn't asking for any money for himself, either.

"Is the wagon solid?"

"If it ain't, the Norwegians will help you fix it up. They'll be grateful to you, and they're damn good carpenters."

Tom didn't usually go out of his way for gratitude, but if gratitude would help him if his wagon broke down, so be it.

This was not what'd he'd pictured for himself in these next weeks and months. The thought of it made him queasy, but the only thing worse would have been to stay still. His skin was already tingling, and nerves were fluttering in his belly. He'd been in danger before, but never as an invalid.

They had to go.

"If you can swing that, I'll get the girl for you," Breeden said, brushing off his coat and moving toward the door. "But we leave in the morning either way."

"Will she be agreeable?"

"Her father is dead. She's traded away nearly everything she owns just to be kept up this long. She might come from . . ." He trailed off, gesturing vaguely. "A long way off, but she ain't no different from you and me." Breeden shrugged. "She needs money to live."

"How much money?" Tom asked.

Breeden hesitated but only for a moment. "Five hundred," he said.

"Oxen?"

"Yeah."

"We're going into the cold," Tom pointed out. He wasn't sure why he said it; that detail couldn't be lost on Breeden, but this wasn't the best time to be getting underway for this sort of thing. Tom was no pioneer, but he knew winter was nothing but trouble.

"Tell that to Fulton."

Of course. The Fultons were rich, and they weren't going to run out of anything. They didn't care if the trek was a little slower. They just wanted it done. The Norwegians, though—they would be in for a long and difficult winter. So would Tom if his leg wasn't doing better by then.

"All right," he said at last.

"You got that money?"

"I do."

"All right, then."

Breeden came back to the bed and put his hand out. Was that relief on his face? Was he really that worried about this girl? Why not? She needed help. Asher hadn't been thinking about learning to fight when he jumped into the water to help Tom; he'd just been trying to help.

It just came so naturally to these folks. Tom didn't understand it.

And he didn't need to.

"I'll tell her. She'll be happier than you can imagine," Breeden said.

This soon after her father's death? Tom doubted it, but he didn't say anything until after Breeden had gone.

"Kid," he began, but Asher was staring at him in horror. "What?"

"Five hundred dollars?" The boy was as white as chalk.

"Oh, for the love of God." Tom pinched the bridge of his nose. "Kid, you are the worst thief to ever walk God's earth." He picked up his pouch from his little pile of clothes beside the bed and shook it at him. "Did you not even think to steal it?"

Asher's mouth was open. "Your tobacco?"

"You ever seen this much tobacco?" Unbelievable. "I knew there was a thief on the boat," he added, giving Asher a meaningful look. "You think I'd just leave my winnings in my room?" Of course he'd kept them on his person.

"Then you have money?"

"It's the only thing I got. I don't even have clothes to wear," Tom snapped. The doctor hadn't really undressed him; he'd just cut all Tom's clothing off. "You might have stopped him from doing that," he added, plucking at the remains of his shirt.

"I was not present."

Tom squinted at him. "What?"

"I waited outside. I was not going to look at you without your clothes."

For a moment Tom just peered at the boy. "Then what was to stop *him* from robbing me if he wanted?"

"But he is a physician," Asher replied. He said it as though it meant something.

Tom took a long, deep breath. Then another one. "Can you read and write?" he asked finally.

"I can." Asher drew himself up and smiled.

"Go find me some paper and something to write with."

"For what?"

"Because we're about to buy a wagon. We'll also need to buy things to put in it," Tom explained patiently. "You're going to buy them. I'm going to give you a list."

The boy's smile grew, and he came a little closer to the bed. "Then we *do* have an accord," he said, putting out his hand again and grinning like an idiot.

"Yeah," Tom said tiredly. "Yeah, kid. We do." He reached out and shook.

The boy had soft hands; he'd never done anything like work before. But Tom's hands were soft too; playing cards didn't build many calluses. His knuckles, though—they weren't so soft.

"You will teach me to fight," Asher said.

"I'll teach you to play," Tom corrected.

"Ah," Asher said, and his smile got even bigger. Instead of letting go, he held on to Tom's hand. "You said that a good cardplayer has to know how to fight. For when the losers get sore."

Tom groaned. "Kid— Yeah. Yeah." He sighed and pulled his hand free. "*Good* players make enemies because they win. You see? You have to win first."

"I will," Asher promised, and his exuberance poured off him. It was like the light coming from the sun. Nothing was hidden at all. His face was an open book, and he wanted to learn to play cards.

PART TWO
POKER FACE

CHAPTER ELEVEN

Anyone could have been forgiven for having a look at Tom in his usual place and seeing a man not much accustomed to hard work. Tom dressed well, paid attention to his grooming, and was a little better spoken than the average man. He had the look of one who belonged indoors, and as long as he didn't open his mouth, some might even see him and think he was educated.

But the truth was that he hadn't always been that way. There had been a time when he hadn't owned a suit, and he'd been no stranger to a day's work. A gun wasn't the only tool he knew how to use, and there was a fair amount of knowledge in his head, even if he hadn't learned it from books.

Now something new would join his other wisdom: handling a team of six oxen wasn't as easy as it looked. It had been a long time since he'd ridden in anything

but a stage or a train, let alone had reins in his hand.
He knew *how* the business was done, but that didn't
mean he could do it, particularly with his leg afire and
the kid to look after. Maybe it was the amount of pain
Tom was in, but Asher's bubbling enthusiasm was
about as irritating as anything he'd ever seen.

The boy was as pleased as anything to be out here
doing this absurd pioneer impression.

The wagon was sturdy at least, if not particularly
fine. And the oxen themselves seemed all right, healthy
and strong. But it didn't feel real yet, and even if it had,
that wouldn't have made it any better.

The wagons stretched away ahead of them; theirs was
very nearly the last of them, and off to the left were the
cows and their handlers, plodding along impressively
contentedly. The men on horseback were far off, but it
was easy to see that they were good at their business.

The chill had subsided, at least. A few puffy clouds
weren't enough to keep the sun from warming the
country, and that was a blessing. It would get cold again
at night, and Tom's leg would get moody to match.

"That's not how you hold it," he told Asher. "You
hold it like this." He showed him, then handed him the
reins.

"I think Columbine prefers it when you have them,"
the boy replied nervously.

"Columbine?"

"That is her name, Mr. Calvert."

"Why are you naming them?" Tom adjusted his hat
and squinted up at the horizon. The Norwegians were
toward the rear of the train. The families of the Fulton
brothers and the wagons full of hay were all up ahead
at the front.

"To tell them apart," Asher replied as though it were obvious. That was reasonable, but Tom had never seen anyone get so excited over oxen.

"Describe the weed I told you to look out for," Tom told him tiredly.

"It has leaves like this." Asher held up four fingers. "And white hairs."

"They aren't hairs. They just look like hairs."

"And the oxen will get very sick if they eat them," Asher finished for him, pointing to the two leads. "I will watch for them. Petunia and Tulip are the ones to beware. The others eat what they eat."

Tom took the reins back. "Find new names for them, kid." Where had he *gotten* these names?

"Why?"

"They're all males."

"Oh." That shut him up. He looked thoughtful. "Really?"

Tom squinted over at him. What kind of a question was that? Did he really need to explain that they were castrated? He didn't particularly want to. There was a lot to teach this boy, and it gave Tom a headache just to think about it.

"Are you well, Mr. Calvert?" Asher had noticed his scowl.

"My leg is shot," Tom replied frankly.

"Is it painful?"

"Not as painful as this." They watched a dog barking madly as it ran in circles around the wagon ahead. Someone in the wagon threw a stick, and the dog bounded off and caught it.

"This?"

Tom sighed. "It's not where I planned to be. Or

what I planned to be doing. That's the truth." He gazed
at the reins in his hand and shifted to keep his leg more
or less straight. It was awkward to sit this way and
drive the wagon, but there was no other way. The kid
wasn't ready to do it by himself for any length of time,
though there wasn't much to it. "I had notions of where
I would be." He shook his head.

"I believe I know how you feel," the boy replied,
and Tom raised an eyebrow. That was interesting to
hear, but the kid had his own circumstances. He hadn't
been out on his own, creeping around a paddle steamer,
for his health. Things had happened, and the kid had
found his way through. Likely not the best or smartest
way, but he was still breathing. The same could be said
of Tom, but it was still more than could be said for some.

"Maybe it would've been better to risk the railway,"
Tom muttered.

"I beg your pardon, Mr. Calvert?"

"Nothing, kid."

Tom tended to sleep when he rode on a stage, but
even awake, there was never much of a view from in
one of those. It was different at the front of a wagon,
even if a good piece of that view was taken up by cows
and other wagons.

"Mr. Calvert?"

"What?"

"Are you angry?"

"No, kid."

The train was grinding to a halt. Tom couldn't tell
exactly what had happened; it might've been something up toward the front or something in the herd. It
was close enough to midday that folks weren't likely to

start it up again for a spell. It was as good a time to eat a meal as any.

Tom had once shared a stage with a fellow who had made very nearly this same journey. He'd been an older fellow, and he'd taken his wagon from Independence all the way to Oregon some twenty years before the rails were finished. Tom remembered the pity he'd felt for that man, purely because of how exhausting it had been to listen to the tales of his slog across the territories.

The joke was on Tom; now he was staring down the barrel of that very same ordeal.

Asher was rummaging in the wagon, and Tom felt only dread about finding the full extent of what the boy had purchased. There hadn't been enough time to make sure he'd done it all properly, not with the train leaving camp at dawn. Tom had never been one to give much thought to faith, so instead it had been a gamble that the boy would have the sense to follow his instructions.

Tom brought the team to a relatively graceful halt and glanced over his shoulder. Stages weren't as tidy as trains for travel, but even they weren't this fragrant. He was only just beginning to get used to it, and the vast herd of cattle wasn't helping.

"Hey," he said, picking up a tin cup and tossing it at Asher. The cup bounced off the boy's head, and he jumped and looked back, expression hurt. His cheeks were stuffed with sweets. "Stay out of those," Tom told him.

Asher choked. "Why? We have so much."

"You'll find out later. Right now you need to help me." Tom searched for his crutch. "Help me down so I can make some lunch."

"No, I will prepare it," the boy replied quickly, swallowing and moving Tom's crutch out of his reach.

The kid *had* done an impressively good job with the provisioning, at least by the look of things.

"You can cook?" Tom peered at him dubiously.

Asher hesitated, then drew himself up and gave Tom an oddly challenging look. "I can. And I will. I wager I am more skilled than you."

"Leave the wagering to me," Tom told him. "Go on, then." He'd rather eat bad food than do the work himself in the state he was in. The boy *had* done a tolerably good job with breakfast. It also occurred to him to approach one of these Norwegian families that seemed hard up to make a deal; surely some of these wives were fair cooks. Why not pay them to do it?

But the kid looked happy, and Tom couldn't help but wonder where he had come from. If someone had told him to cook a meal at that age, he'd have just laughed. He hadn't been one to volunteer for anything, either.

Asher was different. He seemed like he'd been raised right, maybe a little too right; he was so polite and gentle that it was hard not to see him as just begging to be taken advantage of. A man needed to show that he wasn't to be trifled with, and Asher was only a boy, but he'd be a man soon enough. And if he'd been raised right, what had he been doing aboard that boat? And why did he want to learn to fight and shoot so badly?

"Kid," Tom said as the boy set about readying the stove, "what is it about this place? What's it called again?"

Asher looked up for a moment, then went back to what he was doing. "Friendly Field, Mr. Calvert."

"Why're you so hung up on it?"

The boy took a moment to answer as he fumbled with the matches.

"Do you have kin there?" Tom pressed. Was it any of his business? Maybe it was; they were sharing a wagon now after all.

"No, sir."

"Then why?"

Asher looked up after a moment. "It sounds like a nice place. Friendly Field. It seems like a pleasant name."

Tom shook his head. The kid must've heard stories, like the stories of the gold you could just pluck out of the rivers in California.

"Is it a gold town?" That was a nasty thought; what if it was real but already dried up and dead? How would the kid take to that?

"I do not know."

"Fine." This place he was trying to find? For all they knew, it wasn't even real.

The smell of woodsmoke was an improvement, and in fact Asher was a considerably better cook than Tom was. What exactly had his folks raised him to do? Maybe he'd been raised in a fancy restaurant in a city, but he didn't talk like he came from the city.

It made a little sense at least. If Tom's folks had tried to make him talk that pretty and cook, he'd have run away from home too. But that wasn't the case, and he knew it. Asher hadn't said anything, and Tom would never ask. The boy had parents; everyone did, but his weren't aboveground. Tom had been about that age when he found himself on his own.

It was a bad place to be. The kid needed a hand; it

was just a shame he'd chosen a cripple all out of luck to give it to him.

Asher was so enchanted with the oxen that it didn't bother him to take care of them. He took pleasure in it and didn't see it as a chore. That was another clue, Tom supposed—the boy had not grown up on a farm. It wouldn't be long before these tasks would grow tiresome for him, but the team had to be cared for.

The sun got higher, and someone was approaching. It wasn't Breeden.

She wasn't wearing black or anything, but it had to be the girl whose wagon they were using. She was alone—no, she wasn't. There was an older woman a little ways off, by that second wagon up, watching over her.

It was a nice dress that the girl had on, with some bold, pleasing patterns on it, and her apron was embroidered with such detail that Tom would've needed better eyes to really appreciate it. Her hair was paler than gold and braided nicely. She was uncommonly pretty.

"Kid," he said, and Asher looked up from the ox he'd now named Mr. Christopher, "go talk to her."

"Your pardon?"

"That girl over yonder, coming this way. She's coming over here to thank us for buying this wagon. I'm tired. You talk to her."

"Oh." Asher frowned uncertainly. "As you wish."

"Be polite."

"I will."

Tom leaned back and picked up his new hat. Asher had picked it out for him, and the damn kid couldn't judge size for anything. The clothes Asher had picked for himself were too fine for the road, and too big for his body. The ones he'd picked for Tom were sized right, but the hat was a size too big.

That was all right. There were worse problems to have. Tom settled back and put the hat on, pulling it low over his eyes. He folded his arms and settled in as though to nap, but he couldn't help himself.

He opened one eye and peered out at Asher, who had gone out to meet the girl halfway.

It looked like they were talking. Asher didn't appear to be showing any nerves, so that was good. Did he know how to talk to girls? Maybe Tom should've made sure before he sent him off.

Well, it looked like he was doing all right; at least the boy wasn't the type who was too shy to talk to a pretty girl. Tom closed his eyes, but presently Asher returned. Tom lifted his hat and looked up to see the girl moving away. His mouth fell open.

"You didn't walk her back?"

Asher frowned. He looked over his shoulder. "It cannot be but a hundred yards, Mr. Calvert."

Tom put his face in his hand and groaned.

CHAPTER TWELVE

⌒

THE TERRITORY WAS nearly as flat as Kansas, but the going wasn't as easy. Tom had never worried much over the terrain; it was always someone else's job to get him where he was going. That was still partly true now; Breeden led the train, and he had uncountable cows and dozens of wagons to tread the path ahead, which was well-worn. That was good as long as the weather stayed dry. The chill wouldn't slow them much, but mud and snow would.

This land went on forever, just as the plodding journey did. There was so much green that you really could mistake it for something else, something even vaster, looking out at the carpet of grass and the ceiling of sky, two absolutes that filled the eyes like nothing else could.

A third day drew to a close without incident. Tom's luck really had changed.

"Who is that peacock?"

He hadn't meant to say it that way; it was just how the words came out. There was the one cowboy who'd make a point to ride up and down the line clearly just to be seen. It wasn't enough for him to have clean white clothes; the man sparkled, even in the gathering twilight.

"Jake Fulton," Breeden replied, chewing his cigar. The older man was leaning against the wagon, where Tom sat in his usual perch, leg out straight. He'd gingerly braved the ground to go to the stream and bathe, and that was all the moving he could handle.

"If I was the praying sort, I'd pray for lightning to strike him. These damn Norwegians are even worse off than you said. It's cruel to just show them all what an easy go he's having," Tom griped.

"I know." Breeden scowled. "If it gets cold, their store won't hold. I'll round up a few that got some sense and teach them to hunt. There are some fair trappers among them, but they can't shoot for anything. Those snares won't do them no good in the snow."

Tom nodded. "Teach the kid too. Let him help. I have a notion he's never hunted so much as a fly."

Breeden just grunted tiredly. "Don't mouth to Jake," he warned. "He's all right really. But those brothers are a touchy bunch."

"I won't mouth to anyone," Tom assured him.

The bearded man glanced up at him. "I'll bet you won't. It ain't the law you're running from, is it?"

"I doubt it." There was no sense lying; Breeden would've had to be an idiot not to see it. "More personal, I'd think."

"Well, you don't look like no bank robber."

Tom snorted. "I'm a cardplayer."

"It ain't Jake you got to worry about anyways. It's Rodney. He gets stormy from time to time. The others are all right. Eli's downright nice to talk to. Jake's just— Well, you and I've been there." Breeden puffed on his cigar. "Even if he is a damn peacock."

Tom spotted Asher making his way back from up the line. The herd was settling nicely, and dozens of curling trails of smoke had begun to rise. It had been a long day, and while the others might not be in as much pain as Tom was, they all had to be just as tired. He would've expected driving a wagon to be more tedious than tiring, but he'd have been wrong.

The kid never ran out of energy, though. He was probably insane; that would explain a lot. It wasn't as though Tom spent all his time around boys that age, but he'd been one once, and he hadn't been anything like Asher. He had a feeling the boy needed more guidance than he could give.

He was about to ask where Asher had been, but there was a more pressing matter.

"Go bathe," he called out as soon as the boy was in earshot.

"Your pardon?" Asher called back politely, speeding up.

But Tom didn't want him coming closer. "Bathe," he repeated.

"Listen to him, son." Breeden cleared his throat. "I can smell you from there."

Asher stopped in his tracks, his confusion plain. What was there to be confused about? They'd been on the move for three days.

"But there is no bath," he said.

For several moments the two men could only stare. Tom had been about to put a candy stick in his mouth, but instead he patiently pointed it to the north. "There's the stream."

Asher looked mortified.

"Kid, you got all them pretty manners, but you smell like one of them," Tom told him, glancing at the oxen. Asher knew that; he'd been putting something on, something that was supposed to smell good, but it wasn't enough. It couldn't take the place of actual cleanliness. "Go and do it."

"I have never bathed out of doors before," Asher said.

"It's a beautiful night to start." Tom had no sympathy for him. And it was cool tonight, not chilly, so it wouldn't get any better than this; it would only get worse. "If you don't, you can spend the night on the ground."

The kid looked hurt.

Tom just bit down on his candy. Together, he and Breeden watched the boy head off as though he'd been sent to the gallows.

"Shyness is simple enough to get over," Breeden observed after a moment, and he was right. There wasn't much privacy on the trail. Tom and Asher were fortunate; the wagon was big, and there were only two of them, which allowed room to sleep more or less normally. Most of these families were six or eight people, all in that same space or in crude tents on the ground, but once it got properly cold, those tents wouldn't get much use.

Breeden drifted away; he had things to do, and he

couldn't waste all night chatting with Tom. The sun got lower, and Tom settled in to watch it set. None of this had ever crossed his mind. It wasn't where he would have chosen to be, but it wasn't all bad. It was quiet now, with all the wagons halted and the herd calm.

He eyed the team, and they were all grazing contentedly. He'd never owned a single animal, much less half a dozen. They weren't really his; they were Asher's. Tom didn't want them, and it would be good to leave the kid with something when they parted ways. Tom would have to give him some money too. That was all right.

Someone was coming, but even in the fading light, Tom knew it had to be the girl.

He straightened up a bit as she approached the wagon, and tipped his hat.

She drew herself up as though she intended to say something, but clutched at her apron, and her eyes searched.

Tom took pity on her. "Looking for Asher?"

"Yes," she replied, and even that word came out thick and awkward.

"He's bathing. I will tell him that you called," he told her, finding it in himself to say it with a straight face.

She nodded appreciatively, and went back toward her own wagon or the wagon of the family who was sheltering her. This journey would be long and painful for Tom, but it might not be so bad for Asher. That girl had taken a shine to him.

The sky was a sea of stripes, colored by dusk when the kid finally came back, shivering.

"What took you so long, kid? You can't stay in that

water too long or you'll freeze." Asher had taken ages. A suspicion struck Tom. "You weren't sneaking around, trying to look at the girls bathing, were you?"

Asher looked shocked, and he wasn't acting. *Of course* that wasn't what he'd been doing. Tom should've known better.

"I wanted to go apart," the boy replied, pointing, "from everyone else."

Still shy. "You went the wrong way," Tom told him. "You bathe *downstream* of where we draw water."

He blanched. "I will remember that."

Someone else was coming. Asher saw Tom's eyes and turned to look. It was a Norwegian gentleman, an older one. He was part of the party with whom the girl traveled, probably the father. Tom couldn't help but be watchful; he hadn't mixed with anyone but Breeden, but he was learning the people of the nearby wagons by sight.

The Norwegian gentleman held up a hand, and Tom gave a friendly wave.

"May I approach?" The man's English was far better than the girl's.

"Welcome." Tom waved him in.

"This," the man said as he neared, "is for your leg." He held out a packet of brown paper.

Puzzled, Tom reached down and took it. It wasn't large, though it was fairly heavy. The girl must've told him Tom was hurt; or maybe word had gotten around.

"Thank you," Tom told him. "That's real good of you."

The man had nothing else to say. He didn't look exactly grumpy. It was just that he wasn't happy, and how could he be? Tom wasn't blind. It wasn't lost on the

Norwegians that they weren't as well prepared for this journey as they would've liked to be, but what could they do? There was no going back East.

The fellow glanced at Asher, but gave nothing away, then went back. Tom bounced the packet on his palm.

"Nice folks," he said.

"They are," Asher agreed.

"The girl's English isn't so good."

"She does have a peculiar way of speaking," the boy said, nodding.

Tom searched, and then when he didn't find it, he searched a little more. With his patience firmly in hand, he forced a smile. "Help her," he said tightly.

"What?"

"Help the girl with her English."

Asher frowned. "That would be a kind thing to do," he said.

"And then teach her to read and write it," Tom told him. "I know you know how. Did you buy this?" He leaned back and pulled two hard-bound volumes out of the wagon. "Because I didn't."

"I did," Asher replied.

Tom shook his head and looked down at the books. They were two volumes of one novel from England. It wasn't *so* strange to bring something like this; there was some time to read on the trail when one wasn't holding the reins, though other chores had a way of crowding in even when the wagons were moving. But the boy hadn't had a dime to his name a few days ago, and he'd bought something like this? It couldn't have come cheap.

"How is your leg?"

"About the same," Tom replied, glancing at the paper

packet. He eyed the books a moment longer, then put them back. "I volunteered you to Mr. Breeden. He's going to help the Norwegians with their hunting. He'll teach you to handle a rifle."

"It's the pistol I want to learn," Asher replied without hesitation.

"If you want to learn anything, you can learn that it doesn't matter what you want," Tom informed him tiredly. "You bathe because you have to, and you'll learn to handle a rifle because I tell you to."

"Very well, I will." Asher folded his arms, scowling. "What is that?"

"Let's see." Tom opened the packet, revealing a sort of greenish paste. He gazed for a moment as though that might make it less mysterious. When that didn't work, he gave it a tentative sniff.

Asher had his elbows on the seat and was up on his toes to look. "Will you use it?" he asked.

"I gamble for a living. Why not?" It certainly smelled interesting. There was something vaguely like mint in it. "What?"

"May we play cards again this evening, Mr. Calvert? After supper?"

Tom leaned over and twisted; if he did this, he could just see past the wagon, and the country they'd left behind. His luck was holding; there had been no rain, and there was a fair amount of dust. Anyone on horseback would kick up such a column of it that you would know they were coming from miles away.

There was no one back there. Three days.

It didn't mean anything. Word couldn't have reached Carroll yet that Tom was still alive, and there was at least some chance that it never would. And even when it did, there was *some* chance that Carroll would let it lie.

Enough chance to gamble on?

"Mr. Calvert?"

Tom came to his senses and turned his attention back to the kid. "Yeah, kid. We can play."

CHAPTER THIRTEEN

A SHER HAD A good brain. The problem was his face.

Not for that Norwegian girl, whose name was Ida, because it didn't matter that Asher didn't like to bathe, and it didn't matter that his hair looked as though it had been cut by a drunken man with a rusty saw blade. She was fixed on him like the sun was fixed on rising each day. Nothing could change it.

The boy's face was pretty for the girls, but it wouldn't cooperate. You didn't need the *best* poker face to win at cards, but you had to have some kind of control, and the kid didn't. A smile came naturally to him, and his eyes smiled even bigger than his mouth. Nothing could stop them from lighting up when he drew a strong hand or thought he was being clever.

Once in a while, usually in the evening, Tom would catch the boy's mind wandering, and there would be a different look on his face. A bad memory was the only thing it could be, and that was natural enough.

The season was wearing on, and there was still no sign of pursuit, but that didn't bring much relief. The air was getting colder, and everyone knew it; the easy days were numbered. The land ahead wasn't so flat, and cold rains or snow would make the going far more difficult than anything they'd seen so far. Game would be more plentiful, but there would be less to graze for the animals, and the Fulton cowboys were careful to make sure that their herd had the first choice of everything.

Tom had seen more of the Fulton brothers now; only two of them were married, and there was a fair amount of talk among the Norwegians about the one named Jake, who was friendly enough but no gentleman. Tom had caught a few glimpses of him paying calls on the other wagons. The Norwegians were wary of him, but he appeared to take that in good humor. Tom had a feeling he'd win them over eventually, and a few of these daughters would be heavy with child by the time they reached Oregon.

The only other one Tom had gotten a good look at was Norman Fulton, who dressed more sensibly and looked a bit older than Eli. He had a surly disposition, and he'd taken to riding away from the others, on the other side of the train entirely, and near the rear. It wasn't unusual for him to be walking along, leading his horse a mere fifty yards from Tom and Asher's wagon.

He probably just wanted some quiet, away from the hollering of the cowhands and the thudding of the hooves.

Tom would've liked to do the same, but he didn't have that luxury. Asher was fit to hold the reins, though, so that gave him the opportunity to lie in the back of the wagon. It would've been nice if idleness suited him, but it didn't.

"Hell of a gamble," he said. "This Mrs. Bennet. To wager that she'll take ill that way."

"Your pardon, Mr. Calvert?" Asher looked back from the trail; he sat in the driver's seat alone, while Tom lounged in the back with the book. He wasn't completely comfortable, but it was as good as it would get under the circumstances. There were things he could've been doing: oiling the pistol that the boy had bought back outside Omaha or sorting through the rest of Asher's strange purchases. But he chose to read the book. Asher had already read well past this part.

"She made her go on horseback when it was going to rain," Tom said. "Her intent was that she'd take ill and have to stay the night."

Asher made a noise of disgust. "Then you must agree she is wicked."

"Wicked?" Tom raised an eyebrow and looked back at the page. "I don't know about that."

"To do that to her own daughter?" Asher twisted around to give him an indignant look. "To cause her to take ill for the purpose of seeing her married? It is ghastly."

"She's trying to help her out."

"She might have died."

Tom shrugged. "She gambled. I admire that."

"That is very wrong, Mr. Calvert."

He snorted. "Kid, she's the *only* one who can be bothered to think about what's coming. She's looking out for her girls. The dad ain't doing it," he added, shaking the book at the boy. "Not even the older sis-

ters, the good ones. And the younger ones are only
kids. Who else is going to do it? Their dad could drop
dead at any moment, and they got no home. The mom
isn't trying to marry her daughters off for her amusement. She's doing it because their lives depend on it.
They'll have nothing. Isn't that right?" Tom frowned
and considered the book. "That is what they mean
when they say it's entailed away, isn't it?"

"It is," the boy replied.

"So you know about entailing estates but not how to
hitch a team." Tom snorted.

Asher sniffed. "I can hitch one now."

He could. Tom doubted there was much the boy
couldn't do if he put his mind to it.

Asher looked back again. "Do you really like her?"

"Who, kid?"

"Their mother," he said, taking a hand off the reins
to point at the book.

Tom scowled. "Like her? No. She embarrasses her
family. I don't like that. But I respect that she not only
sees what they need, but has the will to do something
about it. She might not go about it the right way, but
she's trying." He put a slip of paper in the book to
mark his place and set it aside. "That's more than a lot
of folks do."

"Are you certain she is not doing it for her own gratification?" the boy asked stubbornly. "To elevate her
position in the neighborhood? You see that surely, Mr.
Calvert. The neighborhood is everything to these people."

"Society," Tom echoed. That was the word they
used in the book. "I know what you mean, but no. It
might look like that, but that's not how it is. It might
not show, but she's doing it for the girls."

"How are you so sure?"

"Because that's how mothers are," Tom told him.

The boy took a moment to reply to that, and even then he just looked over his shoulder.

"What, kid?"

"You have a strange way of looking at the world, Mr. Calvert."

"If it's down to you and me, *I'm* not the strange one," Tom told him firmly.

"Mr. Calvert, do you see that?" Asher pointed toward the horizon.

"I do." The clouds were dark and thick. "We might yet miss it. Or it might miss us."

"It will slow us down if we have to make our way through mud."

"What's your hurry, kid?"

"The concern is not mine," Asher replied, giving Tom a reproving look. "Ida says the other wagons are worried about their stores. They say if there is no game and we cannot reach the next camp in a week, some of them will go hungry."

"Then tonight's as good a night as any. Ask her to have supper with us, and have that fellow with the red tie join us."

"That is Oen. He is Mr. Bergson's brother."

"Then when we stop, ask Oen and Ida to eat with us. We have food to spare. That is, if you aren't too shy to cook for her."

"I do not mind." It was probably true; he didn't seem troubled. That was something to envy; at Asher's age, Tom would've been deathly shy with a girl as pretty as Ida.

Asher had no difficulty, though.

The wagon hit a bump, and Tom winced as pain shot through his leg all the way to his hip. Sucking his breath in through his teeth, he settled back, his ears primed for any change in the creaking of the wagon. It sounded all right.

They didn't stop until there was so little light that it would've been too dangerous to keep on. The Fulton brothers might have been the most important people along for this trip, but Breeden was still leading the train. He obviously wanted to take full advantage of every good day.

Ida and the man called Oen accepted Asher's invitation, and the boy got to work preparing the meal. Someone in the Fulton party, somebody's wife, had seen an opportunity for business and taken it. She had brought along a clay stove, and every evening she had just enough time to bake two pies using canned fruit that she had also brought along. She was selling them for five times what they'd have been worth in any sort of settlement.

The only people with the money to buy them were others in her party, and she was cleaning them out. Breeden had held out bravely, but even he would buy one soon. You could smell them each night, and it had to be torment for the Norwegians, who were already down to beans and hard tack.

Tom had Asher get one; it had been made with peaches. He didn't have the time or the energy to have Asher clean up, but Ida didn't care, and she'd gone to some effort to present herself the right way. There was only so much a girl could do on the trail, but she'd done it all, and she didn't have to do half as much to stand out.

Oen spoke such good English that he'd clearly been in the country for a while. He was more than qualified to teach the girl, but she chose to have her lessons with Asher in the evenings. That was a stroke of luck; Tom had tried to explain to the boy that most girls favored taller men, and that he was lucky Ida didn't.

"A card game," Oen said after they had, rather reverently, eaten the pie. "Not with money." They were gathered around the stove. Ida shivered, and Asher added more fuel.

"That's right," Tom told him. "I want Asher to practice his game. It needs to be a friendly game."

"What will you wager?" Oen asked.

"These." Tom tossed him one of the small bags of sweets.

Oen caught it, and a look of resignation passed over his face. It wasn't Tom's intention to flaunt his means, but there was no getting around it under the circumstances. A game without stakes had no meaning, and three-quarters of this train had very little to lose.

"I think some would be interested," Oen said, handing the bag back. "For their skill, I cannot say."

"That's all right."

"I will make inquiries."

"Thank you. I'm just trying to teach the boy a trade," Tom said, glancing at Asher, who was hanging on his every word, oblivious of the way Ida had inched closer to him and the look of naked adoration on her face. It wasn't lost on Oen, though.

"A trade?" The man snorted but then made an acquiescent gesture. "Perhaps it is. It appears to have provided for you."

"So far," Tom said. "Luck has something to do with

it," he added. It wasn't true, but it was polite to say. "What was in that salve your brother gave me? It was good for my leg." The wound was a better color now, and there was less swelling. It still hurt every moment of every day, but it was a weight off Tom's mind not to see any purple or yellow in it. He wasn't the queasy sort by nature, but it was different when it was his own skin on the line.

"That is a question you would need to ask my brother," Oen replied distractedly, looking back toward his wagon. "Is that Norman?"

"It would appear so," Tom replied, squinting. It was hard to be sure in the dark.

Norman was talking to Oen's brother.

And Oen didn't look happy. Tom could've asked what business the Fultons had with them, but that would've been rude.

"Walk her back," Tom muttered to Asher when it was time.

"What?" The boy looked annoyed. "Mr. Calvert, I am exhausted."

"Walk her back, or I'll shoot you," Tom told him.

Asher sighed. "Very well."

Oen watched them go, then knelt beside Tom. "You want a game enough to give away your provisions?"

Tom shrugged. "I promised the boy I'd teach him. This is how it's done."

There was only so much Tom could do, playing hand after hand with the kid in the back of the wagon at night. He could give advice, tell the boy what he was doing wrong, what he was doing right, and what he should've done instead.

But there were no stakes, and Asher wasn't afraid

to lose to Tom. He didn't feel like he had much to prove.

He had potential, but if he was going to grow, he'd have to do it playing for real. There was no better way.

The boy returned much too soon. This would've been the perfect night for a stroll away from the wagons to someplace private. Hell, it had been two weeks—what was the kid waiting for? Soon it'd be too cold for that.

Asher saw that Tom was about to climb up to his seat on the wagon, and he hurried to help.

"Thanks," Tom grunted, settling in. "You'll get your game."

"You believe it will work?"

"It will," he assured him. "You'll be surprised how fast it grows." At that moment the same three musical instruments were playing, and they were playing the same few songs as they did every other night. These people, Norwegians, Texans—it didn't matter. Even in hardship, there was also idleness.

A card game would be interesting to them. The number of players would rise, and the stakes would rise with them. Tom knew what he was doing.

"You planned it? This is what you had in mind when you told me to buy the sweets? For me to learn?"

Tom sighed. "We shook on it, didn't we?"

CHAPTER FOURTEEN

TOM HAD BADLY underestimated how quickly word of the game would spread among the wagons, and when rain threatened to put an end to it, the other travelers were better prepared than he was. They erected a crude tent, and Tom didn't even know what it was made of. It looked like sailcloth. They'd just put it together on the spot, and they weren't even people planning to sit for the game. They only wanted to watch.

Asher had to be on his own, so Tom stayed with the wagon. It wasn't completely an act of charity for him to front the sweets to the other players; he wasn't really giving them away. A player had to sit for the game to have them, and he could only leave the table with what he'd won.

Asher looked younger than he was; if he kept his mouth shut, he could probably pass for twelve or thirteen. The Norwegians had sent their best cardplayers,

three men older than Tom, and the Fulton party had
sent their kids. The stakes were split; the Texans had
enough provisions that something like this would
make no difference to them. This was a diversion for
them, while it was a more serious matter for the Norwegians.

There were too many people to fit under the shelter,
but they didn't seem to mind, even when the rain started
to fall. Tom was snug under his covering. There had
been one last piece of pie from last night, and he had no
reservations about eating it now that he was alone.

Three of the Fulton brothers had come to observe.

Jake, handsome and glittering, with his arm around
a Texan girl.

Eli, slightly drunk and laughing.

And there was a chance, however slim, that Norman's attention was on some other yellow-haired girl.
One who wasn't Ida. But Tom had made a business of
weighing the odds, and those weren't good ones. It was
no surprise that the Fulton brothers would notice the
Norwegian girls; Tom had known that was coming. He
hadn't counted on the kid being a part of it. He hoped
Norman would move on from Ida, because she'd all
but staked her claim to Asher.

Tom had assumed the train wouldn't mind having one
more party of means along. He hadn't thought about
how he and the kid might affect the balance of things. It
was a pity they couldn't all just be equal, but that wasn't
how things worked. As it was, everyone had to defer to
the Texans.

The game was going well; he didn't have to see the
table itself to know that. The noise rose and fell as the
hands came and went. Tom had a sense that if he'd

been close enough to really watch, he'd only have spent the evening cringing.

It wasn't as easy as just sitting there with the reins in hand, watching the oxen and the wagons ahead. Tom had known it wouldn't be. It was too late to call this off now; he'd been naive to think they could attach themselves to this train without becoming a part of it. The train's problems were their problems.

And he had a sense that there were a few of those brewing.

A little cheer went up from the gathered Norwegians and a groan from the Texans. Tom could just see Breeden's face through the milling people, and he didn't look concerned yet. A diversion like a card game could be a boon to the party, but it would have to be carefully managed. Cards were dangerous. You could make enemies with cards.

That was why it couldn't be allowed to go beyond the sweets. Tom had explained his idea, and Breeden had agreed.

It would be all right.

The sound of a punch was instantly recognizable, and a figure stumbled out of the lamplight and fell to the ground. Tom stiffened and touched the pistol thrust through his belt. It was a Remington Army, big and heavy. It wasn't what Tom would've chosen, but it had been what the kid had been able to get. Whether Tom liked it or not, the gun would work all the same.

Whoever had thrown that punch was hidden by the spectators. The victim was Jake Fulton. He picked himself up, and Breeden was there. That seemed to be the end of it, but it was still several moments before Tom let his breath out and took his hand off the pistol.

Was he really that wound up about a punch? One punch? Hell, they'd been on the trail together a while now, and he was surprised no one had been shot yet. The Fulton party looked at the Norwegians the same way they'd probably looked at their slaves before the war, and the Norwegians liked their hosts about as much as they liked the cholera. There'd be more of that before they got to Oregon, and there was nothing Tom could do about it.

He settled back and took a long breath, wincing as he moved his leg.

Rain pattered on the covering, and the game resumed. That punch would've been the end of a truly friendly game, even though the ones involved hadn't been sitting at the table. The sweets in play made that impossible. No one was going to leave money on the table.

Breeden called the game off before anyone could go bust, and he had no choice. If he didn't, they'd have likely played until morning. Rest was the one thing they needed that they could have as much of as they liked, and he wasn't going to let them miss it. That was a good way to end; no one would leave the table devastated.

Well, Asher would. Tom could see it on his face as he trudged back, and Ida looked on, though Oen was there with his arm around her shoulders to prevent her from following.

And Norman was there as well. Tom was right.

It was better than if it was Jake or Rodney who had taken a shine to Ida. Norman seemed to have a little more sense than those two, and he wasn't blind. Ida hadn't so much as glanced at him, though he'd turned out with that in mind. He clearly wanted to catch *some-one's* eye. He'd even shaved.

Tom felt for him; Ida was the sort to make the heart ache, but Norman Fulton was rich and handsome and there would be other girls. It was no fault of his that a simple misunderstanding had put Ida onto Asher instead. She must have come to believe that Asher bought her wagon with the strict intent of rescuing her; it was the only thing that could've had this effect. The kid had nothing else to recommend him. He had a weak voice, a weak frame, and an abominable haircut; his clothes didn't fit; and he didn't know the first thing about impressing girls. He had good manners, but Ida barely spoke English, so how much of a difference could that make?

This was luck. Asher had it, and Norman didn't. But luck could change, and Norman's would be better next time.

The boy looked as though someone had just shot his dog. Tom wasn't surprised. Without thinking, he leaned down and offered a hand. Asher, also without thinking, took it, and the pain as Tom helped him climb into the wagon was nearly enough to make him pass out. He hissed, and that jerked Asher out of whatever place the game had sent him to.

"Are you well?"

"I'm fine." Tom took a deep breath. "Put on some dry clothes." The boy had walked back so dejectedly that he'd gotten soaked.

Asher climbed past him into the back of the wagon, and Tom watched the people disperse and take down their pavilion. There would be some happy Norwegian children tonight. Ida wouldn't be one of them; seeing

Asher miserable made her miserable. Neither of them would be as miserable as Norman, but Tom had been there, and he'd survived it. Norman would too.

And Asher would survive his loss this evening.

"I have no luck," the boy complained from inside the wagon.

Tom sighed. "Your luck is the same as anyone else's."

"You did not see my cards."

"It isn't about the cards." He had explained this more than once, but the boy couldn't be expected to remember everything. Tom certainly hadn't at that age. In fact, it was a good thing that Asher was so strange. At that age, Tom couldn't have hoped to keep his mind or his hands off these Norwegian girls, let alone learn to play cards. Maybe being blind, deaf, and partly stupid was a blessing in disguise for the kid.

Because though he'd taken a beating tonight, as Tom had known he would, by the time they parted ways, Asher *would* be a tolerably good player. Tonight proved without a doubt that the kid had what he needed: not skill, but he had his whole life to get that. It was the drive to win. That was what separated people who got things done from people who just talked about them. Asher emerged from the wagon, wrapped in a blanket and shivering.

"Tell me about it," Tom said.

"The children did not understand the game well," Asher replied bitterly. "And neither did the three gentlemen. But they were able to win."

"They've been playing longer than you."

"They had to be taught the rules," the boy pointed out.

"There's skill that's about the game, and then there's just skill." Tom patted the pistol in his belt. "This isn't the same model I've carried these past years. Doesn't mean I don't know how to use it. I might shoot best with my own gun, but I'll still be fair with anything I can lay my hands on. A decent cardplayer's the same. He isn't playing the cards. He's playing you."

Asher took that in. "I detected little bluffing," he said.

"Fairly new players would be more inclined to trust their hands. You could've made something of that."

"I attempted it," Asher grumbled. "They saw through me. The gentlemen, I mean."

"You'll get better. It isn't luck. Your cards don't win the game. Your face wins the game."

CHAPTER FIFTEEN

THE TOWN HAD up and moved, although it wasn't much of a town.

Tom wasn't at the front of the train to see when Breeden finally spotted it and all but died with relief. It seemed the camp had flooded two seasons back, and they'd just built it again, a little higher up this time. Tom had expected tents and a hotel if he was lucky. What they found was something resembling a real town, with not one but two streets and plenty of buildings. There were no fewer than three hotels.

It was still called Camp Boles, but it wasn't a camp anymore.

Breeden had been determined to reach it by their sixth week, and he'd done it ahead of schedule, though not by much. There was a proper storm threatening now, but it still wasn't cold enough to have to fear snow. That didn't bother anyone quite so much; if they were to be slowed by mud, it was better to be held up where there were other people. The camp would offer a welcome opportunity to get provisions, although that was only helpful if the travelers had money to spend.

Tom wasn't going to let his sympathy for the less fortunate get between him and what he wanted, and what he wanted was a bath. So did the kid. The boy didn't really have a desire to be filthy; he just didn't like bathing with other people around. In fact, Tom was all but sure that if he asked, he'd learn the kid had been raised Puritan. He wasn't sure which was worse: having to listen to Puritanism or actually believing in it. He saved himself some grief and didn't ask.

"Invite the girl," Tom told Asher as they halted the team, nestled snugly among the wagons clustered outside the camp. "Just you and her."

Asher took off his hat and frowned at the sky, then put out a hand. The air was thick and moist; rain would be falling soon. "Why not have her join you and me, Mr. Calvert?"

"Because it isn't romantic if I'm there."

The boy sighed as though praying for patience. "I am all for showing Ida kindness, but you misunderstand her, Mr. Calvert."

"Oh, you understand her?" Tom gave the boy a skeptical look.

"I believe I spend more time in her company," the kid retorted.

"Do you know why you have to? Why her English isn't getting better?"

Asher suddenly looked interested. "Why?"

"Because she doesn't care about English. She's sweet on you. Nobody's misunderstanding that. And you're lucky she has the patience of a saint, because anyone else would've moved on by now."

Of course she couldn't really do that; they were a wagon train, and the society—if that was the word for it—was limited.

"Mr. Calvert, she has lost everything. She does not need a—a husband, if that is what you believe her to be searching for. What she needs is a friend." Asher gestured, frustrated. "She pretends to be very strong, and she does not talk about her sadness. She smiles at me, but that is because she feels she is a burden and does not wish to be more of one."

"She told you that?"

"No," the boy replied, scowling. "As you say, her English is poor."

"You're way off, kid."

"I think *you* are the one who is sweet on her," Asher accused.

Tom snorted. "If that was true, I'd make her an offer of marriage. If I weren't a cripple, it would be a sure thing. As I am, I give it half odds. And as I've told you, I got my sights set elsewhere. I'm trying to *help* you."

"Well, I would think she has a better prospect in Mr. Fulton."

"Norman?"

Asher nodded. "Last night after the card game, she embraced me, and I saw him look at me." The boy shuddered.

Tom turned that over in his mind as he watched the others begin to set up camp for the night. He and Asher were the only ones still sitting there in the driving seat, holding reins they weren't using.

"I'm glad you noticed that," he said absently. It meant

Asher was starting to learn to keep his eyes open. God knew Tom was trying hard enough to teach him.

Asher looked troubled. "I do not think Ida likes him," he said finally.

"You should be happy about that." Tom yawned. "As long as he takes it like a man."

"What do you mean?"

"I mean a fellow can get sore over that."

"You mean he would have a grievance with me?"

Tom shrugged. "You're stealing his woman. If he knew you were doing it without trying, he'd be even more upset."

"I am not," Asher began; then he closed his eyes and shook his head. "Is that truly how it appears?"

"To everyone but you, kid."

Asher made a noise of disgust.

"You're just slow growing up," Tom told him, putting the reins down.

"What?"

"Listen to yourself. And you don't even have to shave. You'll see soon enough." He waved a hand and grabbed his crutch. "Help me down."

On the ground, Tom tested his leg and set his jaw, breathing through the pain.

Asher still looked worried. "Will I have to fight him," he asked, "if he really believes what you see?"

"Norman? No. You can't ever fight him. You wouldn't have a chance."

The boy looked indignant. "Because you have not taught me to fight."

"Because you're half his size. Now, are you going to leave the girl to eat at a camp stove or with you tonight?"

"Will we eat in town?"

"Might as well," Tom replied.

Asher nodded. "I will invite her. But what if it seems as though I am leading her on?"

Tom leaned on the wagon. "Do you *not* like her? Has she done something to offend you or make herself undesirable?"

He watched the boy flail for an answer. That was answer enough. He gave the kid a push and caught Oen's eye. They'd already worked a deal; Oen would keep an eye on the wagon while Tom and Asher were in town. The Norwegians likely weren't inclined to steal anything, and the Texans didn't need to, but it was a matter of principle.

"I envy you," Oen said as Tom slung a sack over his shoulder and started to limp away.

Tom looked back. Yes, he was going to eat food prepared in a kitchen. And have a hot bath. And spend the night in a real bed.

He'd still have traded places with Oen in a heartbeat. Oen didn't have anyone after him, and he had two legs he could walk on all he liked.

Asher was on his way back toward Tom, and thunder rumbled overhead.

There were hoofbeats, and none other than Norman Fulton drew up by the wagon owned by Ida's new family. He climbed down and swept off his hat, and Tom shook his head. Poor Norman was just five minutes too late with his invitation to Ida.

That was the way of things sometimes.

Tom would've liked to choose the finer of the three hotels, though *fine* wasn't the word for it, but it was already full of Fultons. That wasn't a good idea.

So they crossed the street to the next one, already a little rowdy and smelling of tobacco and sawdust. It was full of men with muddy boots and plenty of memories of the flood, going by the way they all reacted every time the sky made a noise.

"I will have my bath now," Asher told the stooped man behind the counter, "before dinner."

"Not yet," Tom cut in. He counted out some money, and gave Asher a list. "Take care of it before the stores close. And buy something for the girl."

"What?"

"Something pretty. Just do it," Tom said tiredly, and picked up his crutch to drag himself upstairs.

He was ready for the pain of his wound in a hot bath, and it barely bothered him. He soaked until the water was cool and challenged himself to don better clothes. There wasn't much call for dressing up on the trail, but he was tired of loose trousers and floppy shirts. The suit wasn't necessary, and it had never been worn, but he'd made the kid buy it before they departed anyway.

Putting it on was a ginger affair, but he did it without injuring himself. A good suit didn't make for a good figure by itself; it needed to be tailored, and the crutch ruined it in any case, but Tom wasn't trying to impress anyone. He just wanted to convince himself that even now there could still be *something* like what was normal. It felt strange to go through the day without a waistcoat, and it felt better to have one on, more secure somehow.

Downstairs, he arranged for a private dining room with the barman and took his seat at the counter with a hot mug of bitter coffee. The boy turned up, and Tom sent him up to bathe. When he returned, he explained the room, and though the kid obviously didn't care for the idea, by now he knew better than to argue. Tom knew perfectly well he was being a busybody, but it was for Asher's own good. Would the boy have the courage to take the girl upstairs after dinner? Probably not, but it could still be a nice evening.

That silly book they were reading was half the reason Tom worried so much; in it, it became clear that it was dangerous not to show interest. If you didn't show enough interest, the other party might take that as *disinterest*. Tom felt obliged to help keep Ida around until Asher came to his senses. Maybe that would happen when his voice changed.

Asher went to get Ida from the wagons, and when they returned, she looked more delighted than Tom had ever seen her. Tom didn't even look twice at them; he just sipped his coffee and waited for his supper as they disappeared into the back.

A boy put a tin plate of meat and potatoes in front of him, and it should've been the only thing he could see.

He couldn't think about food, though.

Because that fellow in the corner had been watching him since the moment he had walked in.

CHAPTER SIXTEEN

TOM HADN'T EXACTLY *lied*.

A bluff was a lie if you got down to it, but it was also part of the game, and that made it all right. The private dining room for Asher and Ida *was* for their benefit. It was also to keep them out of the way.

The man in the corner wore an old Union jacket that didn't belong to him, and he was shabby all around, but he looked awfully good for a man dressed so poorly. Tom was no stranger to betting, and he was about a hairbreadth from being ready to bet just about anything that the man was a Pinkerton.

He'd been on the lookout when the train approached the camp, he'd been there when Tom had chosen the hotel, and now he was here working much too slowly on his second glass of beer.

If he was still there in ten minutes, Tom would have his answer.

No, that was the same as telling himself to wait until his leg was healed or until the next fort, the next camp, the next stop along the way.

He already *knew*. He just didn't like it much.

Tom chewed and considered the others in the room. There couldn't have been more than one Pinkerton for him.

"May I have a word?" Tom asked the barman, who poured whiskey for a giant of a man, then shuffled over. "Is there a wire here?"

"There is," the man replied.

That wasn't the answer Tom had hoped for. There hadn't been much light when they arrived, and he hadn't been able to see the posts.

"To where?"

"The fort."

Tom considered that. "Does the operator stay late?"

"He's ill."

That was good news. There was still a chance.

"I need to send a telegram," he said.

"He'll open up in the morning."

The food had no flavor, and eating it felt like a chore. Music was loud from the joint across the street, but Tom barely heard it. The man in the corner didn't have a third beer.

Tom had been so sure his pursuers would be coming up behind him that he hadn't given much thought to the notion that they might be waiting up ahead. Carroll didn't mind the expense. There would be a man like this waiting anywhere that Tom might be thought likely to turn up.

For him to be here meant it had crossed someone's mind that he might've joined this train. Carroll couldn't be *sure* of it, or he'd have simply chased the train down; men on horseback would've had no difficulty doing that.

It meant Carroll was being thorough. Tom had hoped Carroll wouldn't care enough to be thorough, but Carroll didn't see things the way Tom did. Tom had no *real* grudge with the man. He wasn't going to seek him out and harm him, but Carroll knew only that Tom had ruined his boat, his plans, likely upset his wife, and then tried to shoot him.

Tom wasn't his enemy, not really. But Carroll couldn't reasonably see him as anything else.

Of course he'd be thorough.

Tom had gained back a little color from driving the wagon in the sun, but he still didn't look fully well. He'd grown something like a beard, though he didn't have the right face for it, and his beards had always been poor. He was dressed like himself, though. That hadn't been wise.

Would Carroll know to look for a wound? He must; the Pinkerton in the corner wasn't watching anyone else. This was Dan's doing. Dan hadn't missed; he'd simply shot to wound, perhaps out of friendship.

Tom's leg throbbed. Friendship.

He pushed his plate away, picked up his crutch, and heaved himself to his feet. He made no effort to hide how he felt. His leg pained him, and though he wasn't as weak as he had been, he was far from strong. He probably looked like a man twice his age as he hobbled this way, and tonight that was for the best.

The Pinkerton did a tolerable impression of not paying attention, and Tom didn't have to pretend to be tired as he dragged himself upstairs, one arduous step at a time. In his room, he sat on the bed for several long minutes before he pulled the pistol out of his belt. It was partly the gun, which was large, and partly his strength, but it felt enormously heavy.

Four times, the boy had pressed him to learn to use the gun. He claimed he was a reasonable shot with the rifle now that he'd gone out twice with Oen to fire it. Tom kept saying no. The boy wanted to learn skills that would help him, and he believed that shooting was one of those skills.

Asher *suspected* that Tom wouldn't teach him because he wasn't well.

Tom held up his hand, then held it out flat. He could see it trembling. Anyone could.

Tom had seen something else: exactly where his trigger finger had brought him. The boy had come to him for help. It would be easy enough to teach him to kill, easier than teaching cards certainly. The kid had it in him. Tom spent enough time looking people in the eye to know that much.

Skill hadn't been the problem. Tom had been more than fast enough. He might even have been faster than Dan, even without the element of surprise. And the problem hadn't been that the pistol had been empty, either. Even if that sixth bullet had been there and Carroll's dead body had fallen to the deck, things would have been no better.

The problem was the decision that he'd made, but he couldn't call it that. It had happened so quickly, as things always did when he was angry.

He turned the gun over in his hands for another moment, then tucked it back into his belt and leaned over to put out the lamp. Enough time had passed. It was dark, though still relatively early, but he didn't look well. No one would be surprised if he chose to retire while the night was still young.

He found his crutch in the dark and hauled himself upright, easing over to the window and standing to one side. He waited for his eyes to adjust.

There was still plenty going on in the street below. A celebration was gaining steam in the joint across the street, and enough noise came out of there to wake the dead. That was good. It was cold enough that though every window was lit, nearly all of them were blocked by heavy drapes to ward off the chill. Very little of that welcoming glow found the street, and none of it found the alleys.

That Union jacket would be all but invisible in that, but the Pinkerton liked his tobacco. If he was out there, the glow of his smoke would give him away.

There was Asher, returning to the hotel. Tom scowled and pinched the bridge of his nose between his thumb and forefinger. The boy had just walked her back after dinner? He hadn't even thought to *talk* a while in the warm hotel?

He waited a moment, willing his ears to sort the sounds from the music. A shadow passed the door, and there was only the slightest creak from the boards in the hall. That would have been Asher; there couldn't have been many others that light up here.

Tom brushed himself off with his free hand, touched the handle of the pistol, then opened the door and stepped into the corridor. He didn't look toward the stairs; he just hobbled down to Asher's room and knocked.

There was a startled bump from inside, and for a

moment, he felt a spark of hope, but no—it wasn't two embarrassed people; it was just one with more than his share of clumsiness.

Presently Asher opened the door.

"Ask who it is before you open it," Tom told him as he limped inside.

"What is the matter, Mr. Calvert?" the boy asked, lost.

"I'm trading you rooms. Get your things and go on down there."

"Now? Why?"

Tom turned and faced him very directly. "Kid, we're partners, aren't we?"

Asher swallowed, taken aback. "Yes?" he replied.

"You have to trust your partner, don't you?"

The boy looked self-conscious. He folded his arms and took a step back. "I suppose," he replied warily.

"Good. I'll explain later. Now, you go down to my room and go to sleep. Lock the door, put a chair under the knob, and don't open it for anybody but me. Do it," he warned, cutting off whatever the kid had been about to say.

"Is there trouble?"

"Yes. But I'm going to handle it, and I won't drag you into it." Tom put his hand on the gun. "Don't make me knock you out cold, kid. But that's what I'll do if you aren't out that door on the count of three. And look normal," he added as the boy hurriedly moved to obey.

Tom didn't *want* to be a bully, but there wasn't time to be anything else. The boy couldn't have any part of this, even if that would've made it a hundred times easier. Asher wasn't Tom's son, but he was *somebody's* son, and there was nobody out there who'd want their boy to turn out like Tom. Nobody at all.

Asher cast a worried look over his shoulder, but Tom just shut the door with enough firmness to seem cross.

A sudden, much louder crash jolted him, and he looked in surprise at the window as raindrops began to hammer it. He scowled. That was miserable timing, but it was already a miserable night. Tom had never heard a single good word about Pinkertons, though he personally had never been given reason to dislike them. It wouldn't be fair to dislike them now; they might as well dislike him for gambling. Everyone had to put food on the table somehow.

Tom hobbled to the window and opened it, letting in a rush of cold wind and rain. Getting wet would have been the least of his worries. He cautiously leaned out for a look. Asher's room faced the alley, so there was no view but of the timbers of the next building. Tom hadn't realized it was quite this tight between the structures. He threw his crutch down and clambered out, doing it slowly and gingerly as though he were twice his age.

His good foot found the top of the first-floor window, and he perched there precariously as the rain poured on his head. Blinking the water from his eyes, he considered the delicate business of getting to the ground. He had to be difficult to see in the dark, and the rain made it unlikely that this peculiar behavior would be observed.

After several moments of pondering, there seemed no better way to get down than to drop. There was an old cart down there, and it stood four or five feet off the ground. If he hung from his fingertips from the window, the fall would be laughably short, at least for a healthy man.

The impact was painful, but he went about it as though he had some sense, taking care not to land on his bad leg. Sore, soaked, and freezing, he clambered the rest of the way down to the alley, where his boots sank in the mud. He found his crutch and peered in through a window. No sign of the Pinkerton near the counter or at the tables.

Tom limped out of the alley and onto the street, going boldly to the door and entering the warmth of the hotel he'd just left. Shivering, he ignored the scattered looks he got from the patrons and went to the foot of the stairs. There, he took care to be discreet or at least to do a reasonably convincing impression of it.

The Pinkerton lurked on the landing, more or less hidden from the room below and also from the corridor. He was leaning against the wall in the shadows, smoking.

He heard the tap of the crutch and looked, but Tom already had his pistol in his hand.

The Pinkerton wasn't blind. He kept still as Tom hobbled a little closer and gestured with the gun.

The Pinkerton didn't raise his hands, but he left his cigarette in his mouth and moved them away from his body with his fingers spread. He looked fairly calm for a man in a bad position, but he was easily ten years Tom's senior, so there was a reasonably good chance that it wasn't the first time he'd had a gun on him.

"Go on, then," Tom said.

The man went down the hallway, and Tom let him into the room. The Pinkerton stopped in the middle, his eyes on the open window.

"Shut that for me, please," Tom told him, "with just your one hand."

He did it, and Tom waved the gun toward the bed.

The Pinkerton sat. "Don't you want my gun?" he asked.

"No," Tom replied, sighing. It wasn't a large room. Any shot made in here would have been an easy one. He perched on the chair with a groan, dripping on the rug. It didn't look like the Pinkerton had much sympathy for him.

"Do you know who I am?" Tom asked.

"I do," the Pinkerton replied. There was a Colt that might've come from the war in a holster down on his right leg, but he wasn't making any move toward it. He glanced toward the door, then back at Tom.

"Do you know why he wants me?"

"Don't make no difference."

"It does to me," Tom said.

"Murder," the Pinkerton said, unimpressed. "You kilt his friend."

"I did do that," Tom confessed. "He did me wrong, and I was holding him to account. He did more than call me a cheat. He attacked my character and lied. I made a mistake when I pulled on Carroll." There were those words again, coming out of his own mouth, not Shafer's. "The other man, though—that was not a mistake. I would do it again. I am no threat to Mr. Carroll. I mean him no evil. He will never see me again in his life."

"Less'n he catches you," the Pinkerton grunted, scratching his nose, which was red from years of drink.

"That may be." Tom looked down at the pistol in his hand and lowered it a bit. "You aren't going to try to bring me in by yourself. Not alone." No, this man had been sent here on the outside chance that Tom happened to appear. His role wasn't to act; it was to report. If he confirmed that Tom was headed west with the train, *then* Carroll could make certain he had men waiting wherever the Fulton cattle drive party turned up next.

Tom used his free hand to take his money out of his pocket. Buying a wagon and a team and provisioning for the trail had been expensive, but there was still a fair amount left. It would be enough to tempt anyone, and it was a good deal more than this fellow could expect to earn for himself by reporting Tom's whereabouts.

"I'll give you this," Tom told him frankly, watching his eyes, but the Pinkerton had a poker face that was wasted on a man in his line of work, "if you never saw me."

"I never saw you," the man replied at once.

CHAPTER SEVENTEEN

TOM HESITATED. THIS did not come easily to him.

"Can you live with that on your conscience," he asked, "letting me go?"

"I can."

Tom held out the money, and the Pinkerton reached for it. Why was it so difficult to do it? Because offhand he could think of exactly six better ways to handle this situation, each one of them snug in the chambers of his revolver? Tom was no stranger to gambling. He'd forgotten more about taking risks than most people would ever know in their lives.

Why couldn't he do it?

Because he was a *good* gambler, and this was a bad gamble.

The Pinkerton struck fast enough that it might've worked if Tom hadn't been a cardplayer. He'd sat down with more than one cheat, and he knew what those

men would do when they didn't want you to see what
they were doing with their hands. Their little tricks
and misdirections tended to work pretty well on people who didn't know what to look for. This man wasn't
foolish enough to do anything as obvious as going for
his gun with his right hand; he went for his knife with
his left instead.

While Tom wasn't really ready for him, he also
wasn't taken completely by surprise. His leg was the
problem; he couldn't move as quickly as he would have
liked.

Rather than his throat, the blade struck the barrel
of Tom's pistol as he leaned back and jerked it up to
block the knife. The Pinkerton was stronger than expected, and the blow sent the gun flying across the
room. Tom recoiled, and now he overbalanced, toppling out of the chair and onto the floor.

The Pinkerton pulled his own pistol, and Tom
kicked out desperately, knocking the other man's legs
from underneath him. With a cry of surprise, the
Pinkerton fell heavily, and Tom saw only black. He had
kicked with his bad leg, and the pain was too much.

The Colt pistol lay there within reach. Tom groaned
and snatched it up, cocking the hammer, but there was
no competition. The Pinkerton hadn't tried to get it for
himself. In fact, he hadn't even moved.

Tom heaved himself to his knees and brought the
gun up, but there was blood. For a moment his mind
was blank, and then he understood. Tom shoved the
Pinkerton onto his back, and there was the knife, buried in his ribs where he had fallen on it.

The Pinkerton gurgled horribly, and his wide eyes
fixed on Tom.

For a moment, Tom's brain stayed frozen; then it took off at a sprint. The Pinkerton opened his mouth, and Tom covered it with his hands, casting a panicked look at the door. His knees were wet; the blood was spreading.

He lunged for the bed and tore the quilt off, pressing it over the wound, then snatched a pillow as well and pressed it over the man's face. Pain like nothing before it shot through his skull as he ground his molars. Just kneeling was agony for his leg even when he wasn't moving, but he didn't feel that; he just felt the fingers pawing feebly at his arm.

Tom could barely breathe, but he pressed until the job was done, and then a moment longer, but that was all he could do.

Gasping, he seized the bedpost with white knuckles, got his good leg under him, and found his feet; then he wavered with a light head. The Pinkerton's body was motionless, with the pillow still covering his face and the quilt wadded up over the knife. The blood on the floor was smeared all over.

Tom caught the table and leaned over as a surge of nausea took him, but he held it in.

The Pinkerton was dead. Tom hadn't exactly killed him, but that wouldn't be likely to matter. He remembered Carroll's stubborn statement on the deck of *Newlywed*, that he trusted Shafer. Sometimes the truth just didn't matter as much as folks might like to think it would.

There wasn't a lawman in the world who would believe Tom hadn't murdered this Pinkerton in cold blood. It wasn't Tom's first mistake, but it had come dangerously close to being his last. This man hadn't been a watchman; he'd been an assassin. There was a bounty on Tom's head, and why not? For all anyone knew, he'd murdered that woman on the boat, murdered Shafer without cause, and perhaps even *attempted* to murder all the passengers, because why not credit him with the fire as well?

Someone who felt as Tom did that he wasn't the villain might have taken the money and kept his mouth shut. But the Pinkerton likely hadn't seen him that way, and nothing Tom might've said would change that.

He swallowed with a dry throat and wavered on his feet but gripped the bedpost. The Pinkerton might have been dead, but that didn't make him harmless. His corpse might kill Tom just as easily as a bullet would if it was found. Lawmen might ride out of this very camp if the Pinkerton had spoken to anyone downstairs, but even if they didn't, the death of a man here would confirm to Carroll that the wagon train was suspect. The man going missing might do the same, but perhaps not, and at the very least it would buy Tom some time. It was already a certainty that he couldn't go all the way to Oregon. At some point he would have to disappear, but he couldn't think about that now.

Sweat dripping from his face, he bent and picked up his crutch, then went to the window. It was still pouring. He opened the window and leaned out, and for once, the cold was welcome. His body was burning up and tingling, and he couldn't get enough air.

It was dark down there. He couldn't see much of the street, but hardly anyone would have been moving around in this weather. Good gambling wasn't so much about taking risks as it was about knowing which risks were worth your time.

Sometimes you didn't have many to choose from. He went back to the body and dragged it to the window. He took a breath, then jerked the knife out and tossed it down. Then he set his jaw and heaved up the Pinkerton, shoving him through as well. He couldn't close his ears to the thump of the body hitting the mud below, and there was also his own hiss of anguish at the strain on his leg. His dark suit was already wet from the rain; that was good. He knew he was bleeding, but if he was soaked all over, at least he wouldn't show the blood so much.

He didn't look down at the body splayed below. Tom closed the window, got his crutch, hobbled around the blood on the floor, and went into the hall. He didn't look at Asher's door as he passed it, dragging himself down to the taproom. There was enough life in the joint that a wet cripple wasn't unreasonably conspicuous. All the same, Tom thumped painfully over to the counter and put coins down, catching the barman's eye and taking a bottle of whiskey. With that under his arm, he limped out into the rain. It wasn't much, but there had to be something to show that he wasn't just coming and going from the hotel at random. If anyone saw anything odd, he would be drunk. It was all he could think of.

The Pinkerton was only a little bigger than Tom, but Tom had never been a strong man, and he certainly wasn't strong now. He set the whiskey on the cart in the alley, then moved through the mud, past the body to the yard behind the hotel, piled with lumber and debris. The outhouse door stood open, but the hotel's rear door was right there, not twenty feet away. Anyone might come out at any moment.

Fear was like a stone growing in his chest, pressing on his lungs and weighing him down. His fingers were slippery on the crutch, and now he was soaked through again and freezing.

There wasn't time to stand around and agonize.

Tom hobbled to the door and wedged his crutch under the handle. It wouldn't hold it against much, but at least it wouldn't just spring open with someone standing there to see what Tom was doing, plain as day. The dark and the rain couldn't hide everything.

With one hand on the hotel to try to keep some of his weight off the leg, he limped back to the alley, but he would need both hands for the body and all his strength. The Pinkerton had grown heavier in death, perhaps to spite Tom, or maybe it was just the water and the mud that clung to him. With his arms around the dead man's chest, Tom dragged him toward the yard. Every step was a monumental undertaking, and his leg felt curiously wrong and warm. That had to be his own blood, but he didn't stop, even when he felt faint and saw double—not that his eyes were blurred, but his hat had fallen off, and he didn't have a free hand to wipe away the rainwater.

He nudged the outhouse door open and squinted in the dark, then let the body slip to the ground. Tom caught himself on the wall, choking on the smell. It wouldn't be as simple as just tossing the body in; it was too big. A few of these boards would have to come up to make room.

He staggered to the seat and tried to lift. The board creaked, but his leg flared. The outhouse wasn't the sturdiest, but it still couldn't be effortlessly pulled apart with bare hands. Tom eased himself to the ground and rolled onto his back, pulling the pistol from his belt. He used the handle of the gun as a hammer, confident that the rain would drown out any undue noise.

He knocked several boards loose, then scrambled up and jerked them out of the way. The smell became a stench, and he held his breath as he fumbled for the dead Pinkerton. Without ceremony or any regard for what was happening in his right leg, he dragged the body up over the boards and shoved it in.

Coughing, he moved the boards back into place and hammered them down. It was dark, but in daylight, someone might be able to see. He scooped dirt and rotting leaves from the ground, throwing them in over top of the body. He didn't know if it was floating or visible, but he wasn't about to look. Only now did he realize he should have weighted it down with something. Maybe he could throw a heavy rock down on top of it—but no, he couldn't even lift a heavy rock. It wasn't in his head; he was weaker now than he had been a few minutes ago. It was like his blood was running away from him, fleeing like rats from a sinking ship.

The rain pounded the roof of the outhouse, drowning everything else out, and there was barely enough of him left to worry that anyone might be there to see what he was doing. He cast a look over his shoulder, and the dark yard was empty, water streaming from the rooftops to puddle in the mud.

That was enough. He couldn't do more. He crawled out of the outhouse and into the rain, which was heavy enough to make a lot of noise, but not so forceful that it would get the mud and filth off him.

There was a rattle from the hotel door, then the bang of a frustrated palm on it. Tom tried to take one more step than his bad leg could handle. He cringed, and his boot slipped in the mud. He caught himself with his hand and his elbow, but the pain from his leg shot through all the right side of him.

From the ground, he looked up at the jiggling handle, but he couldn't see clearly. It wasn't just the dark and the rain. He was going to faint from the pain, like a lady standing too long in the sun in a corset.

Something that wasn't cold enough to be rainwater splashed him, burning his eyes. A shape moved past, snatching the crutch from where it was wedged.

The door banged open, and yellow light spilled into the yard. Asher was between Tom and the man there, shielding his eyes.

"Would you help, mister?" Asher was asking the figure in the doorway. Tom saw the whiskey bottle lying in the mud. "My uncle has been drinking."

There was a noise of irritation, but strong arms and weak ones pulled Tom up.

"His leg is hurt," the kid was saying. He'd used the whiskey in just the way Tom had aimed to.

"All right, all right," another voice grumbled.

And they took him inside.

CHAPTER EIGHTEEN

I T AIN'T GOOD," the doctor said, squinting behind his smudged spectacles.

Tom was in too much pain to give voice to any of the remarks that seemed appropriate in reply to that. The rain was gone, but the clouds were staying; that much was obvious, even in the light before dawn. The air was merely crisp, still short of being frigid, and the rest of the wagon train was waking.

Asher was supposed to be getting the team ready, but he just stood there and watched, worried.

Tom still didn't know how much the boy had seen the night before, and there hadn't been time to talk about it. He didn't remember all of it himself, at least not as clearly as he thought he should have. He recalled stopping the kid from opening the door to his room, the one with the blood in it, and doing what he could to clean it up.

More or less.

"I know, Doc. I was drunk. I fell."

With that big beard to hide behind, it wasn't easy to tell if the doctor was suspicious or not. It wasn't even a quarter mile from this spot to that outhouse. Tom's ears were primed, but there was no indication from town that anything was amiss.

"Hurts, does it?" the doctor asked.

"Yes," Tom replied tightly.

The doctor frowned. In his hand was a stack of cloth strips that was bound to become a fresh bandage, but he made no move to use them.

"I have money," Tom told him. He'd already spoken to Breeden; the train would be back on the move in less than an hour. Tom needed help from a doctor, but he also needed to be away from this place. The air of the outhouse seemed to linger in his nose even though he was away from it now.

"It ain't that," the doctor replied, scratching at his beard. "It's that I don't know if you can keep the leg."

That hurt more than the bullet had. Tom wasn't completely apart from his senses; losing his leg had crossed his mind. He'd known plenty of men who hadn't been lucky in that regard. It was far from unheard of, but no matter how he turned it over in his head, it was something that happened to *other* people.

The kid stared.

"Is it that bad?" Tom asked, forcing a little calm into the words.

"It ain't good," the doctor repeated. "Feller, I simply do not know."

Tom licked his dry lips and caught himself before he could throw a desperate look at Asher. He couldn't do that; he was the one who was grown. The boy could rescue him from a river, but he couldn't rescue him from this.

The doctor kept looking.

"Well," Tom said finally, sucking in a deep breath, "I would just as soon you let me keep it. Unless you're real sure I shouldn't."

The doctor raised an eyebrow. "Could kill you."

Tom saw Asher. The kid was too soft. They hadn't even known each other two months, and now the boy wanted to make that sad face because Tom's leg was in a bad way. The only thing worse than the pain in his leg was that look. He sat up and snorted.

"Something'll have to," he said. "Leave it be, Doc. Unless you're sure."

"Well, I ain't sure."

"All right, then." Tom covered his leg and put on a smile. "You got some linen and something I can try to keep it clean with?"

"I do."

"I'll take it, then."

"Son," the doctor said, opening his bag and handing things to Asher, "if you see a line around here"—he motioned to Tom's thigh—"a line or a difference, like some of the skin ain't like the rest, you find someone to take it off quick as you can."

"All right," Tom replied, and he didn't let any of the queasiness into his voice.

"Quick as you can," the doctor repeated, shaking a finger at him. "You change that bandage every day, and you look at it. You look good, even when you don't want to. You watch it close. And stay *off* the damn thing. And quit drinking," he added.

"I will," Tom promised. He didn't drink, and he never had, but that didn't matter much at the moment.

When the doctor was gone, Tom sagged in the back of the wagon and looked out through the flaps at the sky above, and the gray ceiling of clouds. Asher was there, peering in.

"Quit looking at me like that, kid," he snapped. "I'm not dead yet."

"Do you remember much of last night, Mr. Calvert?" the boy asked guardedly.

"The less I remember, the better. Did it go well with the girl?"

"Ida?"

"Who else?"

Asher scowled at him. "It did. I cannot believe she is your chief concern this morning, Mr. Calvert."

"She isn't, but it's easier to talk about her than my leg," Tom replied, and that was God's truth. "She's prettier too." Of course, nearly anything was prettier than his leg at the moment.

The boy didn't say anything for a moment. "May I help you with the bandage?"

"I need you to, but it would hurt to ask." Tom smiled, and the smile was real this time. "I thought our notion was that I was the one looking after you."

Asher studied his face for a moment. "You told me last night that the notion was that we were partners."

"I just don't like asking for help, kid."

The boy smiled. "I see that."

"Are you going to make me ask?"

"I have already offered my services," Asher replied, a hint of indignation there.

"When you get to my age, you'll forget things too."

"How old are you, Mr. Calvert?" Asher asked, picking up the bandages and moving the blanket. There wasn't much left of Tom's trousers; they'd been crusted with blood, and the doctor had cut away what he had to in order to see the wound. Tom would have to cut the rest off himself, then figure out a way to dress himself that wouldn't leave him dead or in tears. He'd accept the boy's help with the bandage, but the business of dressing was something he'd have to handle himself. If the day ever came when he couldn't, that was a sure sign it was time to give it up and fold.

Folding wasn't losing. Sometimes you had to fold to win; there wasn't any shame in it.

HOOVES THUDDED ON the trail, and a rider who was likely Norman Fulton rode up from behind. He didn't linger, and Tom didn't see him look at Asher before riding on. He must've gotten another shave in town yesterday evening. It wouldn't change his fortunes with Ida, but he'd still spent his time better than Tom had. For these long weeks Tom had spent every second dreading riders out of Omaha.

Now it was riders out of that camp who were on his mind.

The wheels of the wagon creaked and groaned, so they and Tom had that in common. The pain in his leg was back in a way he hadn't felt since that first day out of the river. Something was torn, and he had a feeling he'd be lucky if that was the worst of it.

"This doesn't make any sense," he called up to Asher, who looked back from the trail.

"Your pardon?"

Tom peered at the tiny words in the book, drawing it over toward the light falling in through the wagon's open flaps. "Why's he say he hopes the man isn't sensible? Shouldn't he want him to be sensible? He has to want the man to marry one of his daughters."

"Mr. Calvert, he says that he hopes the man will not be sensible because he knows that a sensible man would never marry his daughters," Asher explained without looking back, "on account of his lack of fortune and their lack of graces and connections."

Tom considered that. "Ha," he said after a moment, slapping his knee and wincing. He groaned in pain, then smiled. "I like him, this dad."

"So do I," Asher said, and he sounded a bit wistful.

CHAPTER NINETEEN

⌒

Wyoming was a hundred times prettier to look at than Nebraska, and a thousand times more difficult to traverse. Even on a trail that had been traveled so many times that it was very nearly a road, the bumps and jolts were painful enough to make Tom see black spots and to make everything swim in his eyes.

"The gentleman Mr. Olaf, he is clever in his way of playing," Asher was saying as they crashed over another rock.

Tom's eyes strayed to the spare wheels lashed together behind their things. At this rate it wouldn't be long before they were needed. Two Norwegians had broken down just yesterday afternoon, and even one of the Fulton wagons had had some trouble the day before. They'd been lucky with waters being low so far, but it wouldn't last. It couldn't, could it?

"He isn't," Tom told Asher tiredly, watching his

breath come out as a puff of white. He pulled his blanket tighter around himself and cast an irritated glance at Asher's back. "He just knows better than to show anything on his face. I've explained it to you enough times." The game last night had been the third, and it had gone poorly for Asher.

Worse, Tom had heard from Breeden that Norman Fulton was making inquiries about sitting down to join the game. He wanted to buy his way in with sweets he'd purchased in that camp a while back. Refusing him would have been best, but that wasn't Tom's decision to make; it was Breeden's. The old man wasn't stupid; there was no winning move. Letting Norman sit was trouble, and so was telling him no.

"Do you see that stand, Mr. Calvert?" the boy called out over the creaking of the wagon. He was pointing.

Tom grumpily leaned over to see for himself. The trees in the distance looked promising, and the time of day was right.

"I expect you'll get your wish," he said tiredly.

Breeden had taken every opportunity he could to round up the men of the Norwegian families and teach them what he could about making the most of this land on the trail. The camp was far enough behind them now that a little fresh meat would go a long way for their peace of mind. It was just a matter of finding the right place to hunt when they stopped for their noontime rest.

Asher had learned to fire Breeden's Winchester rifle, and to hear the bearded man tell it, the kid was a fair shot. Cards were not as interesting to Asher as guns were. He never let a day go by without pestering Tom to teach him to shoot a pistol, and he'd even taken to interrogating him about using his hands to fight.

Tom didn't have the heart or the energy to keep telling the boy he was too small for it; he'd imparted what wisdom he could from the back of a wagon. Asher drank it all in eagerly, though Tom wasn't convinced the boy really understood any of it.

He understood hunting, though. Asher would have no difficulty with that if the game came along, so that was a mercy.

There was sweat on Tom's brow despite the cold, and he wiped it off irritably.

"Mrs. Taylor is ill," the boy was saying. "I heard it from Mr. Breeden."

Tom had heard that as well. "She's young, and she looks strong enough," he said. "She'll be all right."

Where was the harm in saying it? They didn't know the woman well, and Tom could hardly care if she lived or died, but Asher was different. Asher didn't have to know someone to worry about them; that was what had made him jump into the Missouri that night. If Mrs. Taylor died, Asher wouldn't remember Tom's false confidence, but the false confidence might help the kid *now*.

"Do you suppose Mr. Norman Fulton is skilled at cards?" Asher asked.

"I don't know, kid. I doubt it. He's an easy read."

"That is a shame." The kid was cocky; he wanted a challenge.

As soon as the halt was called, the boy fixed coffee for Tom and saw to the oxen more quickly and diligently than he ever had before, and then he was racing off to find Breeden. Tom watched from the wagon with more than a little envy; he'd never cared much for working outdoors, but as things were, he could barely walk, let alone run. It was hard not to resent himself for taking all that for granted.

Tom dragged himself out of the back and into the driver's seat, where he had a better view of things. Fires were being built, and figures were heading for the nearest trees to gather wood. It looked as though Asher wasn't the only one planning to venture out with a rifle.

And there was Ida, waving spiritedly to Asher, who stoically smiled and waved back.

Presently Breeden appeared, looking twice his age. He'd said from the beginning that he didn't like the cold. Tom had told him to go to Texas, and Breeden had told him to go to hell, so that didn't seem like a conversation worth having again.

The hunting party was setting off. Asher had Breeden's rifle, and Tom was a little surprised the old fellow wasn't going along to supervise, but it made sense when he thought about it. Breeden was tired, and he'd put his back into teaching them to get their own game. He'd earned the rest.

He climbed up to the seat beside Tom and settled in with a groan, accepting a cup of coffee.

"Is there no one else in this train you can complain to every day?" Tom asked mildly.

"Not that ain't a damn immigrant or a Texan. Can't say for sure which I hate more."

"Fair enough."

"What is that?"

"This?" Tom picked up the book. "The kid brought it. I never saw anyone so interested in rich women writing one another letters and going for walks."

Breeden took the book and paged through it for a

moment, then handed it back and sighed. "Bjorn Georgenson's boy is sick."

"Georgenson?"

"I can't say his name proper, damn it," Breeden snapped. "His son's real sick. He'll die here fairly soon."

"That's a pity," Tom said. There wasn't much else he *could* say.

"Still a good trail," Breeden replied, a touch defensively. "A charmed one, I should say. Blessed." He looked at Tom as though expecting a challenge. When he didn't get one, he just scowled and went back to watching the families prepare their noon meals. "This is where it gets bad, though. You see that rise?" He pointed.

"I do."

"Every water we've crossed has been low. That one ain't." Breeden stroked his beard. "There's a better crossing, but it'll cost us seven days at least. What do we lose if we cross? What do we lose if we don't?"

"You've already made up your mind," Tom told him.

"Course I have. Don't make me like in no better, though. That ain't the only trouble coming."

"I know."

Breeden jerked his chin, and Tom followed his gaze. "Up yonder, the wagon with the yellow on the rear?"

"I see it."

"That's Gus Burns and his wife and their two girls. Wife's name's Etta, and two nights back, we didn't have a notion where she was for near on two hours."

It was all Tom could do not to groan. "Who was she with?"

"I believe it was him right there." Breeden was

looking at a Norwegian boy from a wagon that Tom hadn't had any dealing with. He couldn't have been more than Asher's age, but he was taller and broader, and he had the makings of a beard.

Tom didn't say anything.

"If Gus is sure of himself, he'll shoot that boy dead," Breeden said, and there wasn't much feeling in the words. "And I won't lift a finger or so much as open my fool mouth. He brung it on himself." The old man shook his head miserably. "I warned him. Best thing you can do is push that girl off, Tom."

"Ida?"

"Asher don't care about her. Let Norman court her proper. If the boy had feelings for her, I'd understand, but he don't. He's making an enemy for no good cause. You *don't* make an enemy without good cause," Breeden said stubbornly.

He was right, of course. About all of it.

"I don't make the kid do anything," Tom reminded him, "not really."

"Like hell you don't. She wouldn't be so led on if you didn't."

"She'd still be sweet on him, though," Tom said quickly. "And if you don't believe it, your eyes are worse than my leg. He'll wake up. You'll see. I reckon it'll be when it's time to part ways. The kid'll realize he doesn't want to be apart. He *does* care. He worries about her. He sits with her. He listens to her though she can't barely speak, and he tries to help her."

"Why are you trying so hard, Tom?"

"Because the boy doesn't have anything," Tom told him, annoyed. "Just like me. Look at me. He's drifting, but he's got no sense, no money, no skill to put his hand

to. I had all those things and see where it landed me."
He pointed at his leg. "I wouldn't be here if I had a
wife and something to worry about. A home I should've
been at instead of the road and the boat. A cardplayer
has to move, though." Tom didn't know why he said it
or even who he was saying it to.

"The boy looks up to you."

"That's the trouble."

Breeden just shook his head in disgust. "He needs a
pa, not a damn matchmaking mother goose."

"Mother hen," Tom corrected.

"Don't matter." Breeden was right. It didn't.

"I won't back down. He'll wake up," Tom repeated.
"And he'll be glad when he does. A girl like that
doesn't come along often."

"She ain't the brightest."

"Hell, you don't know how bright she is. None of us
does because we don't speak her language. She could
be smarter than you."

"Why not? Everyone else is," Breeden grumbled,
patting his pockets for his tobacco pouch.

"What are they doing?" Tom asked suddenly, sitting
up. There were mounted figures in the distance, near
the front of the train. At least half a dozen of them,
and he could see rifles.

They were getting ready to ride out.

Breeden's face had gone stiff, but a muscle twitched
in his cheek. "Intending to hunt, I'd say." He wanted
the words to come out sounding calm for Tom's benefit.

The Texans didn't need to hunt game; they had
more than enough supplies for themselves *and* the
Norwegians, if they were inclined to share. In fact,
Tom was a little surprised they hadn't already. It

seemed a safe enough way to buy a little goodwill, which Norman was keen to get.

Now Norman had a rifle in his hand, and he was riding out behind the others.

It was too many people, and half of them didn't know what they were doing. They didn't speak the same language. Breeden had started to get to his feet, but there was nothing he could do. By the time he got back to his horse, he'd be too far behind them all to be any help, and another body in the trees wouldn't make things better.

Breeden knew exactly what Tom was thinking: that with all of that at work, it would be awfully easy for something to go wrong. Almost too easy for someone you didn't like to find a bullet by accident, or at least you could say it was an accident. Was that what Norman had in mind?

If so, there wasn't a damn thing Tom could do about it.

CHAPTER TWENTY

TOM STARTLED AWAKE, head thick and heavy, hot but shivering. He was tangled in his blanket, and he squinted up to see the clouds. They were just as they'd been a moment ago, only they weren't—they were darker. Was it the clouds that were darker? He couldn't be sure.

The noise to wake him had been some excited shouts from the north. He rubbed his eyes and tried not to groan as his leg gave a spasm and tightened up on him. He gripped the side of the wagon and squinted.

They were coming back, not just to the wagons, but this way. He tried to straighten up as everyone came closer, and there were figures on horseback behind them, but at a distance. That had to be the Texans.

Two figures were struggling under a heavy burden, and there were two more who were laden as well.

Asher was there. For a moment the pain was gone,

and Tom's eyes were clear. Breeden was with the boy, helping him carry a magnificent buck. Someone else moved in to help, and Asher pulled free and broke into a run.

He rushed up to the wagon, red-faced and sweating but beaming. He pointed back excitedly. "Do you see, Mr. Calvert?"

The only people happier than the boy were the Norwegians, and Tom understood. Asher had already promised his kill to them, and that was just what he should've done. They'd even gotten a pair of smaller deer as well. It wasn't nearly enough, but anything was better than coming back empty-handed.

One of the men was speaking excitedly to Ida, no doubt telling him the tale. There *would* be a tale, as there always was at times like these.

And there was Norman, a hundred yards off, just sitting on his horse, watching. None of the Texans had hit anything by the looks of it, and that was a genuine surprise. Breeden had spoken at length of how those Fulton boys could sling guns. How they were faster than he'd ever seen and how they didn't miss.

Gradually, Tom's heart was starting to slow down. He could breathe.

Asher was safe. Norman hadn't done anything. Had it been on his mind?

There wasn't a single reason to think Norman hadn't gone into those trees with the same notion as Asher: to find food for the bellies of the less fortunate in the train.

That much hadn't even entered Tom's thinking. Jealousy and . . . scheming. That was where Tom's mind had gone without any hesitation at all.

Norman was a long way off, but that wasn't why Tom couldn't see his face, even squinting.

"Mr. Calvert?" Asher's voice sounded worried.

Tom shook his head, but the dizziness wouldn't clear from his mind, and the blurry look of things wouldn't leave his eyes. He peered at the boy, who was still smiling the way he *ought* to smile every time he saw Ida. He was still short of breath. Tom was too.

"I see," he said, leaning forward and offering his hand.

Grinning, Asher stepped forward and shook it eagerly.

"That's quite an animal," Tom told him.

CHAPTER TWENTY-ONE

ASHER WAS BETTER with the animals than Tom was, and he got them across the river that Breeden was so worried about with surprisingly little difficulty. Columns of woodsmoke rose up as they all reached the far bank and built fires. Clouds of steam rose from people and animals alike as they all tried to get warm.

There might have been a feeling of relief if the clouds hadn't returned to hang, heavy and menacing, over the river. The river water was cold, and rain wouldn't be any warmer. The noises of the rushing water and the raised voices as they toiled to get everyone across were almost overwhelming, but once the work was done and the fires were built, a thick silence descended over them all.

People were huddled together, shivering just as Tom was in the smoky haze that filled the air. Soon it was as though a white fog had come off the river, and even the people from a wagon just thirty feet away looked like specters.

Asher tidied up after they ate, then climbed to the driver's seat, where Tom handed him a blanket. The boy wrapped himself in it and watched a pack of Norwegians with their fishing tackle making their way down the bank.

"Will they catch anything?" he asked.

"I'm the wrong man to ask." Tom knew nothing at all about fishing.

Asher peered into the wagon. "Is there anything more to dry?"

Tom shook his head, squinting at the ghostly shapes of the cowhands riding among the cattle. One of them was shouting something, but he couldn't make out the words.

"And the books?" the boy pressed worriedly, looking around. "Are they dry?"

"They are," Tom said, smiling despite himself. Of all the things to worry about. He held up both volumes, and Asher took them, looking relieved. He turned to the spot where Tom had marked his place.

"Oh," he said, seeing the page that Tom had been reading. "What do you think, Mr. Calvert?"

"Hmm? Oh." Tom scratched his cheek. He'd done a terrible job shaving; his hand had been shaking. He was lucky he hadn't cut his face to ribbons. He focused on the boy's words and ignored the pain in his leg and the ache behind his eyes. "I think the girl can't see straight."

"I do not take your meaning."

Tom glanced at the book disdainfully. "This new officer's no good."

"You do not think so? Why?"

"He talks too much."

"You can judge his character from only that?" Asher was staring at him.

Tom rubbed his eyes. "First time he speaks to her, he tells her all the bad that's ever come his way? A man doesn't do that, kid." He snorted. "But a grifter's always got a story to tell."

THE NORWEGIANS WERE getting ragged. Up to this point, they'd had enough food to eat, if not as much as they might have wanted. They had been stretched every inch of the way and held up well, considering, but once they crossed that icy water, things weren't the same. Getting cold was a lot easier than getting warm again.

It was one thing to know the winter was coming and another to start to feel its breath. This might've been a good spot to take the time to go in search of game, but no one was making any moves in that direction. Moving might have been the best thing, but it wasn't so easy to get started when there was frost on the ground. The air was sharper and emptier. Birds didn't like the cold any more than people did, and even the buzzards had made off for somewhere better.

Tom had never seen people so tired.

Yet they still found the strength to get the poles and the canvas and put up the big tent. The threat of rain seemed to be moving on, but the tent was part of the tradition now. It was still strange to see people so invested in a game without money, but no stranger than the book that Tom and the kid were reading. People

sat around and played cards because evidently they
had nothing more pressing to do. The notion was
strange to Tom, like something out of a dream that
didn't make any sense.

Night had never been so bright; the fires were built
up bigger and hotter now, but they kept away the dark
better than the cold, which was stubborn and ruthless.

From his seat on the wagon, Tom couldn't see the
game, but he could see the faces of the players. Asher
had his back to him, but he had a good view of nearly
everyone else.

These boys from Texas didn't know how to play cards.

They'd done it before, and unlike Asher, they'd probably even done it for money. Not for real, though. They'd
played for their amusement, and that wasn't gambling.

And Norman—well, Norman wasn't well-known for
his ability to conceal what was in his head. He'd made
it about as obvious as could be that he wanted nothing
in life but to stare at Ida, and he was no more guarded
about his cards than he was about his feelings.

Asher had finally come far enough to see it. Tom
had gotten it through the kid's thick skull that if you
knew how your opponent felt about his cards, that was
as good as knowing what the cards were.

Norman had come to the table, but he wouldn't
make a dent in it. It was those three older Norwegians—
they were Asher's real opponents, and the kid knew it.
That was the tragedy. Norman was nobody's scholar,
but he had to have enough sense to think that he wasn't
likely to impress Ida by playing poker. Maybe he just
wanted to beat Asher at something. Anything.

But he wouldn't. He wouldn't win. Asher was a poor
poker player at best, but after weeks in a wagon with

Tom, he *was* a poker player. Norman wasn't, and that
meant he was outclassed. He was going to lose all his
sweets, and that wasn't even the worst of it. Not only
would he not win the duel he wanted so badly to have;
he wouldn't even get to have it. He might as well not
even have been there. Asher didn't see Norman as a
rival. He didn't see Norman as anything, and his attention was fixed wholly on the three Norwegians, who
were now his only competition.

Norman didn't want to lose, but he couldn't *stand*
being ignored.

Breeden hadn't made any mention of Norman as an
angry man, and Norman had given no indication of it
with his stubborn solitude and staring, but it was there
all the same. It was the stiffness in his body and the
sullen look in his eyes. It wasn't anger—not yet. It was
resentment, but there was a certainty in that. A caterpillar would become a butterfly, and resentment had
only one place to go.

Tom's hand hurt more than his leg did; he saw himself gripping the edge of the seat. He let go and took a
breath, making himself look at the distinctive shape of
Jake's hat in the group. It was too easy to get lost in
thinking on the bad, and that was a mistake. Things
weren't *always* going to play out the way Tom expected,
and occasionally they'd turn out better. Jake was a
good example of that: Tom and Breeden had been all
but convinced that he'd be a terror to the train's wom-
enfolk. He'd initially made good on that, but it hadn't
gone as Breeden had feared and Tom had fully expected. The girl's name was Nora, and it had now gotten around that Jake fully intended to marry her.

Tom hadn't believed it at first, but the weeks had

gone by with nothing to suggest anything untoward. So maybe he'd be wrong about Norman as well.

It was easy to tell when the last hand came, and Tom cringed at the way it ended. He couldn't see Asher's face, but he knew just the look that would be on it. He didn't have to imagine how Norman would react to that; *that*, he could see clearly.

Then something happened that he did not expect. Norman's temper held, after a fashion. He said something, and the people reacted in a hushed manner, but one that indicated surprise, not alarm. Frustrated, Tom tried to sit a little taller, straining his ears.

Norman was saying something to Asher.

Breeden tried to step in, but Eli was there, and Eli said something that stopped the other man. Breeden didn't look happy, but he just grimaced and shook his head.

Asher said something, then leaned forward and put his hand out.

Norman shook it, and it was all Tom could do to keep his dinner down. The people dispersed, and the tent came down; it was later than was wise, and morning would come much too quickly. Tom waited, shivering, as Asher made his way back.

There were things he wanted to say, but he didn't. He'd spent enough time in the kid's company to know that it was never necessary to ask.

"Mr. Calvert," Asher said breathlessly, hurrying up to the wagon, "Mr. Norman Fulton has challenged me to a game of poker."

"Oh, yeah?" Tom replied neutrally, squinting at the people all returning to their wagons.

"Yes. And I have accepted. We will play for money."

Tom winced, and for a moment, his irritation reared up—then it settled down again. Nothing he said or did would change things. Once you pulled the trigger, the bullet could never go back in the gun. Sweets were harmless. Money wasn't. Tom knew it, and Breeden knew it, and no one else seemed to.

"Did you clean him out?" he asked tiredly.

The kid was so happy that his smile seemed brighter than the lantern. "I have walked away with half again what I sat down with," Asher reported proudly.

"You should've gone easy on Norman, kid."

Asher frowned. "Your pardon?"

"Norman. You know he's sweet on Ida. He doesn't like you. You're only making it worse."

"Mr. Calvert," Asher replied, a bit forcefully and with a hint of annoyance, "you have labored to teach me to win. And I have sat down and done it, but even if I had the inclination, I am not so skilled that I can win and lose at will. I played my best hands. With no regard for my opponent," he added, eyes flashing.

Tom groaned. "That's fair, kid. But we have a while yet in his company."

"He is a poor player."

"Don't let it go to your head. You've been practicing, and he hasn't. That's the only difference between the two of you, and even the worst player can knock you flat on a good hand."

But the boy wasn't listening; he was just gaping. "Mr. Calvert, I have done *precisely* what you asked me to do," he said. "*Why* are you scolding me?"

The question took Tom by surprise. He swallowed, and a particularly cruel throb from his leg made his eye twitch. He let his breath out slowly.

Norman and his brothers were nowhere to be seen in the dark. They'd gone with their people, to the wagons at the front of the train. There was barely a sound from the exhausted herd, and the camp itself was well on its way from quiet to silent.

"Because I don't want to see you make enemies," Tom said finally.

"You said that was what winners do," Asher shot back.

And there was nothing Tom could say to that.

CHAPTER TWENTY-TWO

TOM HISSED, WINCING.

Asher stopped what he was doing with the stove and hurried back to the wagon, jumping up to look in.

"Mr. Calvert? Are you well?"

"I'm all right." Tom glanced up at him. "It's just this silly book."

There was the lightest dusting of snow on the ground, barely enough to change the color of it, but the trouble was that noon had come, and it wasn't melting. The sun shone impotently while dark clouds waited in the west.

"What is it?" the boy asked curiously.

Tom made a face and put the book aside, dragging himself out of the back. The kid obligingly got out of the way.

"She just found out the girl's going to marry that preacher."

"Ah," Asher replied, but he paused and gave Tom a funny look. "I would think you would approve, Mr. Calvert. I thought you would say that was a good and sensible thing."

"Well, they have an odd way of putting it to words, but nobody likes him," Tom pointed out. "You wouldn't want to marry someone you didn't like. Someone no one liked."

"She had her reasons. Good reasons. Intelligent ones."

Tom shook his head. "Money? Money for your freedom—that's a bad trade, kid."

"What freedom, though?" Asher glanced at the pot on the stove to be sure it was all right, then folded his arms and met Tom's gaze. "I expect you have forgotten that you and she are not the same, Mr. Calvert. You can do as you please. Go anywhere, do anything. She cannot. She does not see things as you see them."

"Well, obviously. Because I'd never marry someone for those reasons," Tom replied, shrugging.

"She does not feel that she has the luxury of choice."

"Of course she has a choice."

"You might think that, but to her, she might very well see only an unhappy marriage or spinsterhood. Even destitution. In her circumstances, that is not *really* a choice," the boy explained stubbornly.

"Then you would've done what she did?" Tom challenged.

"If I saw the world as she did, I might very well have done the same," Asher replied, unperturbed. He was going to go on, but he saw the look on Tom's face. "Mr. Calvert?"

"Something's not right."

A couple of the cowboys were ignoring the cattle, and Tom could see Breeden speaking to Jake and Rodney Fulton. There were other men from the forward wagons coming together, and several Norwegians had noticed that something was amiss.

"You'd better go see what it's about," Tom told the boy. "I'll see to this."

"Are you certain?" Asher asked, eyeing Tom's leg.

"Go." Using his crutch, Tom eased himself to the ground, keeping his weight off his bad leg. A few weeks ago Asher would've argued. Now he just gave Tom a look that made it clear how he felt, and jogged off.

Tom gingerly saw that the beans didn't burn, then leaned on his crutch and watched what was unfolding. A Norwegian man was taking something wrapped in a blanket out of the back of a wagon. Tom saw him unwrap a massive smooth-bore powder rifle.

That more or less answered his question.

The horses were sensing the agitation, and several of the mounted cowhands brought them around, rifles in hand, their eyes on the distant trees. It was several minutes before Asher came running back, visibly troubled.

"What did they find?" Tom asked, looking back at the trail. There was no sign of anyone back there, but they were very nearly the last wagon. Tom hadn't minded that so much in the beginning. It was no longer convenient, though.

"There is—," the boy began, but paused to get his

breath. He pointed. "A farmstead. You can see it from the fore. It is to the south. Mr. Breeden told me that several men from the Texas company rode out to trade and found no one there."

"Were there signs of trouble?"

"It appears not. No graves or bodies were discovered," Asher reported. "The animals are gone." He paused. "Everyone seemed to know what it all meant, but I do not. What do you make of it, Mr. Calvert?"

"Think about it, kid. Did they just leave?"

"Not without their things."

"Someone took them. Did anyone say how long ago they reckoned it was?"

"Not long, according to Mr. Eli Fulton. A few days at most."

Tom looked to the west. He hadn't heard of anything like this, but the trail wasn't what it had once been. There were no longer so many wagons, no longer so many people passing through this country nowadays. Most folks realized they were better off going by rail.

Without realizing it, Tom had taken out a deck of cards and begun to shuffle.

"Is it savages?" the boy asked.

Tom stopped shuffling. "Most likely," he replied after a moment. "Though I don't know that's what you want to call them. After all, you don't see them shooting one another over a piece of paper," he added, holding up a card. "Or perhaps they do. I don't know. But I don't like that word."

"Are we in danger?"

Tom put his cards away. "No, kid." He indicated

with his finger. "This is a good train. There won't be enough of them to move on us." The fear of Indians was more dangerous than the Indians themselves. It would no longer be safe for anyone to go away from the train alone or even in a small group. Bathing, hunting—everything would be more difficult, but the worst thing of all would be this: what was right in front of them.

The others were all getting their rifles and growing wary. The trail and the winter were enemies enough; worrying about being attacked would only stretch them further. People could worry only so much, and worry hurt more than they realized. Tom liked to use worry and pressure against his opponents at the table, but that was different. Upsetting them, forcing them to make mistakes was a solid way to win games.

These people weren't his opponents, but now their fear was.

Breeden didn't waste his time trying to calm them down; he just got the train moving as quickly as he could. There were those who didn't care much for it, but their desire to keep up was stronger than their urge to complain.

IT WAS A long day under a cold blue sky. Asher asked Tom everything he knew about Indians, which was pitifully little. He asked why Indians would take people from their home that way, and Tom didn't have it in him to answer truthfully. Instead, he shrugged.

"Whose home is it really?" he asked.

The boy looked surprised by that and a little affronted. Then thoughtful.

"What's Friendly Field supposed to be like?" Tom asked. The kid needed to think about something else.

Asher jumped as though startled, and the team noticed. For a moment he struggled to get the oxen back in line; then he cleared his throat.

"What do you mean, Mr. Calvert?"

"Are you really trying to find this place? Or is it just your reason for keeping on the move?"

"I will find it."

"What's it got more than a nice name?"

Asher hesitated. "I have heard there are good Christian people there," he said.

"Who told you that?"

"My aunt."

"Where is she now?"

"She is gone." Asher kept his eyes on the team.

So that was it. The kid didn't give a damn about Friendly Field. Tom had already more or less figured the boy had no parents. His aunt had probably raised him, and he'd lost her too. She'd likely mentioned something about Friendly Field to him, and it had stuck.

Tom couldn't know for certain, but he didn't need to.

"Sorry, kid. You may yet find it."

"I expect I will," Asher replied.

Friendly Field was in question, but the night would always come, and it had changed. The dark wasn't a blanket anymore to help them all to sleep; now it was a cloak for invisible Indians that more than likely weren't even out there.

The fires went up bigger and higher than they had any night before, even colder nights than this one, and the wagons had never been so tightly packed together.

The boy had eaten with a glazed look on his face, saying nothing, which was unlike him. He didn't appear worried about Indians, though.

"Go and find Ida," Tom told him after they'd tidied up. "She'll be as afraid as the others. More afraid, maybe."

Lights were moving in the dark; men on horseback were keeping the perimeter and building up even more fires.

"Mr. Calvert, I do not know what I might tell her that others have not," Asher replied, looking up with a frown. "*I* am afraid as well."

"You don't have to tell her anything. Just sit with her by the fire for a spell."

The boy took that in. Finally he took a deep breath and nodded.

"You are right," he said as he sometimes did when Tom's words pulled him out of his reverie. It wasn't that they disagreed; it was just that the boy had a way of getting lost in his thoughts. Sometimes he had to be reminded of even the most obvious things.

As Asher walked off, Breeden approached the campfire. Tom had been wondering when he would turn up to gripe.

"Almost as though they *want* trouble," he grumbled, settling down beside Tom and taking a bottle from inside his jacket. He took a long pull. "Like there ain't nothing in this world they'd enjoy more than shooting an Indian."

"I expect a fair number of them are bored to tears, driving that herd day in and out," Tom replied.

"You don't look for trouble for idleness' sake."

"You shouldn't," Tom agreed. "Doesn't seem to stop anyone."

Breeden didn't even have words for that; he just made a noise of disgust. "Damn Norwegians. I about talked myself blue, trying to make them understand they have to keep them wagons in close and tight. They won't do it."

"They're a proud bunch, aren't they?"

"Well, they got more sense than some," Breeden snarled, glancing toward the wagons of the Texan party. "But that ain't saying much. Listen to them holler. There's a chance them Indians might not have even known we were about. So much for that."

"They won't bother us," Tom said, yawning.

"I know. But them ones that take you in the night," Breeden said, squinting out at the dark, "spirit you away, take you and don't leave nothing behind—they're the ones you don't want to run into."

Tom couldn't argue with that.

The stars came out, but a thin veil of clouds came along to dull their light. There was something out there, some shape in the hills that did something to the wind, making it loud and ugly as the moon rose.

The fires around the wagons grew higher, and the cooking fires died down. Asher returned, and Breeden shuffled away into the gloom, his rifle leaned over his shoulder.

"Let it go out," Tom told Asher as he started to gather sticks. "Is she all right?"

"I believe so," Asher replied, looking distinctly uncomfortable as he always did after spending time with Ida. He joined Tom by the dying fire. They listened to it crackle and watched the embers dim.

"Shall we retire?" Asher asked.

"Not just yet, kid." Tom rubbed his face for a moment,

then sat up straight and pulled the pistol out of his belt. He turned it over in his hands a few times, staring absently out at the dark. Then he shook himself awake and looked at the boy. "You still want to learn how to use one of these?"

CHAPTER TWENTY-THREE

IF THE LAST camp had exceeded expectations, Croshaw Camp fell well short of them. There was one hotel, though that was using the word generously, and very little else. A vague uncertainty hung in the air with the chill, as though even these few settlers who remained were not fully convinced they ought to do so. There had been a silver mine here, and then there had been talk of gold that never materialized, and now all that was left was fur.

The motley, tumbledown collection of buildings offered little comfort to the approaching wagons, either real or imagined. There was smoke in the air, though, and people were about, and that counted for something.

Normally Tom would have killed for a chance to sleep in a bed. Now that thought was followed by thoughts of getting down from the wagon, entering the inn, and climbing up to a room. It would almost be better to just sleep in the wagon. When had the pain in his leg grown greater than the aches in his back?

Asher was looking at him uncertainly, and Tom handed over the reins. Just the thought of reaching for his crutch seemed like too much. The boy wasn't blind.

"Perhaps we do not need rooms tonight," he said uncertainly.

"No, kid. Best if I don't roll over and fold." Tom reached into the back and got his crutch. "If I go to sleep that way, I may not wake up."

"I do not understand."

"Neither do I. I just feel like if I stop moving, I might not be able to start again."

"Your leg pains you, though."

"So do you, kid. But the sun'll still come up tomorrow. Bring us up over there," Tom said, pointing. "Over by Oen."

He didn't look at his leg, and neither did Asher. It should have been an easy night. The people of Croshaw were glad of the opportunity for business, and they could all rest without worrying about Indians. That was how it ought to have been if things had been simple.

Tom eyed the sad little cluster of tents and buildings, indistinct in the gathering dark.

Asher did a good job positioning the wagon and jumped down to see to the team. Tom hefted his crutch, steeled himself, and prepared to climb down. As he leaned over, his head swam, and his limbs were alarmingly heavy.

But he wouldn't be deterred. He wouldn't be frightened by pain and weakness into just lying down on his deathbed. If he was going to die in his sleep tonight—and he did not *think* that he would, but supposing that was the case—he'd do it in a real bed in that hotel after dragging himself over that patch of icy mud, into that street, through that door, and up those stairs.

He could do that much.

Or not; he started to topple out of the wagon, but strong hands caught him. The moment of faintness fled, and he pulled himself back upright, heart thudding. He could've broken his neck just then.

It wasn't Asher who had caught him; it was Norman Fulton.

The dour young man had a worried look on his face, a welcome departure from his usual expression of general discontent. His eyes went to Tom's bad leg, but he didn't ask after his health; he just drew himself up and fixed Tom with his gaze.

"Hello there," Tom said for lack of anything better. The faint way his voice came out was perhaps the most alarming thing yet.

"Mr. Calvert."

Asher had stopped what he was doing to stare in their direction. Norman noticed but didn't react.

Tom waved a hand. "Keep on," he said.

Reluctantly, Asher obeyed.

"What's on your mind, Mr. Fulton?"

"Is your aim to humiliate me?" the young man asked simply, taking off his hat and turning it over in his hands. He wasn't wearing any gloves, but if the cold bothered him, he wasn't showing it.

"No. I give you my word on that. And it isn't his aim either," Tom added, glancing at Asher, who was still busy with the oxen.

"You seem like a man who ain't blind," Norman said frankly, stepping closer.

Tom saw the gun on Norman's hip, and it wasn't the first time he'd looked at it with a feeling like worry.

"I do not make my feelings a secret," Norman said.

"Have you made a declaration to her?"

"I can't very well do that."

That was true. Tom grimaced and nodded. "I don't know what to tell you. She doesn't hide hers, either. It is what it is."

"I have powerful feelings for her."

Tom believed him, and what was more, Tom sensed those feelings were more or less honorable. It was true that Ida was very pretty, but she was also rather insubstantial. She lacked the womanly curves to tempt a man, and though she was both sweet and gentle, she was also very odd. There were half a dozen Norwegian girls in the party more inclined to draw and keep a man's eye, and not once had Tom seen Norman so much as glance at any of them.

"I wish you would find another girl," Tom said.

"I have thought that myself," Norman said quietly.

Tom could hear the anger under the words, and it was colder than the frost on the grass.

"That is just what I ought to do, and then I see how *he* feels." That was closer to a snarl.

"He's just a kid," Tom hissed back. "He says he's sixteen. Tell you the truth, I don't *know* how old he is. He *looks* twelve. He has no eye for girls. He doesn't mean you or anyone any ill."

"Yesterday she went to kiss him, and he acted like a snake were jumping at him," Norman shot back. "I'd step aside if she got fixed on a man who loved her, but

I'll be damned if I give up for a simpleton who don't even want her. That," he went on, cutting Tom off, "is what I mean to say, and I've told you on account that the boy has no sense at all, and I will not waste my breath on him."

Tom hesitated; then he swallowed his reply. "All right," he said after a moment. "I've heard you, Mr. Fulton. And I believe I take your meaning."

Norman put his hat back on and stalked away without another word. Asher was already finished with his work, but he'd been waiting politely out of earshot. Now he trotted over, casting a worried look over his shoulder.

"What is it?" he asked. "Something to do with our game?"

"No, kid." Tom rubbed his eyes. "He's tired of you."

"What?"

"Of you and Ida. He finally came out and said it." They watched Norman climb onto his horse and head into town at a canter. "You'll have to watch your back."

"Mr. Calvert, I have attempted to distance myself from her," Asher said, frustrated. "At least in that way."

"Did you tell her you weren't interested?"

"No, but I remarked more than once that the Fultons are fine men and that any one of them would make a very eligible husband. I told her very forthrightly that Mr. Norman was in love with her. I told her that I have very little to offer and would be a poor match," the boy said sourly.

Tom was taken aback. He hadn't realized the boy had gone that far. Yet Ida was as deeply in love with him as ever, so it clearly hadn't worked.

"Her reply?" he pressed.

The kid swallowed. "She began to weep and asked me if . . ." He groaned in frustration, and it was every bit as intense as what Norman had to have been feeling. "It does not matter. She was wounded, and I had no choice but to comfort her, and then it was as though I had never said anything. She will not be dissuaded." Asher glared at Tom. "Not *all* young women are this way," he added fiercely.

"Hush, kid. You don't know the first thing about women." Tom snorted. "And it's to Ida's credit that she doesn't care about money."

"Mr. Calvert, she believes *we* have money."

"We do, at least compared to her and her people. But you're right about that." Tom sighed. "Forget it, kid. She's not the problem now. He is. I've seen that look before. A man can be pushed only so far."

Asher groaned. "*I* am pushing no one," he said indignantly, shaking his fists.

"Stop that," Tom told him, swatting Asher's hands down. "And it may not be your design, but you *are*. Hell, you're pushing me too. I've told you at least five times that by now you should have an arrangement with that girl. But leave it be. I still have a hill to climb, and we have the rest of the night to fight."

"I do not wish to quarrel with you, Mr. Calvert. Or with Mr. Fulton. But if I rebuff Ida, *then* I will make enemies of Oen and all the rest."

There was that as well. The Norwegians appeared to take Asher's hesitance as a sign of gentlemanly intent. They all liked him very much, but they also liked the notion of another connection to a Fulton. It didn't matter to them what happened to Asher or Norman or who came out ahead.

But a few of them, like Oen, would all be greatly offended if anyone said or did anything unkind to Ida.

"I must remain her friend," Asher went on. "When the time comes, we will go our way, and she will go hers. In the meantime, she will fare better with me to confide in. You may call it love, Mr. Calvert, but I say she has grown reliant on me as a—a brother, in place of the family she has lost. Even if she does not realize it herself."

Tom didn't know which was worse: that the kid was lying to his face or that he was lying to himself. He knew damn well Ida wanted Asher so badly, she probably cried herself to sleep each night.

It was irksome enough that Tom had half a mind to lay the kid out right there. He put that urge aside and picked up his crutch. "Help me," he said, reaching down, and Asher did his best. Tom's leg hurt enough to bring down a man twice his size, and he didn't have the strength to hold up a silk scarf.

With the boy to help *and* the crutch, Tom started up the muddy slope toward the camp. Asher waved to Oen, who would dutifully watch over their wagon and team. If Tom had enough strength in him to be inclined to hit the boy, there was no better time to make the journey. It might've been possible to coax a few of the other wagons out of the way so that they could drive up a little closer to the hotel, but Tom liked it better this way. Either he'd make it or he wouldn't, and he'd know which soon enough.

Asher shoved the door open, and they dragged themselves into the relative warmth of the camp's best impression of a taproom. Being the only such room for many, many miles, it was appropriately filled with people. Tom should've been able to take the lay of it at a glance, to know how many there were and a great deal about each one—but all he saw were squirming figures, and the noise of it all sounded far away.

"Sir," someone was saying.

"Mr. Calvert," Asher prompted, and his voice came out tight from the effort of supporting nearly all of Tom's weight.

"I'm all right," Tom bit out hoarsely. It was just the effort of the moving and the pain—it had sent him far away for a moment, but he was back. He shook his head. "I'm sorry. We need two rooms if you have them."

"I have the one," the man replied, coming out from behind the counter. He spoke as though distracted, leaning over to peer at Tom's face. "And I could move a girl out of another, though you'll pay for that."

"I will." Tom shifted his weight onto his crutch. "I will," he repeated, even though the clipped words seemed to take all his breath.

"Son, do you need a drink or a doctor?"

Tom grimaced. "May as well send for the doctor."

"I'll do that." The man was older, and his finger shook as he pointed it at Asher. "How about I give you the key for one room now and you take this fellow on up there, and then I'll have another got ready in a little bit. Would that suit you?"

"That will be fine. Thank you," Asher said, and there wasn't enough politeness in the world to hide his worry. For once Tom didn't blame him. Now, with Norman wearing thin, would not be a good time for the boy to have to face the day alone. He'd learned a great deal in the time Tom had known him, but he wasn't ready.

Not yet.

"Sorry, kid," Tom panted as they struggled up the steps. He knew he wasn't being much help, and it was clear how difficult it was for the boy. He was tough, and he wasn't afraid of hard work, but Asher just wasn't growing.

"It is quite all right," the boy bit out. "Only a little farther."

They got through the door, and Tom fell on the dresser. There he stayed, leaning on it heavily. Asher caught his crutch before it could fall. Tom held up his hand before the boy could try to say anything.

"Asher, the notion was that you would help me," he said, "not that you would play nursemaid."

"Mr. Calvert, I fear you have taken a turn for the worse."

"I have, but fearing it's a waste of your time. Go see about something to eat. I'll see the doctor. If you'd bring up some food, I'd be grateful, but that's all I need of you."

Asher looked hurt, and Tom groaned.

"Hell, kid. This long cooped up in a wagon, you're supposed to be glad to have a minute to yourself."

"I am worried for you, Mr. Calvert."

"Worry about yourself. Think about what you're going to do about Ida. Think hard on it. Think about whether or not you want those Fulton brothers for your enemies, because that's where we're going. It's a wagon train, so it's not going anywhere fast, but it'll *get* there. And so will you. Go on." Tom shooed Asher out the door and closed it.

Slowly, he eased his weight off the dresser and onto his crutch.

It wasn't much of a room. The fixtures were poor even to Tom's eye, and he asked very little. Still, it was preferable to the back of a wagon. He wobbled but stayed upright; all of the weakness was with him, but at least there was none of the light-headedness at the moment. He was thinking clearly, though that was no longer a terribly cheerful business.

CHAPTER TWENTY-FOUR

〰

ABOUT FIFTEEN YEARS before Tom took a bullet to the leg on the deck of *Newlywed*, and also about fifteen hours before he first picked up a deck of cards, he'd been Asher's age or close to it and working hard every minute.

Most days he spent working at the K Saloon in Springfield, and when he wasn't there, he worked in the livery. There hadn't been any call on him to fight in the war on account of his mother, who was ill and would be dead within a year, and there was no one else to provide for her.

He didn't mind the livery, but he preferred the saloon, where the wage was a little better. There was also a girl there named Elizabeth who liked him, and on slow days, it was possible to steal away with her for a while.

Yet he also saw the gamblers, who were neither

plentiful nor much good, but sometimes as much as ten dollars might be piled up there on the table for the man who just happened to be holding the right cards to take. To take for nothing, to Tom's thinking.

But he liked the certainty of real work. He was a planner, and because he knew little of cards, they didn't seem to him like a terribly reliable way of providing for a family. He had good prospects of taking over most of the business of the K in a few years, and that would be a fine living. That had not seemed like an unreasonable plan: to move up a little more, propose to Elizabeth, and go from there.

But Elizabeth had disappeared one day. At the time, Tom thought she had run off. As a grown man, he realized she'd likely been murdered by one of her customers—but on that day, the day before he played his first hand of poker, Elizabeth was still alive, and he was holding her hand and then letting go of it to hurry downstairs and get back to work.

That was when a man called Butch Helms came into the K, and everything changed. He was nothing special to look at, an older fellow with a mustache, dressed well enough for a man who looked and sounded like he worked around horses. There was a lot of gray in his mustache, and he had a big Colt pistol in what looked like an Army holster.

He drank just one whiskey, and as the usual men drifted in, the cards came out.

Helms won a hand early against Blake Straw, who was by far the stupidest and most belligerent man of Tom's acquaintance. He liked to hit women and make it clear to anyone who would listen that if not for a long list of injustices that changed from day to day, he would certainly be mayor or president or the Almighty, for all anyone cared.

Blake lost the next few as well and left the table, and that was when Tom started to pay attention to Helms. He'd never seen anyone like this: someone who just sat there with a face like a statue and won hand after hand without any apparent effort—or even interest in what he was doing.

But just like that, in a quarter of an hour, he had taken twelve dollars from these men who played cards every night.

Then he lost twenty dollars and didn't bat an eyelid, even as Fred Simmons got up and danced a jig in celebration.

Tom looked on as Helms took it all back and then some. It was more money than Tom would take home in a month, a good month, and Helms looked ready to fall asleep. There was something about how he handled the cards, though. It reminded Tom of how Franklin the barber handled his razor and his scissors. How many decades had Helms spent doing this?

That was what Tom was wondering when John Hillman called Helms a cheat. He hadn't noticed them taking a break from the game, or John speaking quietly to Blake outside the saloon, or any of the other things that might have served to give him a fuller picture of what was unfolding, but he still put it together. That wasn't difficult to do when it was all happening right in front of his nose. The accusation was a formality really. Nothing was meant to come of it, because as John said the words, Blake aimed to shoot Butch Helms in the back.

Poker hadn't always been a game, as such. Even before that night, Tom had seen it go bad. He'd seen teeth sent flying and broken glasses and even a knife drawn once. All the same, none of those moments had given him a sense of just how quickly it could happen. Like a candle being blown out.

Even if he wore no uniform, the days were still filled with the war or at least talk of it. And more, he had seen the result: wounded men and all that went with them. Tom thought about war and battle, not murder. Murder was another matter entirely. One moment you could be counting your money, and the next—that was what a bullet in the back could be.

Of course, Helms wasn't content to be murdered. He must've had a notion of what was coming—that or he'd used the mirror behind the bar, but there were only two shots fired that evening, and neither one of them struck him. Blake toppled through the door, back into the street with a bullet in his belly first, as Helms had fired under his coat before turning the gun on John.

John put his hands up with wide eyes, but Helms wasn't interested. He didn't even allow John to speak, let alone give any thought to his words. He just pulled the trigger and sent John on his way, all in the space of a heartbeat.

And his poker face held all the while. The face he wore when he won a hand, lost a hand, and shot a man through the heart—they were all the same.

Later, when Tom picked up the cards for himself, he decided that he would *not* die the way that Butch Helms had almost died that night. He would be careful, like Helms. That was why he'd taken care to keep his eyes open and clear, unclouded by smoke or drink or anything else. That was why he'd spent countless hours and even more bullets with that gun of his. Because the life of a cardplayer was a lonely one; you had to be able to handle your own business. It was all well and good to have someone to watch your back, but you couldn't count on that any more than you could count on the inside straight. So it struck him as interesting that he'd given so little thought to where he would die, when he'd given so much thought to where he would *not*. Tom had been as careful as a man could be to avoid a bullet in the back; breathing his last in a creaky, half-rotted bed on the second floor of a third-rate hotel in a place that could only charitably be called a camp—well, he hadn't seen it coming.

It *was* coming, though. Maybe in this bed or in the back of the wagon when he nodded off.

He stood where Asher had left him, leaning on his crutch and gazing at the bed.

It was time to face it. Each day he changed for the worse, but his thoughts were the same: that he would wait and see. That perhaps he would get better and perhaps he would not. He liked to think he was being reasonable, but that wasn't the truth. He was just trying to make it all into another day's problem.

But it was a problem for now, because he knew.

His wound had gone bad. No matter what, he would not show it to Asher. If only Tom knew, and no one else, then it wasn't completely real. But if Asher knew and Tom saw the look on his face when he learned— then it would be real in a new way. A way he wouldn't be able to avoid.

And he didn't much care to. It would be better to just die one of these nights and never go through that.

He snorted. A wound gone ill could run its course, but he'd seen enough during the war that he also knew the other side of it. Could he live if he let the leg go? Was there still time?

There was a tap at the door, and that brought him out of his brooding memories. Was Butch Helms still alive? If not, how had he gone? At rest or at the table?

Tom opened the door for Asher and the doctor, only it wasn't them. Of course it wasn't. It had been only a few minutes. Even in good health, Tom didn't need long to spend an eternity basking in the pale and sickly light of the past.

Dan Karr held a revolver in his hand.

It was a moment of clarity. There was no lightness in Tom's head, nothing to stop or slow his thoughts. He had one chance, and only one, to take his shot. The big Remington pistol was in his belt and loaded. The odds weren't in his favor, but he didn't have his usual luxury of twisting them to his liking.

This was it. Was he faster than Dan? At his best, he had a feeling that he was.

He let the moment pass, but Dan didn't pull his trigger. He just looked at Tom with a funny expression, chewing his lip.

Presently, he gestured with the muzzle of the pistol. Tom wasn't really blocking the door, but he shuffled aside. Dan let himself in, pulling the door shut quietly behind him.

"Tom," he said.

"Dan."

Tom had never seen this look on his face before, and it was an odd one. He snorted.

"Something on your mind, Dan?"

"You aren't well, Tom."

"That's no mystery." Neither was how Dan had gotten here. He'd been waiting. That Pinkerton in the last camp hadn't been found, but his disappearance hadn't gone unnoticed. It wouldn't have been difficult to figure out the train's next stop and head it off, though Dan might've saved a little time by simply riding out.

"Why not just catch up to me?" Tom asked curiously, making sure his crutch was steady and leaning on it. Dan had probably been downstairs, just sitting there watching, and Tom hadn't even noticed him. The thought of dying was frightening. The thought of having a head so fuzzy that he couldn't see like he needed to, think like he needed to—that was terrifying.

"I thought you might do the sensible thing and split off."

That had crossed Tom's mind, but it was easier to talk about it than to do it. Breaking away from the train with just the boy? Where would they go? Now that it was all behind them, it was easy to pick out things they might've done differently. The truth was, Tom had spent most of those days feeling as though he was barely getting through them. Shaking it all up hadn't really seemed survivable.

"I suppose you didn't come this far to let me go."

Dan stepped forward and took Tom under the arm, helping him to the chair. Tom groaned and sank into it, and Dan took the Remington away, tossing it onto the bed.

"I was awful surprised," he said after a moment, leaning against the dresser, still wearing that melancholy look, "to see you try to kill Mr. Carroll like that. Awful surprised," he repeated.

Tom just sank back, rubbing his eyes. "You heard him, same as I did. He said he trusted Jeff Shafer. How's a man that stupid get that rich?"

Dan looked vaguely sympathetic. "Tom, he ain't the one that called you a cheat. You oughtn't have done it."

"I know that, Dan. But I can't take it back."

"It's a waste, Tom. It's a damn waste. You oughtn't have done it." He'd already said it, but this time he said it with all his frustration in it.

Tom felt a pang of guilt, not for the bullet he'd have liked to have fired at Carroll, but for what Dan was going to have to do. Dan *would* do it. He didn't have many brains, but he had integrity to spare. Dan wouldn't enjoy killing Tom. In fact, it looked as though it bothered him to do it.

"It was a mistake," Tom admitted though he didn't have the strength to shrug. There was a wrinkle in the rug, and he watched Dan straighten it with his foot. "And it wasn't my last, Dan. I don't know what else to tell you."

The other man just shook his head in disgust. "Least you own it," he said finally. "I ain't seen that in a while. Most of 'em want to blame it all on someone else."

"Oh, I'd like to as well," Tom assured him, mustering a smile. "But we know better."

"We do."

Tom looked at the gun in Dan's hand. This was more like it. He wasn't on his feet, but at least he wasn't in bed. Or, worse, in the back of a wagon. And though it was too late for it to matter, he was beginning to realize that he really did like Dan.

"Why didn't you pull, Tom?"

"What's that?"

"You ain't even got the strength to lift it?" Dan glanced at the gun on the bed.

Tom looked over as well, then scowled and shook his head. "I reckon I do. But what's shooting you going to do for me, Dan?" He took his hat off and placed it on the arm of the chair. "At first I thought I might slip through." He saw the Pinkerton in his mind. Tom saw him alive, and he saw him as he'd been when he fell on his knife. Tom saw his limp, leaden body slipping into the dark of the outhouse. "Look at me. How much running do you think I have left?"

Dan didn't say anything to that; he just looked around the room in obvious distaste. Tom didn't know when the other man had become such a snob; he hadn't always worked for men like Carroll. Tom had often wondered what it would be like to be a bodyguard in the room with all the cardplayers taking home all the money. Would they resent the players? The money?

Not today. Clearly, Dan was the one who'd had it right. Instead of trying to take the big hands, he'd been content with the steady ones. He still had both legs and, more important, a future. That was the nature of it, though, wasn't it? High risk, high reward. Tom had been a gambler, not a rancher.

"You going to do it while I'm still young?" he prompted, and that seemed to wake the other man up.

Dan straightened and put his gun in its holster. He picked up the Remington from the bed and tucked that into his belt, then reached around to the small of his back and pulled out another gun, one Tom recognized. It was his own pistol, the one he'd given up to go aboard *Newlywed*.

"I already did," he said, placing Tom's gun on the

dresser. "I killed you on the boat. I don't have to pre-tend I never saw you. I don't have to lie."

Tom felt a flash of irritation; so that *had* been Dan's bullet to put him here.

"You sure?" He raised an eyebrow. "What if Mr. Carroll sees me again someday? What'll he have to say to you then? I'm not dead yet, Dan. I'll see another doctor. I may even give up the leg."

"The man I shot wasn't blind or stupid. A doctor can't help you, Tom." Dan brushed himself off and let out a long sigh, then went to the door. He paused with his hand on the knob. "What you need is a priest."

CHAPTER TWENTY-FIVE

⌒

IT WAS LATE when the tap came at the door. Late enough that the night outside was as black as it would get and the creaking of the beds from the neighboring rooms had gone quiet.

"Come on in," Tom said from his chair.

"I apologize for the delay, Mr. Calvert," the doctor said as he entered, and it might've been the sickness, but he was the best-looking doctor Calvert had ever seen. He was young but not young enough to cause suspicion and suspiciously well-dressed in a gray suit that had clearly felt the touch of a gifted tailor. He put his bag on the dresser and came straight to the chair. "I was delayed by some trouble outside town. Your nephew very nearly ran himself to death to bring me back here."

Indeed, Asher looked as bad as Tom, sweaty and disheveled.

"It's all right," Tom replied, giving Asher a reassuring smile. "Thanks, kid. Why don't you go down and have something to eat?"

Asher was winded, not stupid. He didn't look happy, but the doctor gave an encouraging nod, and he let himself out.

"The boy told me you'd been shot some months ago."

"It's true." Tom straightened a little. "It was healing all right for a while, but then I had to exert myself," he said wryly. "And it hasn't been so good since."

"You opened it, and it took a new infection." The doctor came close and started to look him over, peering into his eyes and mouth. He touched Tom's forehead and winced. "How long have you had this fever?"

"I can't rightly tell you, Doc."

The doctor's poker face held, but he needn't have bothered. Tom had a sense there wouldn't be any more surprises for him tonight.

"Let me have a look, then."

Tom had already cut a slit in the cuff of all his trousers so they could be rolled up easily. The doctor produced scissors and cut away the day's bandage. Tom wanted to look, and in a strange way, he felt as though he ought to—but he didn't. He closed his eyes and kept them that way, hissing when the doctor touched the wound.

Something stung and burned, and Tom just set his jaw. In a moment, he was being wrapped in clean linens, and he opened his eyes.

"Have you been examined by any other physicians?" the doctor asked.

"I have. The last fellow didn't seem sure if taking the leg would help or not. I'm ready now, though."

The doctor shook his head. "That'll kill you for

sure, Mr. Calvert. What you have is a wound that wants to heal, but can't for fear of sickness. If I take your leg, what am I doing but giving you another wound? You're too weak. And the wound is too high." He gestured at Tom's thigh. "I personally wouldn't be confident in my hand in taking this even if you were strong as an ox."

Tom sighed, but he was smiling. "That's it, then."

The doctor looked up at him, and seeing Tom's expression, he gave what might have been a nod.

"Most likely," he replied. "We could nail you in this bed so you don't exert yourself. Keep it clean, change that bandage each day. Make sure you're eating right. Your strength might return. Or you might just wither. I've seen it go both ways."

"I'd just be throwing the dice."

The doctor shrugged. "I like to think that how much you want to live plays a role in it, but I'm a physician, not a theologian."

Tom let out a bark of laughter. "And if I go back on the trail?"

"I'm not a palm reader, Mr. Calvert. You look as though you already have a notion."

Tom did. He pointed a finger at his head. "I keep seeing these spots, Doc. It makes me think there's someone there when there's not. And sometimes I can't think clearly. Can you do anything about that?"

"No. If you want to think clearly, stop drinking whiskey."

"I don't drink whiskey."

"It's the fever, then." The doctor passed his hat from one hand to the other. "It'll break."

"If I live long enough."

"I will be in this camp for another month at least. I will be happy to care for you if you remain."

Tom would have as good a chance with this doctor as with anyone, but chances weren't what they'd once been. He turned feebly to look out the window, and there was nothing to see out there but the slats of the tumbledown stable. If he stayed, the kid would have to carry on with the wagon train. There was no way around that.

Asher's future waited to the west, not here. Ida would carry on west, and Tom chose to believe the kid would wake up, given enough time. But he'd been thinking that for weeks, and it still hadn't happened. Hell. It was too late to change his mind now, and he'd just as likely die before he could be proven wrong.

"The boy wouldn't let me stay," he said finally.

The doctor frowned, uncomprehending.

"He would stay as well. He's the worrying type."

"You would want him to leave you?"

"He has to. He won't find what he's looking for sitting here, watching me drag my feet into hell."

The doctor nodded. "Or to see you mend."

Tom lifted his hand from the arm of the chair. It was trembling. Not *shaking*, but still . . . The doctor glanced at the gun on the dresser.

"What do you do, Mr. Calvert? You don't seem like a robber or any of the other sorts who wind up on the wrong end of the pistol."

"I play poker."

"Ah." The doctor sighed and got to his feet with a groan. "Easy come, easy go. Shall I call on you again in the morning?"

"No. We'll make an early start. Tell the kid I'll have my strength back in a month."

"It won't be long before he knows. If he doesn't already."

"By then we'll be far from here."

Tom made the doctor take some money, and he left the room. Barely a minute passed before Asher was pushing his way in, a look of suspicion on his face.

"Mr. Calvert," he said uncertainly.

"Yeah, kid?"

"The doctor said your prospects were not so dire."

Tom waved a hand. "It doesn't matter what he says. Nobody knows. I could be dead in the morning or up and dancing. No way to find out but to wait and see."

"Then we will not remain here?"

"Of course not. There's nothing for us here."

"He seems a very good doctor."

"If Friendly Field is out there, you won't find it by staying here. And I *know* you don't want to leave Ida alone. Think how she'd feel without you." It wasn't fair to say it, but Tom wasn't feeling especially compassionate.

Asher scowled. "Your health is more important," he protested.

"You see that, kid? Out there." Tom pointed at the window.

"What? There is nothing."

"Exactly." Tom looked meaningfully at the ugly slats outside. "That isn't going to be the last thing I see."

CHAPTER TWENTY-SIX

T HE MORNING CAME, and the doctor called even
  without being summoned. He changed the bandage and helped Tom to his feet, putting his crutch in
his hand and closing his fingers over it.

The trail was waiting, but Breeden wasn't. Fortunately, Oen was willing to help with managing the
wagon. Asher had the will, but not the strength, to do
it all himself. It wasn't painless getting back to the
wagon, and Tom's pride hurt more than anything as
Asher worked himself to the bone to get them rolling
along with all the others.

Black spots danced in Tom's eyes as he lay in the
back, taking a peculiar sort of comfort in the bumps
and jolts of the rattling wagon. Each spike of pain in
his leg was a reminder of a few more inches crossed.
Though he wasn't convinced there was anything in it
for him, a part of him had become very curious to see

the end of this trail. For months he'd watched the Norwegians struggle through each day, much as he and the kid were, but it was different for them. Tom and Asher had means, while the Norwegians had nothing but their hopes to push them forward. He wanted to be there when it all paid off for them. Of course, he didn't know that it *would*. Dreams were often lovely, but they weren't always honest.

However it might shake out, it was hard not to feel a little melancholy, knowing he wouldn't be around to see it.

Tom waved his hand, but there were no flies—it was much too cold for that. It was just the spots in his eyes. Tom pulled his blankets about himself, feeling like an old woman in her rocker. He moved a little closer to the light from the flaps and picked up the book. He had to squint to make out the words, and it made his head hurt, but he did it anyway. He might not see Oregon, but he'd be damned if he died before he found out what happened to these five ridiculous Englishwomen who had nothing better to do than go to balls, write letters, and take strolls through the countryside.

What was the English countryside like? What if he'd run in the other direction? Gone east and boarded a ship? What a thing to think about.

Breeden did not come by so often, and that couldn't be held against him. Sitting to chat with a dying man could hardly lift a man's spirits, and Breeden had enough on his mind. All the same, he made his way to the rear of the train from time to time to share gossip.

One such day under a clear and icy blue sky, with the air full of haze from steaming breath and woodsmoke, Breeden appeared at the wagon while Asher prepared the meal. He lifted himself onto the seat and pulled the flap aside, leaning into the wagon.

"I wager there's game to be had there," Tom said, pointing past him at the hills covered in trees.

"I think not," Breeden replied sourly. He looked around, then leaned close and pulled something out of his coat.

Tom took it, frowning. It was a belt of thick leather and quite dirty. He reached the buckle, which was . . .

"Cavalry," he said, his heart sinking. "Where'd you find it?"

"About two miles back in the dirt. Tracks too." Breeden scratched his beard irritably. "They're here, Tom. Close by, I expect."

"No hunting, then. We'll have to stay close."

Breeden's frustration was plain to see, but Tom didn't know what to tell him. It could've been worse; the Texans didn't *want* to slaughter their cows for eating, but they would if they had to. And they'd do it to feed the Norwegians if it came to it.

"We have beef," he said.

"It'll complicate things later," Breeden told him.

"I know that. But there's something to be said for having a later to worry about."

"Oh, just die, then."

"Dead men have no worries," Tom pointed out, smiling.

"You said it. Hell, I've half a mind to come with you."

"You planning on telling anyone about that?" Tom asked, handing the belt back.

"Don't see what good it would do."

"I think the same way."

"Well, then, I know it's the wrong decision. Eat your

meal." Breeden nodded to the west. "We have to get through that ravine while it's still light. They won't come at us in the open, but in that position and the dark, it wouldn't take but two or three of them to put us all in the ground."

"Send riders up," Tom said, pointing. "Let the Texans cover us. They got enough rifles."

Breeden shook his head. "Not without knowing their numbers."

Tom sighed. "You're right."

They shook hands, and Breeden moved on. Tom settled back and looked at the columns of blue smoke standing out starkly against the white sky. He looked around at the distant trees, the bluffs behind them, and the plains. If they were out there, those Shoshones or whoever they were, they knew how to keep a low profile. He squinted, but all he saw was the sky and the little spots swimming in his eyes.

He shook his head, and Asher brought him a steaming bowl. He must've purchased some new seasonings in Croshaw, because Tom could think of no other way that the boy was making the same few meals taste different over the weeks.

"That was a nasty way to end a story," Tom remarked as they ate, gazing at the Fulton brothers, who were out among the herd. "With it all going to hell that way. Her little sister going off a fool and ruining their name." He shook his head. "That's no way to end it."

Asher looked up, then let out a long breath. "Mr. Calvert, the mistake is mine." The boy looked guilty. "I made a foolish purchase in that novel."

Tom raised an eyebrow. "We got your money's worth out of it. You didn't know how it would end."

The boy looked properly embarrassed as he rubbed his cheek, which had turned a little pink. He licked his lips.

"I was mistaken, Mr. Calvert. That is not the end of the story."

Tom blinked. "What?"

"I believe there must be a third volume."

A moment passed, and Tom let out a bark of laughter. He grinned and shook his spoon at the boy.

"And you just bought the two?" He snorted. "*That* is a good joke." To tell the truth, he was relieved. At least this way, he could imagine that things ended better for those sisters. He spent a lot of time thinking wistfully about them, about what it would be like to have nothing more to worry about than marriage. Not that marriage was a trifling worry, because it wasn't— but it still struck him as all being very privileged.

The boy looked frustrated with himself, and Tom couldn't blame him. It was a mistake anyone might have made, and Asher had been even more taken with the story than Tom. He'd rushed through those pages as though nothing had been more important. This, at least, explained why the kid had looked so mopey when he finished reading. It hadn't been Tom's health that had done that to him; it had been that the novel had left him on such a bleak note.

Tom was still shaking with mirth, and he kept on for several moments. Maybe it was his light-headedness, or maybe it was just that it had been a while since he'd had a laugh.

"What do you suppose becomes of them?" Asher fretted.

"Oh, I expect there's a happy ending," Tom told him, waving a hand.

The boy didn't look convinced. "Things had taken such a turn," he said.

"It's just a story, kid. And if you don't want your story to take a turn, there's something I want you to do for me."

That took the boy aback, but this was as good a time as any for this talk, and the kid really was broken up about the book. Best to take his mind off it.

"What is that, Mr. Calvert?"

"Call off your game with Norman and the boys. It might embarrass you, but just do it. It isn't worth the risk."

Asher looked annoyed. "Do you think I am not ready?"

"You are, more or less. It's a different sort of game from what you've done up till now; I haven't taught you to settle a personal score or to play against people who know you or know of you. But you're a fair enough player to muddle through against the likes of those Texans. The game isn't the business at hand, though. There's still too much trail left ahead of you to make any more of an enemy out of Norman Fulton than you already have. Truth is, I think he may be a little closer to taking his shot at you than you know."

"You think he would shoot me in cold blood?"

"I don't know about that. Things have to be settled. Shafer couldn't beat me at the table, so he came at me another way. Norman'll find a way to hurt you if something doesn't change. That would be one thing if you really wanted Ida for yourself; then you'd have no choice. Taking a risk for something you want is all right. Taking one for no reason—that's not good business, kid. Forget the game and his challenge. Tell him you're a coward. Their good opinion of you doesn't matter."

"I am no coward," Asher replied, and Tom groaned in frustration. The kid wasn't hearing him.

"I know that. And you know," he said, lowering his voice. "And that's what matters. These people and their notions—they don't matter."

"I mean to play this game," Asher said stubbornly. "I have not learned these skills not to use them. It is only a game of cards."

"Money as well," Tom pointed out. "And I won't give it to you."

"You will not have to." Asher reached into his waistcoat and produced some neatly folded notes. It was the money Tom had given him for pulling him out of the river. "Did I not earn this?"

Tom scowled. "You did."

"Then it is mine to lose. And I will lose it willingly if that is what is needed for me to hone this skill."

For several moments, Tom wrestled with his temper. It wasn't the same, uncontrollable temper that had made him draw his gun on the deck of *Newlywed*, but it put up a fight all the same.

"Is that your aim?" he asked, keeping his voice even. "To learn?"

"Of course."

"Then play the game. And lose it."

The boy looked disdainful. "Mr. Calvert, you are not well."

"No, kid. I'm thinking straight. The only thing harder than winning a game is controlling it. Were you paying attention when you watched me play that night on the boat? I wasn't playing to win. I was playing to make sure that stranger didn't win while I took his measure. *That* is a display of skill. If it's skill you want and not your name you're trying to protect, then play the game and make sure of two things: that you lose and Norman wins. It's that other one, Eli—you'll have to make sure he loses."

Asher narrowed his eyes, and someone shouted from one of the other wagons, but he wasn't distracted. He stared at Tom.

"Kid, I wouldn't lie to you. Hone your game and protect yourself at the same time." Tom waved a hand. "That's how you do it. Protect Ida too. Think how it would be for her if something happened to you."

Nothing followed that shout, so it couldn't have been anything too important. There was no breeze, and the white ceiling of clouds wasn't moving. It was as though the day itself had frozen solid. It was certainly cold enough.

"Play the game," Tom pressed. "And give it to Norman without him knowing that's what you're doing. And when he walks away with your money, hang your head. That's how you take care of yourself and Ida *and* get your practice. It's like you said. It's your money. And I'm not your dad. I can't tell you what to do."

Tom fell silent there and waited a moment, just looking at Asher.

"But I'm asking you." He put his hand out. "If you want to get yourself killed, wait until after I'm dead. Don't make me bury your body."

Asher didn't look happy, but after a moment, his expression softened. He rolled his eyes. "Very well," he said, and shook Tom's hand.

CHAPTER TWENTY-SEVEN

TOM HAD HEARD men speak of having a dream that was always the same. He couldn't imagine that; it had never happened to him. Now it was, though it wasn't as simple as just seeing the same thing again and again. He'd dream that he was back on his feet and walking into a town, but unable to remember if anyone in that town knew him by his name. Or he would dream that he was renting a room for the night, but he was unable to recall if his pursuers were one day behind him or two.

Then he had one where he just wanted to look at a map to figure out where it was safe to go, but the wind caught the map, and he chased it into the street or tried—but his bad leg took him by surprise, and he fell into the dirt.

He woke from that to a cold gray light before dawn. Those dreams were becoming more frequent, happening a couple times a week now. They didn't bother him after he woke, but while he was in them—he didn't like that much.

And it was *unusually* cold, or there was something different about the cold—something that wasn't right.

Tom gently levered himself up in his nest of blankets, careful not to move too quickly; he didn't want to wake the kid. Only the kid wasn't there. He reached back and moved the flap to let in a little of the predawn light, just to be sure. No, Asher's blankets were there, but the boy was not.

The first notion to come to mind was that the boy had had to relieve himself, but they'd shared this wagon for months, and Tom knew damn well that the boy was a stubborn and heavy sleeper. Asher *never* woke before Tom for any reason.

Panic struck harder than a bullet could. Tom scrambled up to sit, then dragged himself to the rear of the wagon and peered out. No sign of Asher. Tom turned and struggled to the front, crawling out onto the seat.

The camp was uncannily still. No smoke, no fires. No one was awake. The animals were scarcely even stirring.

Something moved, and Tom looked over sharply, but it wasn't an Indian; it was one of the Norwegians with a bucket of water.

"Hello there," Tom called out, waving. He didn't hesitate, though it was rude to raise his voice with everyone sleeping, and there were those who wouldn't take kindly to it. He didn't care.

The fellow frowned, or it looked like he did—it was difficult to be sure because of his beard, but he put down his bucket and made his way over.

"My nephew's gone," Tom told him, and at once he

knew the man didn't speak English—there was no comprehension on his face. "He's gone," Tom repeated anyway, pointing fruitlessly at the wagon.

The man looked past him, expression blank.

It was pointless. Tom snatched his crutch, and that got the Norwegian's attention. He said something Tom didn't understand and stopped him from trying to clamber down. He said something else and pointed a stern finger, then made a gesture with his hands that had to be an order to wait.

Heart thudding, Tom watched him turn and jog away.

Had those Indians snatched the boy right out of the wagon? Why hadn't they taken Tom as well? The crutch was still in his hands, and his knuckles were white, but he knew what the Norwegian had been able to see so obviously: that there was no sense in him getting down. He wasn't going to chase or find anyone by hobbling around.

Someone else had to do it for him, and the only thing that hurt more than his leg was watching other people carry his burdens.

Oen was coming, but he looked curious, not alarmed.

"It's the boy," Tom told him, showing him the back of the wagon. At that, Oen's face went stony, and he turned away, scanning the horizon with his hand on his pistol. He started to speak, but the bearded man touched his arm and pointed. Tom twisted around to look at the two shapes in the distance.

There wasn't enough light to be certain of anything, but it couldn't have been Indians. Whoever they were, they weren't very large—and that was enough to make Tom's heart lift. He started to breathe again.

It was Asher and Ida. They were shivering and looking rather worried, probably because they'd hoped not to be discovered, but they were safe and whole. Tom wanted to laugh, but his heart was still thudding, and he could still feel that panic in his chest.

Without a word, Oen put his arm around Ida and led her away. The other fellow followed, and Asher paused a few paces away, teeth chattering. He looked up at Tom.

"I did not think you would wake," he said finally, a little abashed.

"You scared me, kid. I thought you'd been taken by Indians." Tom shook his head, and now he could laugh a little. "Good thing the Norwegians didn't notice the girl was gone. They'd have thought the same."

"We only . . . ," Asher began, but Tom laughed again, louder this time. The relief was hitting him almost like a strong drink would.

"I know," he said, wiping his eyes. "I know what you were doing."

That seemed to surprise Asher. "You do?"

"Nothing I didn't do myself when I was your age. Come on, let's have some breakfast."

But the boy just frowned. "I thought you told me you knew nothing of herbs," he said, and Tom paused in the act of reaching for the flaps.

"What do herbs have to do with anything?"

"We were gathering them." Asher gestured meaningfully. "For your leg. Mr. Svensen knows how to make a poultice. It helped you before, and he said those trees"—Asher turned and pointed—"were of the right sort to make looking worthwhile."

Tom stared at him. By now he knew the boy well enough to know he wasn't lying.

Asher was dead serious, but he was also freezing. He started to build the fire.

"Well, did you find any?" Tom asked, handing him the cooking set.

"We did, though they were sad to look at," the boy replied, adding more wood. Other camps were coming to life as well. "It is too late in the year, I believe. I hope there is enough for Mr. Svensen. Ida has the herbs," he added.

"Course she does," Tom replied, scratching his chin. It *was* a little cold to be stealing away into the woods just for privacy. He shook his head and picked up his crutch, easing himself down from the wagon.

With the utmost care, he stood with the crutch for a few moments before wavering. Asher lunged to catch him before he could fall, helping him sit beside the fire. Tom kept a hiss of pain from getting out and wiped away the sudden icy sweat that had appeared on his brow.

"I do not think that is wise," Asher chided, but Tom ignored him. He had to move his leg, and he had to get down from the wagon *once* in a while; otherwise the leg would just waste away. Even so, he could barely walk three steps without danger of falling, and there was still considerable pain.

As they ate, Tom studied Asher's face. The boy appeared to be miles away, and Tom couldn't even guess what he was thinking about.

"Is it that you don't know what to do?" Tom asked suddenly, frowning.

Asher looked up across the fire at him. "I beg your pardon, Mr. Calvert?"

"Once you get her out of her dress," he clarified. "Is

it that you don't know what to do—is that what's got
you too scared?"

The boy's mouth opened, and the pinkness in his
cheeks from the cold spread to the rest of his face so
quickly that it was almost worrisome.

Tom groaned. That *was* it. The boy was educated
and polite; he liked his manners and his airs. He didn't
want to look ignorant.

"So that's it. All right," Tom said, sighing. Asher
started to say something, but Tom cut him off. "Shut
up, kid. Listen. Here's what you do."

It wasn't as though it was a terribly complex matter
to explain, and it didn't take very long, and that was
good because the boy was getting so red that he was in
danger of fainting away.

"That's how it's done," Tom told him frankly. "It's
nothing to be afraid of. You just listen to her when she
tells you something." He shrugged. "Understand?"

Asher nodded mutely.

"Don't look like that," Tom warned, shaking a finger at him. "Heed me. If you listen to her, you'll always
know what to do, and if you don't, she may not be inclined to repeat. You see?"

The boy swallowed. "Yes, sir."

"Good. Course it won't do you any good at all."

Asher stiffened. "What?"

"Kid, there're Indians out there. It was good of you
to think of my leg, and I am grateful, but if you sneak
off again, you might as well not bother coming back,
because if you do I'll shoot you myself."

CHAPTER TWENTY-EIGHT

S NOW HAD ARRIVED, but it wasn't yet falling too thickly. It was pretty to look at, but no one could see it without thinking of other things, like how to keep their teams and their families fed through the miles ahead.

The Fultons spent a fair amount of time boasting of their ranches and their cows, and Tom could see that wasn't all bluster. They managed the cattle with a great deal of skill, and the cows were faring a good deal better than many of the teams. The snow was what they all saw and worried about, but it wasn't the snow that would be the problem; it would be ice. That was what would make wagons brittle and prevent them from getting any purchase on the hills. The going would be slower from here.

Most everyone was too cold to be worried about Indians, and the Texans were already melancholy due to one of the hands being trampled two days ago. Breeden still kept his rifle close to hand and his eyes on any distant hills or trees. No one had seen anything to suggest there were Indians close, and no one had any reason to think there *weren't*. There were no other signs of the Army or anyone else.

And Tom hadn't seen Norman Fulton once today.

"Tonight's the night," he said to Asher, who was hunched over pitifully, trying to cocoon himself in his coat. It was cold, but the boy seemed to feel it more keenly than Tom, likely because of his small frame. His size really was a shame, because it always ended the same way when he badgered Tom to teach him to fight. Tom would give him some advice and then warn him that none of it mattered because he wasn't big enough. The boy argued that he'd gotten stronger since the journey's beginning, and that was true, but it didn't materially change anything.

Instead of asking what Tom meant or startling out of his reverie, Asher just nodded slowly.

"Yes," he said, and he didn't look as though it bothered him. Tom had worried or perhaps hoped that the boy would feel some nerves as he neared his showdown at the poker table with Norman. Maybe the kid would lose his nerve and back out. Normally Tom wanted to see him strong, but this was one duel he was better off simply not having.

The boy thought he was ready, and he was right. He'd learned the game well, and he had a mind of his own; he thought of his own tricks, which occasionally gave Tom pause. Tom could beat Asher with his eyes closed because he knew him, but if Asher were a stranger who walked into a game—Tom could see himself losing some money in the time it would take him to figure the boy out. Asher wasn't good at a true poker face, hiding everything—but he could be distracting enough with his words and his expressions that he was almost more difficult to figure out. He *knew* the power of distraction, and that was a strange thing to see in someone his age, but he was grown-up in a lot of ways.

There was Jake Fulton now, riding down the line.

Tom straightened up a little, wondering if this journey would leave him with a permanent hunch. It was a good worry to have; his leg was doing better, and if he was worrying about the future, it meant there was still a part of him that thought he had one.

"Mr. Breeden tells me we'll draw up just five miles yonder," Jake announced with a wave. It would be an early end to the day's drive. "Might be a good night for a game of cards."

Jake wasn't a subtle man, but neither was Tom.

"Sounds good," he replied, tousling Asher's hair. "The kid's ready to take all your money and your brothers' too."

Jake snorted. "We have an appointment," he said, tipping his hat.

"You remember how you lost to me when you first held cards?" Tom asked Asher as the other man rode away.

"I do," the boy replied.

"Tonight you lose that way. You lose bad. Stay in it an hour. Then throw it all to Norman."

"I know."

It wasn't a perfect plan, but if the boy insisted on playing, it was the only thing worth trying. Tom worried, though. What did it mean that Norman had sent his brother to propose the game for tonight? Was he feeling nerves? Did it mean anything?

Tom watched a few lazy snowflakes falling and pushed it out of his mind. Worry could be a powerful weapon; men who worried were the ones who planned, the ones who exercised caution. A plan wasn't always much, but you were generally better off to have one than not. The men who didn't think to worry were the ones stumbling from one crisis to another day in and day out, usually troubles of their own making.

But worry could also be a liability.

The boy's eyes were on the pale horizon. Asher wasn't worried, and when a man had that look on his face, you didn't worry about him; you worried about whoever might get in his way. There was a piece of Asher missing; that wasn't entirely lost on Tom. The boy's eyes didn't match his face or his frame at times like these. They weren't the eyes of boy of thirteen or fourteen, but Asher couldn't be *much* older than that. Time wasn't the only thing that could age you, but Tom understood those other things to generally be less than pleasant.

The kid had seen hardship, but he was still looking for more. Stowing away, setting off alone across the country—not backing down from trouble with men like Norman Fulton. Well, if he wasn't going to protect himself, Tom would do it for him. Asher had pulled Tom out of that river and done the work of two men keeping their wagon rolling this long. He'd bought himself that much.

CHAPTER TWENTY-NINE

I T WASN'T THE usual tent. There were no Norwegians at this table, only Asher and the Fulton brothers. The Texans hadn't even planned to put up any cover, but the snow got worse as soon as Breeden called the day's halt. The Norwegians had always thoughtfully erected their tent close to Tom's wagon, but the Texans weren't as considerate.

There was even more of a crowd gathered for this game, if crowd was the word for it; the train had begun with ninety souls, and it was down to eighty-seven, one lost to the cattle, one to fever, and another to an illness no one had been quite sure what to make of. Of those eighty-seven, at least half were keen to watch the game. Tom expected that the majority of the train, and likely even the cows, understood what was going on better than Asher did.

Oen helped Tom down from the wagon, and though it was a journey of only about a hundred feet to the nearest of the Norwegian wagons, it nearly put Tom in his grave. His wound appeared to be back on the mend, but the long months had left his leg with so little strength that the combined weakness and pain made it difficult even to hobble.

But Oen's strong arms pulled him up to the wagon's seat, and he had a good view of the proceedings. The Texans had carried out a beautiful table. It must've been an heirloom or important to somebody, because it was much too heavy to be practical to drag it across the country.

Asher was already at the table, and so were the Fulton brothers. They'd all dressed in their best, and the boy's grubby clothes and small stature made him look distinctly out of place.

All the same, he sat there at the table, and he didn't look back. There wasn't even one glance for Tom, though Asher's nerves were written all over his back. He was apprehensive, but he was still there, and Tom was struck by it. Would he have had the nerve to sit at that table when he had been that age? It would've been simple to call off the game or walk away; it was easier to avoid eyes than it was to face them.

The kid was facing them, though. If Jeff Shafer had had even a fraction of the grit that Asher had, he wouldn't have been at the bottom of the Missouri right now. A few months ago, no one ever would've been able to convince Tom that he would sit out here under the vast Wyoming sky at the end of a fall that felt like winter, kept warm by the pride he felt that a pitiful little stick of a boy was about to lose a poker game.

It made him want to laugh.

Oen had gone to join his family, leaving Tom alone, but Breeden was making his way over. The older man still had his rifle leaning on his shoulder. Most of the party was more interested in Asher and Norman than in Indians, but Breeden had a little more sense than most.

"I do not care for this." Those were his first words to Tom, and it was a sentiment he'd repeated often. Breeden knew perfectly well that Tom felt the same way. He shook his head and leaned on the wagon, glancing up at Tom. "And I believe I saw Norman at the drink before he sat down."

"How much did they bring?" Tom asked. "The whole wine cellar?"

"They drink it like water, particularly that oldest one. He can't even get up in the morning without it, or that's what I been told."

"That's a pity," Tom said, meaning it.

"I reckon they bought more at that last camp. Norman ain't a drinker, though."

That was worrisome, and it might make Asher's job more difficult, but it wouldn't stop him. The first hand ended, and it wasn't clear to Tom how it had gone. He wasn't paying close attention; the early hands didn't matter much.

The lines on Breeden's face looked deeper than ever.

"I am sorry," Tom said. "Course, if the boy had gone the other way, we'd have just as much trouble. Those Norwegians are mighty protective."

"As they ought to. You know she ain't got the sense to protect herself."

"Nor does he."

Breeden snorted and shifted his rifle, then climbed up to join him. "Tom, I got no grudge with you. Truth is, this train's got less strife than any I worked before. If old Norman and your boy are the worst we got, we'll be all right. There is always someone and something to give us grief. The difference 'tween your boy and most is that he don't mean no ill."

It was easier to read a man from across the table than from fifty feet away, but Tom's vantage point let him see more or less what was taking place.

Eli was scooping chips toward himself. Tom had told Asher the truth: losing was easy, but losing to a particular player by design—that was difficult, even for Tom. True, Asher would do himself the most good by making certain that Norman left the table happy. In the end, it wouldn't matter which of the Fulton brothers won the game, and if Asher did manage to throw it all to Norman, that would really be something. Tom had to wonder about the boy's future. If Friendly Field was real, would anyone play cards there? Tom hoped so, because it would be a waste for Asher to stop now.

Tom saw him throw down his cards. A little theatrical to his eye, but he wouldn't complain. He shivered and hunched over. There was nothing wrong with his coat, but the winter seemed colder when he spent all his time in one place, never moving around much. Freezing was only slightly less appealing than making the trek back to his own wagon.

Breeden was searching his face. "I seen men die from such wounds," he said after a moment. "Tom, if you was dyin', you would've already."

Tom smiled. He was inclined to agree, but it felt good to hear it from someone else. It made him feel as though he wasn't just telling it to himself. He didn't want to be like the men who rushed west all but certain they would strike it rich. The odds were Tom's bread and butter, and all he needed was his eyes to tell him there were a lot of fools. A few were rich, but most were poor. Gold wasn't as easy to find as people liked to tell themselves.

Tom didn't want to just *tell* himself that he would pull through this.

Asher was giving up more money. The plan had been to drag it out a little, but Tom wasn't going to give the boy any trouble over it. Luck *did* play a role in a card game after all. Just not as large of one as people liked to think. Tom couldn't know what was really going on at that table unless he was sitting at it.

And that was what he would do if this wasn't good enough for Norman. Tonight's game was supposed to be about Norman and Asher, not about money. But if these Texans wanted to play any more after this, they'd play with Tom, not Asher. *He* would ensure everyone left the table satisfied. And when they got where they were going, then he could take all that money back and settle any bad blood that might come of it.

"It's the rivers that'll get us," Breeden predicted, squinting up at the night sky. There was no sense in watching for Indians tonight; the dark was enough, and though there weren't *so* many snowflakes falling, they were big ones. "Normal times the water gets low when it's cold, but there's one"—he pointed into the gloom—"now but two days." Breeden shook his head. "That one don't never seem no lower, and it is cold." His breath came out as a white plume, and he looked as though his teeth would begin chattering.

Something changed in the air, and they both looked toward the game. The onlookers had quieted. Tom held his breath.

The players showed, and Norman Fulton took the money.

Asher was getting low, and some of the Norwegians didn't care for that. Even if Norman might offer better prospects to Ida, many of them still preferred Asher because *Ida* preferred Asher. That and there was less resentment all around for Tom and Asher, as they didn't ride up and down the train as though they owned it, nor did they flaunt anything in front of those who were clearly struggling.

Tom wasn't worried that this gambit would further sour the Norwegians' view of their traveling companions. The general dislike wasn't malicious, and the game wouldn't change that.

"I reckon I know what you're doing," Breeden said, lowering his voice though no one else could possibly hear. "How much is it costing you?"

"I'm not doing a thing," Tom replied. The other man knew he was lying, but about the only thing that could ruin the plan for Asher to lose was if the Fultons found out about it. Breeden would never give it away deliberately, but it was best not to talk about it at all.

Breeden smiled, and applause startled them both. Tom looked over in surprise to see Asher taking a large pile of money.

Tom couldn't see Norman's face, but Jake looked taken aback—and worried.

Eli Fulton was dealing again.

"Kid," Tom muttered under his breath. Could it have happened by mistake? Tom didn't see how.

Breeden raised an eyebrow. "Maybe I had you wrong."

Tom wasn't listening. The snow was still falling, but he didn't see it, and he didn't hear the murmurs from the Norwegians. He could see Asher's hands and the money. He saw Eli slide Asher one card.

The seconds went by.

They showed, and Asher took the money again.

"Stop the game," Tom said.

"What?"

"Stop them," he repeated, and Breeden couldn't fail to take the urgency—but he hesitated, stricken. "It ain't my place," he said, "to go crosswise with them Texans."

Cards slid across the table, and Tom knew without seeing it all for himself that Norman Fulton had just thrown down his hand.

Tom started to get up, and Breeden grabbed his arm to stop him.

"All right," he said, climbing down. "All right." He snatched up his rifle and hurried stiffly toward the table. Breeden pushed through, and the people parted, giving Tom a better view from the wagon.

Norman was saying something to Asher, who replied.

Breeden intervened, and he spoke loud enough that Tom could make out the words.

"That is nonsense, Norman Fulton. The boy don't mean to insult you no more than I do. You asked him to play this game, and he done it. Ain't no part of that where he promised you not to win!"

"It ain't that he won! It's how he done it!" Norman snarled, pointing across the table.

"You calling him a cheat?"

"No, I am calling him a son of a bitch!"

At that, Asher got to his feet, startling everyone. He said something that Tom couldn't make out. There was a murmur from the spectators, and several of them moved back from the table.

"You don't mean that, son," Breeden said.

"I believe he does," Eli Fulton said obstinately, and Breeden pointed a warning finger at him.

"Don't go making it worse." He turned to say something to Norman, but the younger man was already on his feet. Asher moved past Breeden before anything else could be said, and there was a moment of pure shock on Norman's face.

Tom knew why. Asher had just offered to fight him. And then he'd taken the first step forward, *toward* a man nearly twice his size. Anyone would expect him to run *away*. It was a peculiar thing to see and surely more so through Norman's eyes.

That moment of shock hung in the air but not for long.

Norman knocked Asher off his feet with a single punch. The boy tumbled into the snow and lay still. It had happened so quickly that it was unlikely Breeden could have done anything about it.

Ida rushed forward, but Oen caught her and pulled her back. Norman barely hesitated a second before striding forward and delivering a kick to the boy's face, though Asher was clearly already out cold.

Breeden didn't even make it a step before Eli shoved him to the ground and stood over him, one hand resting on his pistol. He wouldn't allow him to intervene.

Norman kicked Asher in the head again, and that was as far as he got. He and everyone else turned at the shot from the pistol.

Tom was splayed out on the ground, and the gun was pointed at the sky. He had been too hasty, and his leg hadn't been strong enough to hold him when he let himself down. No one had heard him fall into the snow, but they heard his Peacemaker. The warning shot had its intended effect; the snow kept falling, but the people were all locked in place.

Tom groaned as they all stared at him, lying there in the dark. He jammed the pistol into his belt and got his elbow under himself, worming forward and forcing his bad leg as well. When the knee bent, it felt as though his whole thigh just split open, but he did it and rested his weight—and overbalanced. His elbow hit the ground, and the pain shot through him like forked lightning would shoot through the sky.

No one said anything. Tom planted his palm on the frozen ground and set his jaw, putting out his other arm for balance.

Ponderously, Tom rose to his feet. His right leg quivered every inch of the way, and there was a warmth that he knew could only be bleeding, but there was no time for that.

"That's enough," he bit out, barely able to get enough air for that much. "He's beat. You won." He turned his eyes on Asher. Was he even still breathing? There was blood in the churned-up snow.

It was no good, though. Norman's temper still had him. "I know that," he called back.

"Don't touch him again," Tom warned.

"And if I do?" Norman snarled, watching him waver. Tom saw black spots and fought to stay on his feet. He looked down at his right hand, red, stiff, and hurting.

Tom sighed, and when the cloud of his breath cleared, Norman and his three brothers were all still there staring him down. It wasn't a dream he could wake up from.

"I'll kill you," he said truthfully.

Norman hesitated but only for a second. He went for his gun, but Tom was faster. His bullet punched through Norman's belly before the other man's gun was even clear of his holster. He stumbled back and fell over with the same look of disbelief that his three brothers were wearing.

There was just enough time for the shot to die away over the black plains before all three of them came to their senses and went for their pistols. Tom's gun thundered twice and came to bear on Jake Fulton.

The handsome brother hadn't even managed to get his pistol pointed in the right direction. So the gun and the leather were just for show. Jake froze as Eli and Rodney fell dead, one on either side of him.

Tom stared at him. There was a strangled sob from one of the Texan women.

Jake tried to bring up his barrel, and Tom shot him through the heart. He toppled over onto the table, sending the cards and the money to flutter with the snowflakes in the air.

The echoes faded, though the ringing in his ears didn't. Tom lowered his Colt.

Jake had been right to try his luck; Tom couldn't very well have let him live after killing all his brothers. That would have been leaving the job half finished. It would have been like hanging out a sign saying he *wanted* a bullet in the back. He might get one of those yet regardless; Tom eyed the other Texans for a moment, then blinked the spots from his eyes and limped forward.

Asher *was* breathing.

So was Norman. The dying man looked up at him, unable to speak, both hands clutching his belly. There was no physician in the train, and nothing that medicine could have done for him anyway.

"You're in luck," Tom told him, pulling the hammer back to set the last cartridge in the revolver. "I got one left."

PART THREE
CALVERT'S LAST BLUFF

CHAPTER THIRTY

TOM DIDN'T GAZE wistfully after the wagon train, though there was a part of him that wanted to. He just peered west for a moment, then went back to feeding the fire, building it up as high as he could. It was a bad decision, but that was hardly uncharted territory. Dan had given him a pass on his sins, so Tom had just gone on and committed some new ones. It figured.

A tower of smoke reached for heaven, a clear marker for the single solitary wagon sitting on the vast field of pale brown grass. Anyone within five miles would see it, including Shoshones, but Tom didn't care. He had to keep the boy warm, and that meant a fire.

A big fire.

He felt a wave of faintness as he reached for more wood, but there wasn't any more—only there was. But no, he couldn't use *that* wood; that was the remains of the broken wheel. It would've been ungrateful to look back on that moment, when that cowhand had taken his ax to the wheel, as misfortune. It wasn't misfortune; it was great fortune.

Even exhausted, hurting, and unable to think clearly, Tom knew they were lucky to have been left behind rather than simply shot. Of course there had been only four Texans who had been in a position, so to speak, to render judgment. And they were all dead.

That meant the decision was Breeden's. The older man had taken mercy on them, even though right now he was no doubt cursing the moment he ever laid eyes on Tom Calvert and his young so-called nephew. Tom hadn't meant for this, and Breeden knew it, but he also knew that Tom hadn't done all he could to prevent it. No one was blameless, but Tom deserved the lion's share, and that wasn't lost on anyone.

The kid kept breathing, though he didn't move, and he didn't come around. He hadn't so much as stirred since last night. His face was swollen up bad, but his skull all seemed to be in one piece. There was no telling how long he would sleep, if sleeping was what he was doing.

He had to be kept warm, though.

There was just enough snow on the ground that it was a simple business to melt it for water, but fuel for the fire was another matter.

Tom leaned over and used his elbow to drag himself back toward the crippled wagon. There was no one to see him do it, and it wouldn't have mattered even if there was. He gripped the spoke of a wheel that was still intact and dragged himself upright, laboriously making his way around to the back. His crutch had gone missing in the night, and if that was the worst the surviving Texans meant to do to him, so be it.

He got out the rifle and the ax, slinging the rifle over his shoulder and letting the ax serve as his cane.

There were two stands of trees in sight, both at least a mile away.

He started to hobble, leaving an odd sort of trail in the snow, a footprint and swath where he dragged his right foot along. Over the weeks the miles had been the ones to come and go, but now it was just yards.

His foot came down, and there was nothing there but snow. At least it was soft, and it caught him when he fell. There was a slope here, and the wind had come and blown the snow to make it all appear level. Luck was on his side again; he hadn't fallen on the ax, but it took longer to get up this time.

The better part of an hour of limping brought him to the trees, where the ground was flat and there was a fair amount of dead wood already on the ground. Tom began to gather it, the quiet wrapping him tightly, pressing on his ears.

Dizziness came, and he dropped the branches and planted both hands on the ax, leaning on it and taking deep breaths.

It passed, but he stayed there with his eyes closed. He knew it was a bad idea, but it felt good to stop after the slog and the work—work that wouldn't have made him break a sweat before all this, not that he'd have done it. He had no house to mind, just a lot of hotel rooms that were all someone else's problem. He swallowed, enjoying the dark behind his eyelids and the stillness.

It wasn't easy to see it that way, but it was a beautiful day. The snow had covered the signs of the cattle's passing, making the world white down below and up above. Every spindly black branch in this forest gleamed with ice.

He could see himself sitting down, maybe over by that big tree, and just staying a while.

A twig snapped, and he looked up to see a doe not even thirty feet away. Carefully, he got the rifle into his hands and put it to his shoulder. The sights blurred, splitting apart into two and going wide to the left and right. With a monumental effort, he made his eyes draw them back together, finding the bead.

But the doe was gone.

When he had as much wood together as he dared try to move, he knelt with painstaking care and tied the bundle of sticks together. He put the rope around his waist and tied it, then began to trudge back toward the wagon.

As soon as he left the trees, the wind picked up, lifting a white haze from the ground and hiding the distance from him. It could have been worse; he wouldn't lose his bearings as long as he had the tower of smoke from the fire to guide him. After a while he realized he wasn't so much using the ax for a cane as he was treating it like an oar to drag himself forward. His fingers and ears had gone numb long ago, and when he looked back, there was nothing but the occasional spot of blood on the snow. His leg had opened up again, and he hadn't even noticed.

The rope around his middle went tight, and he'd lost just enough feeling that the fall didn't hurt so much as having the breath knocked from him. His sticks had caught on something back there. He tried to look back, but he couldn't see. That was all right; the snag could wait. He just needed to rest first.

CHAPTER THIRTY-ONE

THE CRACKLING OF the fire was a good sound to lull one to sleep, but there wasn't any comfort in it; this had to be as close to hell as one could get. For all Tom knew, that was exactly where he was, but hell was supposed to smell like sulfur, not woodsmoke.

He came awake with a startled curse and jerked away from the fire, patting furiously at the scorched arm of his coat.

Asher had been in his way, kneeling there beside him, dozing. Now they both fell in the snow in a smoking tangle. Tom pushed the boy off and checked to be certain no other part of him was alight. He sat up, weathered a rush of light-headedness, and looked around at the gray world. It was evening.

Asher's face was in poor repair, but his eyes were as worried as they'd ever been. He scrambled up, the color flooding back into his face. Tom opened his mouth, but Asher just threw his arms around him and squeezed. Startled, Tom found the strength to pry the boy off and push him back.

For a moment, they stared at each other.

"Hell, kid," Tom said finally. "I know it's cold, but did you want to cook me alive?" He looked meaningfully at the fire.

"I was so worried."

"You and me both. You got a knot on your head bigger than a teacup." He deflated. "And don't go hugging people like that. It's rude and overfamiliar."

"I am sorry, Mr. Calvert." That was where Asher's relief seemed to end, and there was no blaming him for that. He must've woken up by the fire, alone and confused, when Tom had been out there in the snow.

Tom looked back toward the distant trees. So he'd made it far enough that the boy had been able to see him lying out there and dragged him back. And his sticks too, which were likely burning now and what had kept him from death.

"What happened, Mr. Calvert?"

A branch popped in the fire, and Tom shielded his face from the sparks. He brushed them off his coat and moved back a little more. He was still cold, but he could feel all his parts, so he was as well as could have been hoped.

"We had a disagreement with the Fultons."

At that, Asher's face went stony. After a while, he lowered his eyes. "I did not plan to win," he said. "I saw the opportunity."

Tom arduously sat upright. He shook his head, and after a minute, he snorted.

"Kid, you aren't the first to go wrong for greed.

That'll happen to the best of us." He shook a finger, though his heart wasn't in it. "It was trying to fight him that I can't forgive you for. I spent months telling you so."

"You taught me so much."

"I can't teach you to be six feet tall." Tom rubbed his face tiredly. "But it doesn't matter now. You lost. He knocked you cold with one punch."

"That is a lie, Tom Calvert."

Tom flinched. "It is?"

Asher pointed at his own face. "I do not believe this is the work of a single punch."

"He didn't stop until Breeden stepped in."

The boy swallowed. "And they left us when the wheel broke?" He looked past Tom at the wagon.

Tom hesitated. "That's right."

Asher didn't look convinced, but that was his own business. Tom's head was clear, at least for the moment, and in some ways, that was worse than a fainting spell. The wind moaned over the plains, bringing with it a chill haze of fallen snow. Tom looked away, and Asher shivered.

"Can we mend this wheel?" the boy asked finally.

"Doubtful."

"We do have another wheel, do we not?"

Tom scratched at his beard. "We do." But the two of them couldn't make the repair. Tom knew more or less how it was done, but between the two of them, did they have the strength? He shook his head. "We would have to lift that up," he said, pointing at the rear of the wagon. "I don't know that we can. I don't know that we could even if I had two good legs still."

Asher looked thoughtful. "Mr. Calvert, you and I

are not terribly strong," he said. "But they are." He indicated the team with his eyes.

Tom turned to look, and his brain took longer with the problem than it should have, but he got there all the same. The oxen weren't bothered by the cold or the hard work. They were as strong and lively as ever, and if anything, they looked pleased to finally be away from the herd.

It was true they wouldn't have had much difficulty lifting the wagon if there was a means to engineer it. And there was—it would be simple enough, though it would take some finesse not to tip the entire thing over.

"That's a good notion," he told the boy. "Let me think it over. Where was that good thinking when you tried to fight Norman Fulton?"

Asher gave him a look. "He accused me of mocking him. He accused me of taking pleasure in his humiliation. He claimed that it was all by my design."

"So?" Tom asked, bewildered.

"I told him that I was sorry to have occasioned pain to him and that it was unconsciously done," the kid replied, spreading his hands.

Tom groaned. There was Asher again, quoting that idiotic book. Or at least it sounded as though he was.

"He would not have it," the boy went on, and the expression on his face told Tom that he wanted him to understand.

"You got sore when he called you a son of a bitch."

The boy was defiant. "I do not take kindly to those words regarding my mother."

Tom turned to look at the fire, and his desire to argue left him.

"Nor should you," he said, and that was enough. Neither of them could change the past, and blaming the kid wouldn't get them anywhere. The boy was reminded of his folly every time he opened his mouth or even tried to blink. He probably hurt as much as Tom did.

The dark was gathering around them. The fire was the only light, and the plains were vanishing, swallowed up in the night. It was just them. There wouldn't be any stars tonight, and the way ahead didn't look much brighter. Tom still felt only relief. Even cut short, that had been a bad beating for the boy to take. He might not be as pretty anymore, but his brains weren't scrambled, and that was what mattered.

They moved closer to the fire, and Asher put his hands out toward it. It wouldn't burn through the night; they'd have to bundle up in the wagon soon if they didn't want to freeze, but Tom didn't feel up to moving. There was a fair amount of crusty frozen blood from his leg, but he hadn't bled out obviously. He still felt even weaker than before, maybe weaker than he ever had in his life.

Just saying anything more to Asher felt like too much work, but he did it anyway as he watched the boy stare at the wagon.

"Tomorrow, kid. We'll fix it tomorrow."

CHAPTER THIRTY-TWO

Tom DIDN'T REMEMBER making the promise, let alone wondering if it was the last one he'd ever break. A little snow had fallen in the night, but there was none of that now. The clouds were gone, and the sky was blue.

Asher added more wood to the fire, and Tom felt his frustration as much as he felt the heat.

"I'm sorry, kid." The words came out like a sigh.

"It is all right," the boy lied, moving to make sure the blankets were snug. Asher wanted to try to repair the wheel himself, and Tom could see him going over it in his head. The boy couldn't do it alone. In theory the oxen could lift the cart, and only one pair of hands would be needed to position the new wheel, but that would never work in reality. Someone had to mind the oxen so they wouldn't simply pull the entire wagon over. That same person had to pay attention to the wagon itself to be sure the oxen didn't inadvertently pull it apart.

Tom had been weak when he came around last night, and he'd just assumed that at least some of his strength would return to him in the morning, as it always had before. This time it hadn't, and he could still feel it in his chest; he *still* wasn't warm, wrapped in blankets and lying by the fire.

"We'll fix it," he said.

"I know, Mr. Calvert."

"Best to just do it."

"A little later on."

"No, I'm dragging my feet." He tried to roll over, and Asher stopped him, and Tom tried to push him off—only he couldn't. Hard work for weeks on end had made the boy stronger than he had been, but that wasn't the problem.

Tom sagged back on the ground, and his teeth chattered as he looked up at the sky. "Hell," he breathed, and the boy leaned in.

"Your pardon."

Tom wasn't about to repeat that or try to. If he hadn't had the breath to make it heard the first time, he certainly didn't now.

"All right," Asher said after a moment, awkwardly patting Tom's shoulder. He rose to his feet and looked around, then glanced at the fire, then at the wagon. He disappeared for a few moments, and Tom could hear him with the team.

The clouds of his breath came and went as he lay there.

The boy returned, the rifle under his arm. "Mr. Calvert," he said, gazing down at him.

Tom snorted, and it turned into a cough. "Going to put me down, kid?" But the words didn't come out loud enough to hear.

Asher cocked his head, then knelt. "Mr. Calvert, I recall when you told me you would shoot me if I was to go off on my own, on account of there being savages about. By my reckoning, I am in as much danger from them abroad as I am by your side. I intend to go for firewood and game, and I will not be dissuaded. Furthermore," the boy went on, speaking over Tom's attempt to reply, "I know that you issued that warning in my best interests. I do the same for you." He gave Tom a meaningful look. "If you try to get up, I shall shoot *you*."

With that, he rose and stepped out of view.

He was right, of course. Even with half his brain frozen to sleep, Tom knew that much. If the Indians decided to show up now, there wasn't a damn thing he could do about them. Feebly, he wormed a little closer to the fire, snug in his cocoon of skins and blankets. It wasn't right for the kid to be in charge, but there was no alternative. Tom couldn't think or speak, let alone do anything useful.

All those long hours sitting in the driver's seat or lounging in the back of the wagon, he had bemoaned his reduced state, thinking of how much he'd been able to do with both his feet under him and all his strength and no fever. Now he lay and thought of all he'd been able to do when *all* he had to trouble him was his leg and the fever. He could still walk if he had to, more or less. He could hold a conversation. He could do the cooking or even handle the team.

He'd been able to manage a clean bit of shooting, even with a cold hand. Granted, it was a good thing

Dan had returned his pistol to him. Tom didn't know that he'd have been fast enough with that unfamiliar Remington. That was in the past.

Now he was just the most pitiful caterpillar under the sky.

A NOISE OF DISTRESS woke Tom, and he was immediately blinded by the sun, now directly overhead. There were two suns, and they became four. He turned his head vainly, only for there to be two horizons. Tom shut his eyes and opened them, and now he knew what he should have from the beginning: that noise had come from an ox.

But he was facing the fire, and the team and the wagon were somewhere behind him. He rolled, or tried to, and saw the white canvas of the canopy shaking, but it wasn't the wind. The movement was going the wrong way. Or was it? Was the wind even blowing?

No, that was the blood rushing in his ears. Sweat stung his eyes, and he squeezed them shut, but didn't have the strength to open them again. The sun was so bright that it seemed to cut right through his eyelids, leaving him not in the dark, but in a world of flaming red. That color burned without a sound, and there was nothing but the low buzz in his skull, echoes of the shots that had punished his ears the night he gunned down the Fultons.

There had been a time when that sound had tormented him when he tried to sleep. Now it just sounded far away.

CHAPTER THIRTY-THREE

A SHER MADE TOM drink, not that he was resisting. The water was freezing cold, and much of it was spilled in the dark beside the crackling flames, but he got some down.

The boy's hand came into focus, and Tom saw the bandage on it, stained with blood.

The moon shone between the wispy clouds up there, but it didn't give enough light to do anyone any good. Tom couldn't see much regardless. The water was so cold that it hurt to drink, or that might've been the dry tightness in his throat.

Sweat rolled down his face, and he shivered in the snow. He coughed on smoke—smoke full of the scent of charred venison.

Patiently, Asher fed him, waiting for the meat to cool. It was overcooked, and only God knew if the boy had done it right otherwise. A fragment of Tom's brain remembered seeing the kid with the knife kneeling beside the deer, hesitating to do the work. Tom would've done it for him if he only could.

He couldn't, though. He could barely chew.

"He shouldn't have done it," he said later as the boy sat by the fire, gazing at it.

Startled, Asher looked down at him. "Mr. Calvert? I am glad to hear your voice." It sounded like he meant it. "Is your strength returning?"

"He shouldn't have done it," Tom repeated.

"Done what, Mr. Calvert?"

"Let the girl go."

"Mr. Calvert, are you referring to the novel?"

"He should have listened to the other girl. The sensible one."

"Yes." Asher nodded. "I agree."

"He should have listened," Tom went on. "Just because he's her dad and she's his daughter doesn't mean she isn't right. He really put his foot in it."

"Yes. I think you should rest now."

"I am resting."

"All right."

"And she wants to blame herself because this man ran off with her sister and she didn't tell anyone what she knew about him? It doesn't even make sense. There are things you blame yourself for, kid. Having good manners and doing the decent thing isn't one of them."

"I am glad you are so talkative this evening, Mr. Calvert."

"No, I'm tired now."

* * *

THE SNOW WOKE Tom.
    The sun was already up, but it was difficult to
know how late in the morning it was. He sat up, and
because he'd been doing it all his life, it didn't stand
out to him as much of an accomplishment.

It was, though. Tom took a deep breath and rubbed
his eyes, peering around himself blearily. He was hot,
and his thoughts were thick and sluggish, but he *had*
thoughts. He'd been dreaming, but already he'd forgotten what about. The air was cold, but that was good
because he was sweating. He shed a few of the blankets
and wiped his brow, looking around through the falling snow.

The wagon stood on four wheels.

For a moment he could only stare at it. One of the
oxen had turned to look back at him, almost pityingly.
He shook his head, but he wasn't imagining it: the
wheel had been fixed.

Snow crunched, and a figure hurried toward him
through the snow. It had to be Asher, though the boy
had swathed his face with a scarf under his hat. He'd
always been that way, colder than he needed to be. A
breeze would blow, and Asher would be chilly.

He was carrying a rabbit and the rifle, and seeing
Tom sitting, he ran forward.

"Mr. Calvert! How are you?"

"Awake." Tom wiped his face again and pawed
around for his hat, but didn't find it.

"I am so glad."

"Stop that. You sound like a damn girl." Asher stiffened at that, but Tom ignored him and turned to point at the wagon. "How in the hell did you do that?"

"With the utmost care. I did not wish to drive on until you had inspected my work, but I feared . . ."

That Tom wouldn't be able to. Yes, the camp was all packed up—the kid had been planning to put Tom in the wagon and get going. He'd been about to risk it. Maybe it was the fever, but Tom wasn't worried. The kid probably *had* fixed the wheel right. It wasn't so complex that a sensible person couldn't manage it, and the boy was plenty smart when it came to anything but girls and using his fists. He was so good with animals.

Tom shook his head in wonder.

"Are you well enough to travel?" Asher pressed.

Even if Tom wasn't, what was the alternative? They couldn't sit here forever.

"What is it?" the boy asked, seeing Tom's face. He sank to a crouch beside Tom, all concern.

It was the fever. Tom would've held his tongue otherwise.

He just looked at the boy. "I'm sorry," he said.

"For what?"

"I don't know where to go."

"We have the means to navigate."

"No, kid." Tom looked at his hands. They trembled but not so badly. He was afraid to look at his leg. "That's not it."

"Mr. Calvert, you appear to be on the mend."

He wasn't. The fever came and went. It had its back turned now, but it would rush him again at any moment. Tom breathed deeply while he could, and shook his head.

"The law's behind me." He sighed. "And now likely ahead as well." He couldn't remember his dreams or really much of the past few days.

But the night he'd killed the Fulton brothers? That was clear in his mind. His pistol wasn't in his belt anymore; it was in the boy's—he'd taken it.

Tom could still feel the grip in his hand.

Asher frowned. "Ahead?"

Now Tom's breath was going. "Yes," Tom said, feeling as though he'd just run a mile. "Ahead. They didn't leave us behind because we broke down, kid. They broke the wheel. They left us here because we weren't civilized enough to travel with them. Because of what I did."

"What did you do?"

"I killed them."

"What?"

Tom looked meaningfully at the pistol.

Face white, Asher pulled the revolver out and opened the gate, turning the cylinder to tip out the shells.

They were all empty.

Asher swallowed.

"You killed Norman Fulton," he said, "because he beat me in a fight?"

"That wasn't a fight," Tom told him, reaching out and taking the pistol. It felt frighteningly heavy. Was he *this* weak? Yes. Still, stronger than he'd been yesterday. Maybe eating all that venison had helped. He remembered *that* clearly; he hated deer meat. Always had.

"And I didn't kill him for what he did, because you probably deserved it. I killed him because he wouldn't have stopped. I think he meant to kill you." He was parched and trying to swallow. His throat hurt as much as his leg. "Couldn't let him do that, kid."

Asher licked his lips. Now his face was tinged with green.

"And I couldn't very well leave his brothers alive," Tom added, resting the gun on his thigh. "They all drew on me. And even if I let them go, it wouldn't be settled. *Now* it's settled." Only it wasn't; those men had families. The oldest had children.

And the next law the train came across was going to learn what Tom had done. His side of the story wouldn't matter; the law would hear it from the families of the dead.

Asher drew up his composure remarkably quickly. His face went hard. "You defended us," he said finally.

"In a manner of speaking. It won't matter, though." Tom shielded his eyes and looked up at the sky. "I'll hang. And I'm afraid you might as well. Depends on what they tell the lawmen."

Asher sat back on his haunches. He looked to the west, and Tom knew what he was thinking. He'd probably thought that his biggest problems would be Tom dying and getting the wagon fixed. Asher had believed they could just carry on west.

"I got them on all sides now," Tom said, rubbing his thumb along the pistol's grip. "I brought it on myself, kid. You shouldn't hang for it. And I worry that if you're nearby when they get me, that's just what'll happen."

"What do you mean by this, Mr. Calvert?" Something about the calm way the boy said it should have worried Tom, but there were other worries now.

"I mean," Tom replied, but fell silent. He looked toward the wagon, then toward the west. "I suppose I mean to say it's about time you cut me loose." It surprised him to hear the words from his own mouth. It wasn't something he'd expected to say and certainly not an eventuality that he'd pondered. It stood to reason, though. Tom was as good as dead, but the boy wasn't.

There had been times enough in the past that he'd said to himself that he'd played his hand. It was different this time. He didn't regret it: making a deal with the kid, buying the wagon. It hadn't been the worst plan. Not the best, either, but dwelling on that never helped anyone. A bullet in the leg could go either way, and this one might well have gone differently if not for all the things he'd gotten up to. Trouble with that Pinkerton and the Fulton brothers.

Tom hadn't wanted to die in that cramped hotel room, but there was nothing cramped about this place. The country was vast to look at any time, but blanketed in white, it seemed even bigger. The sky and the ground were the same color. Tom looked at Asher kneeling beside him.

"Kid, you didn't hurt anybody. If you go and you tell the truth, the whole truth about what happened, you'll be all right if anyone catches you up. You tell them Norman knocked you cold, and Tom Calvert gunned down the Fulton boys. And if they ask why you left me behind, you tell them you signed on to learn cards from me, not to see killing. You do that, and you'll be all right."

The boy took that in. Then he got to his feet and lifted the rifle, leaning it on his shoulder. The sun was up there, and Tom had to squint in the glare; he couldn't see Asher's face clearly.

"Mr. Calvert," the boy said, "did I understand you correctly when you said you killed all four of the Fulton brothers?"

Tom groaned. "I did it. And I regret it now, though I don't know what else I could've done at the time."

"Were they all armed?"

"They were, though Norman never moved for his gun. And I don't know that Jake even had the stomach to fire his."

"Then you shot and killed four armed men before even one of them could present a defense?" Asher asked.

Tom closed his eye. "I did."

"That is a feat." The boy snorted. "Then I could not very well leave your company before you have taught me to do the same," he said.

CHAPTER THIRTY-FOUR

T HE KID WAS thoughtless. He didn't heed a word Tom said, and he didn't know what was coming to him if he didn't let go of this pigheaded desire to learn the rough skills instead of the gentle ones. Maybe it was what had happened with Norman that had made him this way, even more determined to learn how to do harm. If he thought that would help him, he was even blinder than Tom was.

Only his eyes worked fine, and he was the first to notice that someone was coming.

He shot to his feet in the gathering dusk, coughing on the smoke from the fire and looking to the southwest. Arguing about where to go and how to get there was good and relevant business, but now it would have to wait.

Asher spoke first. "Shall we see who this is?"

Tom squinted at the shapes moving in the fading

light, but he didn't trust his eyes. Were there three riders? Or six? Or more? No, those were pack animals trailing behind. Lawmen gunning for him wouldn't have baggage like that.

"You had better. They'll come to us otherwise."

It was a bad situation no matter how you looked at it, but keeping strangers at arm's length was best. There wasn't much light left for traveling, so these people would be making camp soon. Tom wasn't willing to have people camped nearby without knowing who they were. "Take this." He held out his pistol, and Asher accepted it, checking to see that it was loaded. "And let me have that."

The boy gave up the rifle, and with an effort, Tom shifted away from the fire.

"Go on," he said, rolling onto his belly and taking aim.

Asher tucked the pistol into his belt, then adjusted it nervously. He took a deep breath.

"Then I will return shortly," he said.

"It's all right, kid. I'll look after you," Tom said. It would take more than this fever to break his poker face. Bluffing—he could do that until they nailed him in his coffin. Of course by now the kid probably had his measure, so he might see through it.

Asher started off at a jog, and Tom settled down with the rifle. Like as not these folks wouldn't want any trouble, but there was no saying out here, this far from any law to speak of. The Fulton brothers certainly hadn't expected to be catching bullets, but that was what had happened to them all the same.

Tom breathed through his nose slowly. He wasn't much of a shot with a rifle, though there wasn't much to it. He'd just spent all his time with the pistol because he lived at the table, where that was what you expected to have to use. But it wasn't his skill that worried him; it was his eyes. Even when he could think clearly, he occasionally felt dizziness or saw double.

Tom flipped up the sight and considered the range, then made up his mind and worked the lever, closing one eye and steadying his hand.

The boy was still running, though now the riders' lamps were moving toward him. They met a good three hundred yards from the campfire, and they were all just shapes. Tom couldn't see well enough to know if anyone made a wrong move; he just had to listen for a shot or see some sign of distress from Asher. And if something did happen? He supposed all he could do would be to rain down fire in the hopes that it might allow Asher to find cover.

The minutes crept by, and Tom relaxed, taking his finger off the trigger. He didn't have to be up close to them to know that whatever was going on, it was civil. He glanced down at the rifle and snorted quietly in the gloom. It should've been liberating to know he was about through. It was always a relief at the card table—when his mind was made up, and he was determined to see how it played. Decisions were hard; everything else was easy. Once you'd given up thinking, you were free.

Only it wasn't like that now. This was all the kid's fault. Tom had worried about himself for so long, and that had always seemed like enough grief in itself. He'd forgotten what it was like to have someone else to fret over. He didn't like it much, but that night on the Missouri had soured his disposition all around. There'd been a time when he thought of himself as an agreeable sort of fellow, but these days he couldn't remember why.

After what had to have been nearly half an hour, the boy returned slowly. It was all but dark now, and as he drew close enough for Tom to see, it became clear that he was sluggish because he was burdened.

Asher laid down his sacks and dropped to his knees, his breath coming out in big clouds. He broke more branches and added them to the fire. Tom tried to sit up, failed, and tried again, this time managing it.

The boy was out of breath, and there was a little redness to his face that wasn't just from the exertion of hauling all this back with him. He looked pleased.

"What a thing, Mr. Calvert," Asher said, and he sounded a little shaken.

"Yeah?" Tom still had the rifle close to hand. He looked at the distant lights of the other camp. "They all right?"

"Very reasonable," Asher replied, putting his hands out to the fire. "They are traveling merchants."

"Did they have coffee?"

"They did. Among other things." The boy looked smug. "Our provisions are considerably bolstered."

He really was happy; the kid would talk this way, using words from that novel when his spirits were high.

"Good deal," Tom grunted, laying the rifle aside.

"They also had with them a number of books."

The kid's poker face wasn't holding up. Tom hadn't been born yesterday.

"Oh, hell," he said, though his face was smiling. The boy held up a book.

"Can you imagine the odds, Mr. Calvert? He had

only the third volume." The boy gave a little laugh. "Almost as though it was meant to be."

Tom was tempted to lecture Asher about man's foolish tendency to assign meaning to simple coincidences, but he didn't have the energy. Instead he just let himself smile in the firelight.

"It's a stroke of luck, kid."

"Two of them," the boy said, barely able to contain himself. "It was not the goods these men carried that were of the greatest interest to me. It was the news."

"What news?"

"Friendly Field."

Tom's brows rose. He'd all but forgotten about that place, so wrapped up was he in more immediate concerns.

He saw now how wrong he had been. He had just assumed that Friendly Field was an idea, a notion, something to keep the boy putting one foot in front of the other. A destination to talk about so he wouldn't have to talk about where he had come from. Like a kid so sure his pa would come back one day because it was easier to repeat than to face what really was.

That wasn't what the kid was doing. Or if it was, he'd been doing it so long that it had become real. He hadn't forgotten Friendly Field, and sure enough, every stop they'd made, every chance he got along this trail, the boy had been asking about it.

No one knew about Friendly Field, and Tom had taken that to mean it really was a fairy tale. That hadn't bothered him any; he was lying low, so it didn't matter where they went or when they got there.

Or it hadn't at the time. Now things were different.

"They knew where it is?"

"No," the boy said, and for a moment he was crestfallen—but only a moment. "No, but one of them had heard it mentioned."

Just that was enough to put a smile back on the kid's face.

"Why's that place matter to you so much?" Tom asked bluntly. He knew damn well it wasn't any of his business, but he asked it anyway. He'd probably be dead in the morning, and he wanted to know.

The boy didn't have an answer for him. No—that wasn't it. He didn't *want* to answer. Tom watched him turn away to add more wood to the fire. When he turned back, he was smiling.

"Mr. Calvert, do you have somewhere *else* to be?"

Tom snorted. That was fair. "Fine. Where'd he hear of it?"

"A prospecting camp to the southwest. He said it would be reachable by wagon," the boy added quickly. "Though it would take us from our trail."

"What are you holding back, kid?" No reason not to push, and Asher's attempt at omission was as obvious to Tom as the moon hanging big and low in the sky.

"The gentlemen did express concerns," Asher admitted, fingering the handle of the pistol in his belt, "about the Indians. Shoshones, they said."

"What about them?"

"They said they heard tell of some trouble near here."

"That's all?"

"To the effect that the Army had killed a great number of them, and a few of the survivors were hunting whites for retribution." Asher rubbed his hands together and looked up at the moon.

"That doesn't scare you, kid?"

"I do not begrudge retribution to anyone," the boy replied. He turned to look squarely at Tom. "I intend to make for this camp."

Tom was impressed, though he wasn't sure why. It wasn't as though he hadn't already known the boy had spine. He'd known.

It was brains Asher didn't have.

From the start, Tom had intended to leave the road to Oregon. It was his only hope of staying free. Staying free was no longer a concern, though. He had the law on all sides, and he didn't have a strong preference for his leg or a noose if it came down to it.

The kid was going. There was no stopping him, even if Tom wasn't a sick cripple.

"You know the way?" he asked.

"I have committed the guidance I received to memory." The boy took the pistol from his belt and held it out to Tom. "Would you like to accompany me?"

As he said the words, the boy split into two, then floated hazily together back into one.

He would just load Tom in the wagon even if he refused, and Tom could feel the dizziness coming.

Tom pushed the gun away.

"Keep it," he said. "You're calling the shots now."

CHAPTER THIRTY-FIVE

THE SNOW WAS getting deeper, and there was enough of it that clearing it to build a fire to sleep beside was more work than it was worth, and they'd probably wind up buried by morning.

So they sat in the back of the wagon, cozy and covered, with cards in their hands. Tom was propped up, and he thought he could probably sit up on his own, but earlier that day he'd thought he could pick up ten pounds of beans to hand to Asher, and he'd been wrong about that.

He peered at the cards, watching the hearts become the diamonds. Or maybe they'd been diamonds to begin with.

"Mr. Calvert?" the boy prompted.

Tom put more money in and drew one card.

They showed, and he leaned over to get a closer

look at Asher's hand, but he overbalanced. The boy caught him and helped him back into position.

"Thanks, kid. I think I'm done for the night."

"Yes, Mr. Calvert." The boy put the cards aside and began to divide up the money. Tom shook his head.

"You won it," he said. It was all Asher's anyway; there was no one else Tom wanted to have it. They had enough left that the kid would have a good leg up wherever he landed. It was supposed to be another week to this camp at the pace they were making, slowed as they were by the snow. If Tom lasted that long, it would be a miracle.

Asher sat back against the other side of the wagon, looking around to be sure everything was in order. He liked to be tidy. At one time Tom had as well, but somewhere along the line, it had ceased to be quite so important.

For weeks the kid hadn't been able to keep his hands off the revolver, but now he had the buck knife in his hands, turning it over. He'd used it a few times now, once on the deer he'd taken and to clean a few rabbits.

He'd been queasy in the beginning, but he wasn't anymore.

"How old are you, kid?" Tom asked.

The boy looked up. "What would you guess, Mr. Calvert?"

"You look about twelve, but you aren't."

Asher nodded. "A runt," he said, "is the word I have heard used. And I have learned what you wanted me to learn, Mr. Calvert. I will not attempt to use my fists again."

"Don't use that, either," Tom replied, glancing at

the knife. "Put it down and pick up that book. I know that's what you want to do."

"I would rather talk with you, Mr. Calvert, though I see that you are tired."

He was, but that was always true lately.

THE WAGON JOLTED, and Tom reached for his gun, but it wasn't there. He threw off the blankets, pawing for it.

"Mr. Calvert!" The kid was over at another table, calling out to him. "Mr. Calvert, what is the matter?"

"Shafer just flipped my damn table! Where's my gun?"

Suddenly the boy was there, pushing him back to the floor of the wagon and dragging the blankets over him. Tom spotted the revolver in the boy's belt and grabbed for it, but Asher caught his hand.

"We hit a bump, Mr. Calvert."

There was no hotel. No game. No cards, no other players.

Tom saw the canopy and the daylight coming through the flaps. His strength left him, and he collapsed so abruptly that Asher didn't have time to help. He scrambled to get the rolled blanket under Tom's head and to tuck him in.

"All is well, Mr. Calvert," he said, using a rag to mop Tom's brow. "Mr. Thomas!" he said sharply, addressing one of the oxen.

Looking after the wagon and the team had to be— Well, at least Tom wasn't really in a card game. That was odd; he felt as though that was what he ought to want, but he couldn't think. If he couldn't think, he couldn't win, and if he couldn't win, he wouldn't want to play. That would be frustrating.

"You are delirious again," Asher said soothingly.

"I'm not," Tom croaked. He'd just gotten confused, that was all. The boy helped him take a sip of water.

"I wish you could see it," the boy said, but Tom had.

A sudden warmth had come and melted nearly all the snow. He had seen the dazzling lake reflecting the mountains, which appeared almost orange in the midday sun. And all the distant trees and the rolling hills.

He'd seen it. He still saw it when he closed his eyes. It felt as though he'd been laid up in this wagon for years.

"Are you calm now?" Asher asked.

"Yes."

Asher looked relieved. "Here, Mr. Calvert." He pressed the book into his hands. "Read the book."

Tom just looked at him, though. He had the breath; he just didn't want to use it. He didn't want to hear the words in his own voice. He'd have loved to read the book to pass the time; he'd enjoyed that in the beginning of the journey.

But he couldn't make out the words anymore.

A SHOT BOXED TOM'S ears, startling him out of the warm haze.

The cold rushed in, and the snow that had disappeared was there with it and the dark. The wind howled outside the wagon, and the canvas billowed in the night gale. He shivered, and another shot rang out.

Tom tried to work up the saliva to call out, but his mouth was too dry. For a moment, he lay, thinking hard, before he remembered that the strap of one of the canteens was around his wrist so he could always find a drink of water. He felt it there, but the canteen was too heavy to lift.

Another shot.

The boy was out there in the dark, practicing. He was shooting at bundles of sticks that he'd put together himself. Today—no, yesterday. Or even the day before, or perhaps Tom had only imagined it. He thought he'd cautioned Asher about this, about how a gunshot would be heard for miles.

He tried to lick his lips.

Maybe the boy thought this snowstorm would cover it all up. Or maybe Tom had never warned him.

There was a fourth shot, and he saw Butch Helms pulling his gun in the K Saloon.

Asher fired a fifth time, and Tom saw Helms' second shot in his memory.

He didn't see Shafer, and he didn't see the surface of the black Missouri reflecting the lights of *Newlywed*, the last thing he remembered from when he had gone over that railing. He didn't see the Pinkerton, and he didn't see the Fulton brothers, not even Jake, though Jake still lingered on his mind.

He wished he hadn't shot Jake.

The sixth shot from the revolver in Asher's hand died away, and Tom heard the boy shaking the spent shells out of it.

Shooting Shafer had been a mistake as well.

Snowflakes were blowing in through the flap, which wasn't tied just right, and if Tom wanted to, he had a feeling he could count up all the snowflakes before he'd get finished counting his mistakes.

Outside, the hammer clicked, and the gun fired. The sound didn't startle him anymore; in fact, it was almost a lullaby. It was foolish to shoot, but he couldn't even form the words to tell that to the kid, let alone convince him to stop.

Maybe the storm would be enough, the powerful winds and the clouds of snow—maybe that would keep it all from the Shoshones' ears, if there even *were* Shoshones to worry about. Tom wished he could have been like Asher. The boy seemed to view Indians, or rather the notion of them, as he would the tumbling of dice. Asher couldn't hold their grievance against them, so in his mind, that seemed to mean that if he was killed by Indians, that was all right.

Tom understood, but he couldn't see things that way, and that stood to reason. He could barely see anything at all now.

Maybe he'd have more strength in the morning. Maybe things would be different.

CHAPTER THIRTY-SIX

"D ID IT END well?" Tom asked. "The book?"

Asher glanced over his shoulder into the back as the wagon bumped along. The daylight was hazy, or maybe that was Tom's eyes.

"Yes, Mr. Calvert. All ended well. They married well, just as they wished, both of them."

Tom let his breath out, shivering. "That's good," he said.

"It is," Asher said. "It was as good as anyone could hope."

It wasn't like that most of the time. Tom had never been a reader, but he'd seen a few plays and things, and often those ended with everyone dead or miserable. For a time he'd wondered why that was, why people would make that choice—because with things that were written down, someone had the power to choose.

They probably did it because that was how things

tended to be in life, and that stood to reason, more or less. He watched the canopy swim and pulled the blankets tighter around himself.

"You would have enjoyed it, Mr. Calvert. When the fancy lady from earlier in the book paid her a visit, you might say she employed a poker face in the encounter. It was very nicely done."

"The bossy one? The one that the preacher liked so much?"

"Yes."

Tom cleared his throat. "All that bossiness gets under my skin. Boxes you in. Everyone waiting for their lives to happen, waiting for someone to come along and marry. Can't do anything unless their folks say so. I know the mother was only trying to do the right thing, or what she thought was right, but I'd have run away rather than be smothered that way."

"I think there is something to be said for having a parent or two, even if they are overbearing," the boy replied. He chided one of the oxen, then cleared his throat and went on. "I believe there is value in having someone to consider one's best interests."

"Maybe so, but can you think what it would be like to live with that bossy lady? I could barely read it, let alone think of doing it. I keep trying to think about what it would be not to be able to make your own way."

"You mean to say you would not wish to be a woman."

"What?" Tom frowned up at the canopy.

"Mr. Calvert, the role of the daughters is to be married. That is their only path in life."

"I suppose," he replied, though he didn't really follow. "They should be able to do as they please."

"It was not so long ago that you were bemoaning that one of the daughters was allowed the freedom to disgrace herself," Asher pointed out. "You believed her father should have stopped her."

Had he? Tom tried to think but didn't succeed.

It was coming; he saw the shadows around his eyes and the creeping darkness though it was barely past midday. He turned his head to see Asher's back. He couldn't sleep, but he knew he didn't want the feverish sleep to take him. He didn't know which of these days he would close his eyes for the last time, and he wanted a little while more yet with Asher. He opened his eyes and tried to sit up, but his leg protested too much. He moved over and grabbed the side of the wagon, hauling himself up a bit.

That was as much as he could do. He sagged against the wood and moved the rear flap, peering out at the trail behind. He saw the hills and the trees, all covered in sparkling ice. It blinded him, and he found the strength to lift his hand to shield his eyes. Stars and streaks of light overwhelmed his senses, but he looked anyway.

Something moved, and he didn't know if it was a trick of the light or the silhouette of a man on the hilltop. Maybe it was Jake Fulton, back to ask why Tom had shot him when there'd probably been another way. And Tom wondered if he could get enough breath into his lungs to explain how it wasn't reasonable to kill three brothers and expect the fourth to let the business lie. He'd *had* to kill Jake. It had been wrong, and he hadn't liked it, but it had been necessary. Otherwise he'd have been looking over his shoulder the rest of his life.

Only the rest of his life wasn't going to be very long, and he was looking over that shoulder regardless, be it for Shoshones or the law or . . . whoever else he was worried about. Shafer? No, he was dead. There was someone else, but Tom couldn't remember him.

He shook himself out of it, blinking several times, but there was no one out there on those hills. Just trees and ice.

"I believe that Jeff Shafer is following us," he said calmly.

"That may be, Mr. Calvert. You have mentioned that before."

"Have I?"

"You have. I will not hand you the rifle."

Tom squinted at the hills. "I don't want to shoot him, kid. I want to apologize."

"All right."

"I think he's back there. That way." Tom tried to point, though the boy probably wasn't looking.

"Yes, Mr. Calvert."

"I only want to apologize."

"We may deliver your apology when he catches up to us," Asher suggested over his shoulder. "Would that suit you?"

"I suppose it'll have to." Tom rubbed his face and settled down, letting the flap fall back into place. He shivered and reached for his blankets, trying to get comfortable, but his back was sore again, and he was getting sleepy. Only he didn't want to sleep.

He wanted to apologize.

Brooding about it wouldn't help, but there was nothing else to do in the back of the wagon. And without realizing it, he'd slipped down, so he was no longer sitting. No, there was nothing to do but wait for Shafer and all the rest to catch up to him.

He knew the kid didn't believe him, but that was all right. Tom knew, and that was what mattered.

They *were* back there, and they were coming.

He opened his eyes and coughed, then looked toward the front, looking hard. "Kid?"

"Yes, Mr. Calvert?"

He frowned, thinking. "Did you finish it?"

"Finish what, Mr. Calvert?"

"The book."

Asher turned back, but Tom couldn't see his face clearly; there were two of him again, but he was getting used to that.

"I did," the boy said. "It ended well. They married. Just as we would want them to. The both of them."

"Good," Tom said, relieved. "I was worried. I can't read it for myself. I can't see the words."

"I know. It's all right."

"You got something in your eye, kid?"

"No," Asher replied, quickly wiping his face with his hand. "No, Mr. Calvert. I am quite well. You should rest."

"And you should stop being a mother hen," Tom replied grumpily, but he laid his head back with a groan. "I will, though."

CHAPTER THIRTY-SEVEN

TOM WAS ALONE.

He knew that because the kid snored. Luckily, in all the weeks of their travels, it had never been a problem because the boy was so small. Even snoring uproariously, he didn't make much sound. But the boy never woke easy, and the light told Tom that it was early.

He turned his head, blinked away the doubles to see that he was right.

Asher's blankets lay empty.

Tom listened, but there was no crunching in the frost, and nothing from the team. The wagon creaked quietly, and he could smell the freshly fallen snow. His leg was on fire and so was the rest of him, but that was nothing to take note of. He'd only be surprised to find himself not in pain.

The side of the wagon was cold to his touch, but he

got a grip and dragged himself up to sit. With a mighty effort, he shifted to the rear of the wagon and looked out, then down.

A dark smudge waited on the ground—no, lots of them. They doubled and tripled, then shrank. They couldn't be counted; they were no different from the snowflakes or the stars in the sky—only it was morning so there shouldn't have been any stars. The stars were in his eyes.

No, these were footprints.

Tom's eye twitched. Shafer and the rest of them had caught up in the night.

"Kid," he said, though the word came out quiet and weak and probably carried about as far as his breath did, a pitiful little cloud. "Kid!"

There was no reply.

Tom gripped the side of the wagon, and his teeth ground. Those cowards.

They had finally found him, but instead of settling their business with Tom, they'd gone after the boy. Why? Because they didn't have the spine to face him themselves?

Swearing, he reached up and took hold of the frame, using his good leg to push. For a moment, he wasn't sure he'd make it, but he did.

The snow rushed up to meet him, and he crashed to the ground. It wasn't as much snow as it looked like, and it did little to cushion his fall, but the cold did him good. Sweat was dripping off him, and his arms made wide swaths in the snow, ruining the footprints as he fought to get himself righted. He got his hands on the wheel and then his leg under him; then he was on his feet.

Wobbling, he cast about blearily in the gray light.

The snow was different in that direction, to the south—that was where they'd gone, leaving these foot-prints behind. They'd taken the boy into the trees.

Fine. They wanted to come this far out and follow Tom? He could follow them too.

For a moment, it was as though there was only the one set of prints, but then they were all there again, hundreds of them. Tom stumbled but kept his balance, dragging his bad leg behind him until it gave out.

He caught himself on a tree and looked back toward the wagon.

The sun was just coming up, bringing a pink haze across the horizon. He felt the heat and dizziness com-ing and shook his head, shoving away from the tree and staggering into the woods. He batted icy branches away and called out to the kid, only no sound came out.

He paused, took the time to get his breath, and tried again. "Kid!"

There was his voice, but it was all alone, and it died away all too quickly.

Tom looked over his shoulder, and Shafer vanished behind one of the trees. Tom raised a finger to point.

"I'll deal with you later," he promised.

Shafer wasn't important, and he never had been. The kid was the one who mattered, and it wasn't lost on Tom that he'd come around to it much too late. He'd spent all his time thinking enemies were important. Knowing he'd make them, and making sure he was ready when he did.

He might just as well not have bothered with ene-mies at all. The joke was on him.

"Kid!"

Tom looked down at the footprints, but there were no footprints on polished hardwood. He didn't have time to play cards; he had to find the boy. Only he wasn't sure where the door was; Asher was in the woods, so clearly Tom had to leave this hotel first.

He went to the stairs and gingerly started to make his way down, only his leg wasn't having that. It gave, and Asher leapt to catch him before he could go tumbling down the slope, filled with rocks and branches.

But Asher was small and Tom was— Well, Tom was a bit larger, and Asher couldn't possibly keep him upright. They both sank into the snow.

"Hell," Tom said hoarsely, peering at the boy.

"Mr. Calvert," the boy replied, wide-eyed. "Did you walk all this way?" Asher was appalled.

All this way? Tom snorted; the wagon was just over there. He turned to look, and all he saw were trees. Maybe it was a little farther back.

"Mr. Calvert?"

"They didn't hurt you, did they?" Tom asked, turning back to him and overbalancing, but Asher held on to him.

"Hurt me? Mr. Calvert, you are half frozen. And you are feverish. Here. Here," the boy repeated, trying to get Tom's arm around his shoulders. "We must have a fire. I was not able to find any herbs. I believe it is too cold and they are all frozen."

The boy tried to get up, and Tom tried to help him but something went wrong, and they didn't even make it halfway. Asher groaned in frustration and set his jaw. "Please help me, Mr. Calvert."

"It's all right, kid. Just give me a second. And you," he said to Jake Fulton, who was watching just a short distance off, "laugh all you want. He's all right. I got my whole life to settle up with you."

Asher frowned and turned to look, but Jake stepped behind a tree and out of sight.

"Mr. Calvert, it's time for us to go," the boy said gently.

But Tom wasn't listening. He pointed at the tree Jake was hiding behind.

"You tell the same to Shafer and the rest. I've seen to them once, and I'll see to them again. Just because I know it ain't right doesn't mean I wouldn't do it all the same again!"

With that, Tom was finished. Scowling, he allowed the boy to haul him upright.

"Hiding," he grumbled. "They all want to hide. Call me a cheat when I'm not. Start a fight with a kid. Tell lies. Why couldn't we just play like civilized people?"

They limped forward, the pink light of dawn came through the trees, and Norman Fulton was right in front of them, coming out from behind that tree so fast with his knife that Asher cried out and recoiled, but Tom knew he was coming. He'd seen Jake hide, and he'd seen Norman and the rest of them as well. Things might have been a little blurry, but he'd spent his whole life honing the skill of noticing little things.

An ambush. Tom didn't know why he hadn't seen it coming farther off; a fair fight wasn't in any of their nature. If it had been, they wouldn't have been here now.

He jerked the pistol out of Asher's belt and knocked the blade away, then struck Norman down, only his leg couldn't be counted on the way it had been once. They both crashed to the snow.

Asher was there and Norman's knife flashed toward the boy, but Tom caught his arm and twisted around with the pistol at arm's length to take aim at another man. He fired a single shot, killing Shafer a second time where he was, just five feet away, rushing with his own knife. All these men had learned to move so quietly and quickly after they died. If they'd been this quick the first time, things would've been different.

Norman jerked his wrist free of Tom's grip and threw him off. Tom fell into the snow and kicked out with his good leg, taking Asher's feet from under him. The boy fell, and a knife spun through the air where his head had just been, burying itself in the tree. Tom fanned the hammer of the pistol, shooting Norman in the belly and rolling over to put his next bullet through Jake Fulton's head, only he got his shoulder instead—so he pulled his hammer back and sent another through his chest.

The handsome cowboy toppled into the snow, and Tom shoved Asher out of the way as Eli Fulton swung his ax. Tom shot him dead, then wrenched his torso around to fire his last bullet.

Ten feet away, Rodney Fulton fell back against a tree with a hole between his eyes.

A bullet to the gut wasn't enough to stop Norman Fulton, though. Of course it wasn't; this was about a girl. Those were always the worst kind of grudges. Asher was trying to pick himself up, but this was Tom's fight.

Tom forced himself to his knees, flipping the empty revolver in his hand to take it by the barrel. He struck, knocking the other man's knife into the snow. They grappled, and Tom should've won, but it was the same feeling as when he walked away from the table short. Of course he felt he should've won.

That wasn't real, though. Everyone felt that way when they lost.

Asher rushed in to help, and Norman struck out with an elbow and the boy fell, limp and without a sound. Norman, bleeding from his belly, turned his attention to Tom, who was flat on his back in the snow and seeing dark spots.

Norman hit him. Then he hit him again, and he looked as though that meant something to him. Maybe it did. It didn't mean anything to Tom.

He had been hit before.

Norman came in close, intending to straddle him, but Tom dealt him a headbutt that sent him reeling. He dragged himself up to his knees and shoved the other man into the snow, taking up his pistol and raising it, intending to put Norman Fulton to bed with a blow to the temple, but the black spots were back.

And the dizziness.

The gun slipped from his hand, and he sagged on his knees, gasping as the black circled him. He slumped onto his side beside Norman, who groaned and clutched at his belly.

It needed to be finished, but things never wanted to stay finished. Tom lay in the snow, and there was Carroll, walking toward him. So he'd caught up with Tom in the end. Well, if Asher didn't want to hold a fair grudge against someone, Tom shouldn't, either.

Carroll had a legitimate grievance after all.

And Tom was out of bullets in any case.

CHAPTER THIRTY-EIGHT

⌒

ASHER HAD NEVER stopped wanting to reach Friendly Field.

He had become distracted by other things during the journey, but he never let them get between him and that goal. He never forgot to ask every person he came across.

Tom had misjudged him about that.

He opened his eyes and sat up. Snow was falling, though very little made it through the trees. The pain had now taken up residence in his face as well as in his leg, along with the general soreness in the rest of him.

He blinked and took a breath. He touched his forehead, and all that came away on his fingers was blood and snowflakes.

No sweat.

He looked at the dead Indian beside him, the skins

he wore smeared with dark blood. He turned left, then right. Then to look behind.

There were five dead Indians and no sign of the boy. Tom didn't call out. He just shook his head and searched the snow, but his pistol wasn't there. Teeth grinding, he found that even his good leg wasn't much good. The shin was badly bruised, but he used it anyway. His hands were all but numb, so he didn't really feel the tree branch he used to drag himself upright.

Standing, he looked down at the clearing and the bodies strewn about it.

Not for long; he was already frozen and still shivering and chattering. The fever had been good for something, and now that it was gone, he almost felt as though he missed it. Being able to think clearly wasn't always a blessing; if it were, people wouldn't drink so much whiskey.

But Tom had never had any use for it. Vices were best left to his opponents, and as for opponents—there was one more thing that snow was good for.

The tracks stood out clearly.

Tom tottered to the nearest body, that of the biggest Indian—the one dead of a shot to the belly. He leaned over gingerly and picked up the stick from the ground. It was polished and shaped a little oddly, but it had good heft. A sort of club apparently.

He didn't want a club; he wanted a gun—and if he couldn't have that, he'd settle for a cane.

Shoshone was what people had called these people. Tom didn't know a thing about them, but he recognized his own handiwork. He supposed these men had set upon them because they didn't much like whites, and Tom could only say that if he were in their place, he'd very likely have done the same. And Tom?

He didn't remember it clearly, but speaking generally, he didn't much care for people attacking him. Right or wrong, what had happened here was already in the past, surrounded by his other mistakes.

There wasn't any blood on the ground that couldn't be accounted for.

Asher had left this clearing alive.

The sun was up there, but Tom couldn't be sure exactly where beyond the clouds. He didn't look up; he didn't dare take his eyes off the ground. He was clearheaded but weak, and even just a fall might have been the end of him.

He limped where he could with the help of the club. Where he couldn't, his arms had to do all the work, and their protests were of no interest to him. Muscles burning, he made his way back up the hill. The ice on the branches had started to melt, giving it all a dull glitter.

There were four-and-a-half sets of tracks: three walking and one being half dragged. Tom was no tracker, but he didn't have to be to interpret the signs of their passing.

The clouds were clearing. There would be no more snow today.

Sparkling droplets of water fell from the branches, and he saw the embers in the air that night on the Missouri. The fire and the chaos. Smoke everywhere.

Asher had left his home, wherever that might have been. In Omaha he had stolen something, Tom was certain. He had boarded *Newlywed* to put distance between himself and whatever trouble he thought was following him and also to steal more to provision himself for his journey to Friendly Field.

Tom's actions had cleared the way for him. If the boy had had any sense, he'd have robbed the boat blind while all that was going on and slipped into the water alone.

The memories weren't clear, but they lingered, and Tom had the powerful impression in that icy water of the boy's tiny hands scrambling for him and of something being lost.

Tom was convinced that Asher had given up his spoils from the boat to save his life.

THE WAGON WAS gone.
  Pristine white was really something to look at, even more so with nothing at all to mar it. It was the void that Tom had never known to long for, and now he preferred it to anything he could remember. There was more beauty in those distant mountains and lakes than in even the finest hotel. The best church even, and Tom had been in a few of those.

This white wasn't pristine, though.

It was a sight to picture: Indians driving a captured wagon, but why shouldn't they? Tom hadn't thought twice to take something from a fallen enemy, so why should they? Why not help themselves? How long had they stalked the two of them as they made their way alone across this vast emptiness?

Tom stared at the tracks from the team and the wheels left in the snow. It wasn't a trail to be followed; it was a road made just for him. For once he didn't have to worry about mistakes; this wasn't one of them. There was only one way to go.

The sun passed him by.

It got lower in the sky ahead as the light started to fade, and Tom looked back to see the footprints from his left foot and the long snake from dragging his right.

Of course the sun could outpace him, and a wagon might as well—but a wagon wasn't *so* fast as to be lost entirely.

There was a hill up there with a single tree at the top. The tracks from the wagon showed a wide cut around it. Tom broke from the trail, plunging his makeshift cane into the snow and pulling his bad leg with him every step of the way. A full day's walk on one leg was no trifling business, but Tom had grown to hate the back of that wagon so fiercely that this pain had become a relief.

It caught up with him at the foot of the hill. Exhaustion could be fought, maybe for a long time indeed, but it could never be beaten. On his first step up, he lost his footing and found himself in the snow.

He might have liked to just lie a while if he hadn't spent the past few weeks doing just that. He lifted his face out of the snow and clawed forward with his elbow, making his way up one inch at a time.

Arms burning, he reached the top, looking out over the plain on the other side.

His wagon was there, some five or even six hundred yards out.

Figures were moving, bathed in the purple and orange coming from the west. Three of them and a fourth, smaller one—they were struggling. Tom's eye twitched.

He rolled onto his back, patting himself down. He came up with his derringer, the pearl grips catching the light of the sunset. With numb, quivering fingers, he tipped it open. The barrels were both empty. Of course they were. He'd never even owned bullets for the tiny thing, let alone taken the trouble to load it. He had it for luck, not for killing.

He leaned back and took in a deep breath. The Indians didn't *know* the pistol was empty.

But it was too small to be seen at this distance, even catching the light. That sort of plan wouldn't work, but it stood to reason that it was his first thought. He smiled and rolled back over, crawling forward and giving himself the push that he needed.

The hill took care of the rest, and he found the bottom on the other side without too many rocks to make it difficult.

Three Indians.

He got his hands in the snow and put his palms on the ground, and his good knee. He'd done this a time or two since Dan's bullet found his leg, though he wasn't sure he'd ever done it when he was quite this tired out. It was all right; this would be the last time.

Tom got to his feet and drew himself up. He wavered, but he stayed upright.

They were out there in the distance. He didn't have to be able to make them out to know that Asher was putting up a hell of a fight. One kid against three.

He looked down at the club in his hand, then limped forward.

Tom didn't get far before one of the Indians noticed him. All three turned to see the man in the distance, brushing off snow in the twilight.

The struggle ended as the three of them looked in disbelief. Asher was on the ground by the look of it, but Tom had eyes only for his opponents. You had to win the hand before you could worry about anything else.

He was out of strength, even to take another step. Tom stopped there, the club hanging at his side.

That book that the boy loved so much hadn't been about marriage or wealth or any of it, though that was how it seemed at a glance. It had been about the notions people had from one another when they first met. That was where all the problems came from—every misunderstanding that had brought all those people so much grief in those pages. Those first impressions.

He hefted the club, opening his stiff fingers one at a time, then closing them to squeeze the handle tightly.

Nothing could make the heart race like a fight, but Tom's was as slow and steady as if he were sitting in a barber's chair. The beats went by, and he waited.

One of the Indians broke and ran, and the other two followed without any hesitation at all.

Tom watched them go, faint silhouettes in the dusk, reflected in the snow that shone like a mirror over the plain. His legs waited until they were gone before they gave out, and he sank to his knees. He let the club go.

In time the distant shape of the boy rose out of the snow. It took him a while to reach Tom, and Tom didn't mind. He'd been enjoying the sunset.

Asher was bruised and all but in tatters: his clothes were torn, and he held them about himself, shivering as he staggered closer.

The *Mr. Calvert* that Tom had been expecting didn't come. The boy just fell into the snow and threw his arms around him. It was thoughtless; Tom was in no better repair than the kid was, but he went ahead and used what little strength he had to hug Asher back.

The noises were muffled by Tom's coat, but it sounded like the boy was a little choked up. Just today, Tom decided not to give him any grief about it.

"Hell," he said, squeezing Asher back. "I don't know what you were worried about. I bluff for a living."

Though seeing that Tom had spent the past few months dying, he supposed one could argue that he wasn't much good at it. Somewhere along the way, someone had told him that if his leg was going to kill him, it would've done it already. It was starting to look as though they'd been right. Maybe he'd get to see Friendly Field after all.

There was something between a sob and a laugh from Asher.

"Mr. Calvert," the boy said, wiping his eyes and giving him a direct look, "I do not believe your skill at cards was what sent them away."

"What, then?" Tom asked, frowning.

"I believe they were afraid, as anyone would be," the boy told him, "to see a dead man come back to life."

Tom took that in and tried to give it a fair shake.

In the end he liked it better his way, but he was done arguing with the kid.

Ready to find
your next great read?

Let us help.

Visit prh.com/nextread

Penguin
Random
House